The Merry Heart

Heart Series, Book Two
Louise's Story

Books by Peggy Lovelace Ellis

Regency
Heart Series
The Uncertain Heart (Book One)
The Merry Heart (Book Two)

Short Stories
Silver Shadows, Stories of Life in a Small Town

Anthologies
Challenges on the Home Front, World War II
(Second Edition)
A Beautiful Life and Other Stories
Lest the Colors Fade

The Merry Heart

Heart Series, Book Two
Louise's Story

Peggy Lovelace Ellis

Faraway Publishing
Black Mountain, N.C.

Peggy Lovelace Ellis
76 Wagon Trail
Black Mountain, NC 28711-2565
https://www.peggyellis.com

First Edition
2023

Cover Design: SelfPubBookCovers.com/dianecostanzastudio

Published by
FARAWAY PUBLISHING
125 Spring View Drive
Black Mountain, N.C. 28711

Printed in the United States of America

ISBN: 979-8-9881761-0-7 (pbk.)

Library of Congress Control Number: 2023940387

The Merry Heart
Heart Series, Book Two
Louise's Story
By Peggy Lovelace Ellis

1. Historical Romance; 2. Regency Romance; 3. Regency Morals and Manners; 4. The Regency *ton*; 5. Napoleonic Wars; 6. Wellington; 7. Regency Nobility; 8. George III; 9. The Prince Regent; 10. Regency Slang; 11. Child Labor

In memory of

Georgette Heyer
(1902–1974)

Regency Author Extraordinaire

No One Comes Close

Acknowledgements

First is my husband, James T. Ellis. He has been my support in too many ways to count throughout our fifty-four plus years of marriage, especially during those times when my mind was so busy with characters vying for my attention that I didn't hear him.

No one produces a book without considerable help from others. I'm fortunate to have known and worked with people who willingly listened to me as I droned on about my stories.

Dawn Aldridge Poore (author of Regency mystery and romance series (https://www.amazon.com/Books-Dawn-Aldridge-Poore) and my niece, who chooses to remain anonymous, did major jobs on nitpicking the final draft.

Elgin and Melissa Cook gave expert assistance on the cover picture. https://www.melissacook.us

Randolph Shaffner shared his publishing expertise in the publication of this book.

My endless appreciation to all.

An Overview of the Heart Series

In 1774, three ten-year-old girls living in Somerset, England, made a decision which had a far-reaching effect on their lives.

Bright sunshine had found its way through the barred windows of the nursery at Shelburne Park, reflecting on the tousled curls of the three young misses sitting on the window seat.

Becca, the fair-haired pampered daughter of the earl who owned this estate, held sway over her two visitors, Louise the raven-haired only child of a duke, and Marie the auburn-haired offspring of a vicar.

Suddenly, Becca clapped her hands. "I have the most wonderful idea! When we grow up, we will each have a daughter and give her all three of our names. They will be best friends just as we are."

"Will the names not be confusing? I mean, with mother and daughter having the same name?"

"No, Marie. We will give our daughters our own names as their third name." Becca continued without waiting for another question. "My daughter will be Marie Louise Rebecca. Your daughter will be Louise Rebecca Marie. Louise's daughter will be Rebecca Marie Louise."

After some squabbling over the best order of their names, both girls capitulated to Becca's insistence.

Years passed, as years will do. These three girls became young ladies and entered adulthood still the best of friends.

Table of Contents

Prologue

An Orphanage in Hampshire, England, 1800

Louise looked up from her picture book when the door opened, revealing Mrs. Dysart holding a little girl by the hand. She had the bluest eyes Louise had ever seen.

"Girls, a new friend has come to live with us. Is that not exciting?" At the sound of the matron's voice, an assortment of little girls looked up from their play. They stared at a chubby child with a finger in her mouth, her black hair a mass of curls, tears standing in her big blue eyes.

"Yes, Mrs. Dysart!" The reply came in concert. Some of the children could barely walk, while others were school age. The eldest, who appeared to be about ten, appointed herself the leader, shepherding the small children in front of her until they clustered around the matron.

"This is Rebecca Black, who is six years old. Her mama has gone to heaven, so she has come to live with us." Mrs. Dysart glanced at the older girls, "We will all let her play with our toys, will we not?"

"Yes, Mrs. Dysart!"

Louise elbowed her way through the other children to the side of the newcomer, who moved closer to Matron. "Rebecca. That's one of my names. Do you have any other names?"

Rebecca opened her quivering lips. "My name is Rebecca Marie Louise."

The other child's hazel eyes grew wider. "Oh! Those are all my names, only in a different order. My name is Louise Rebecca Marie. Is that not right, Mrs. Dysart?"

"Those certainly are your names, Louise. This is an interesting coincidence. Rebecca, this is Louise Tracy. She is also six years old, so you have two things in common already."

Louise tossed her red curls back across her shoulders and took the newcomer by the hand. "We have the same names, so we will be special friends. Come see our picture books. Can you read yet? I can teach you. We will be bestest friends for always!"

Chapter 1

Louise Asserts Herself

Somerset, Autumn 1812

"Good afternoon, fair lady."

"Good afternoon, sir," Louise Mansfield answered, as she attempted to pass him only to find his horse blocking her path. Glancing into his twinkling blue eyes, she stated the obvious. "You are obstructing my way, sir. Please allow me to pass."

"My auburn-haired beauty, I don't recall seeing you in these parts. Have you lost your way? I am most willing to take you up before me. Assisting you to your destination would give me great pleasure."

"Your assistance is unnecessary." Turning away, Louise felt no fear. She soon learned her mistake, if she believed her words would discourage him.

He dismounted to pace beside her. After she refused to give her name, he regaled her with a variety of anecdotes covering the possibilities of which muse she might be.

Louise concealed her laughter as long as she could before ripples of merriment burst forth. That was when she made a mistake, or so she told herself later. She turned her face upward toward his. Before she knew what was happening, he slipped an arm around her waist, pulling her against his chest. For one heart-stopping moment, they gazed into each other's eyes. He lowered his lips to hers.

A feathery kiss, akin to a butterfly landing for only a moment on a flower, she thought. Until it deepened. Unaware of anything except the feel of his mouth on hers, Louise clung to him while her heart soared into the cloudless blue sky. When he drew away, they were both short of breath.

Louise blinked her eyes, unable to focus. "I wonder if Matron would say I should slap your face," she murmured behind fingers caressing her swollen lips. "I shan't, though. It must be acceptable to kiss a gentleman who makes me laugh."

"You laugh delightfully too," he assured her.

His husky voice brought Louise to her senses. She backed away, her eyelids lowered until, turning on her heel, she hurried away. Behind her, the audacious gentleman called, "Until we meet again, fair maiden, keep me in your thoughts!"

When the hoof beats faded into the distance, Louise slowed her pace. *So that's what kissing is like. He laughs too.*

Louise could hardly wait to tell Rebecca that a gentleman had kissed her. That thought gave way to another. Such behavior would appall her childhood friend whom she had known since they lived in a Hampshire orphanage. Ladies do not allow strange gentlemen to kiss them, Matron had told the girls on numerous occasions.

Louise must keep her delicious secret to herself. Keeping the secret didn't stop her thoughts of him. Nor the kiss. Would she have responded in such a wanton way to any of the men she met in London earlier in the year? Toby Williams, for example, was a likable young man, yet her heart did not flutter at the thought of kissing him.

She scolded herself. *Just listen to you. You're gloating over a stranger's kiss when you should be asking yourself why you didn't push him away. You not only didn't try to get away, you clung to him.* To take her mind off her embarrassment, she thought back over the afternoon.

Louise Tracy, as she thought of herself, was trying to come to terms with being Lady Louise Mansfield, granddaughter of the Marquess of Granville, the daughter of his late son, the Earl of Mansfield. Having grown up in an orphanage to age eighteen, Louise rejoiced, on the one hand, to have a family. On the other, the knowledge they had disowned their only child distressed her. Why would they want this unknown grandchild?

In the lull of mid-afternoon, Louise had decided to enjoy the sunshine in a stroll around the grounds of Shelburne Park. She needed to give serious thought to her situation while her hostess, the Countess of Shelburne, contacted these unknown grandparents at the nearby Granville Manor.

Only a few days had passed since she and Rebecca had visited the countess in her London townhouse, hoping to learn the identity of Rebecca's family. They had. In the process, Louise's own world turned upside down. Content with the few memories she retained of her parents, she was unprepared to learn they were not who she believed them to be, John and Marie Tracy, who had died of influenza when their only child was six years old. Their closest neighbors couldn't afford to feed another mouth—they had several children of their own, so they took her to the orphanage patronized by the Duchess of Dorchester.

The sound of hoof beats coming in her direction had brought her footsteps to a standstill, her thoughts to the present. Louise had inclined her straw bonnet when the gentleman tipped his high-crowned hat, pulling the big roan to a stop only a few feet from her.

What followed was his fault.

If she had not seen him, been kissed by him, laughed with him, Louise might have been content to join her newly found grandparents at Granville Manor.

Now she dreaded the thought of leaving Shelburne Park because she might never see him again.

Drawing close to the Shelburne house, Louise forced her thoughts to her present dilemma—living with her unknown grandparents who might not want her. Rebecca also was trying to adjust to a new name, including the title of Lady, as well as a new position as granddaughter of the Duke of Amesbury. Rebecca would understand.

Not for the first time, Louise shared her concerns with her old friend, almost a sister since the day the vicar brought Rebecca to the orphanage with the information her father was not in evidence and her mother had died of a fever.

"According to Lady Olivia, they did not want my mother. They even disowned my father in part because he preferred horses to the classics. Why would they want me? What happens if they reject me out of hand? What will I do? Maybe I should return to the City, not put my fate to the test."

The girls sat on the flagstone terrace at Shelburne Park, where a slight breeze eased the heat of Somerset on this early autumn day. Rebecca clasped Louise's hands to calm her.

"They *will* want you. You love the classics, which must count with your grandfather. They will soon come to love you for yourself." Rebecca paused. "Don't you think they regret losing their son? I mean, after the first flash of temper was over, during the passing years, they no doubt wished to find him to make amends. They couldn't know he was dead because he had lived under an assumed name after they disowned him."

Louise's naturally buoyant spirits asserted themselves. "It will be stupendous to discuss the classics with someone as knowledgeable as the countess said my grandfather is. He might have some books I've never read too. Oh yes, life with my very own grandparents will be stupendous."

"*Stupendous*, yes."

Louise accepted her teasing, even admitted she must stop using the word on every occasion. Avoiding the word shouldn't prove too difficult because she would no longer spend time with the piano students whose consistent use of the word had influenced her.

At that moment, some five miles distant in the study of Granville Manor, Lady Granville read the lengthy message a footman had delivered from Shelburne Park.

"Jonathan's child has come home. If she really is his child. We might know that woman's offspring would be a female. Beyond doubt a sniveling illiterate like her mother. I suppose we must acknowledge her?" Lady Granville appealed to her husband. Both were conscious of their position in England's aristocracy. They believed themselves to be at the top of the list, based on their lineage. An inelegant sniff was their only acknowledgment of those German upstarts who called themselves Royalty.

Miss Hortense Augusta Tracy, upon her marriage to the Marquess of Granville some forty-five years previously, had considered she was wedding a person who was *almost* her equal. Although she did not have a title, her ancestry predated William of Normandy. They had, in point of fact, welcomed the Conqueror to England's shores. That ancestor refused a title because he considered titles obsolete. His proud descendants followed his lead. Hortense Tracy had resisted sullying family history by contracting a *mésalliance*. However, upon careful study, she realized the marquess was closer to her equal than any other gentleman was.

After much searching, Henry Jonathan Mansfield had chosen a wife whom he believed to be *almost* his equal. Her family did not possess a title, which meant his chosen marchioness was lesser than he, therefore not a challenge to his lineage.

With those private thoughts, they had managed to rub along together for nearly half a century. Their conceit had not diminished during those years. Instead, their pride had increased with the birth of a son to carry on the family name.

Their son, Jonathan Augustus Tracy Mansfield, was the light of their eyes until he refused to be a party to their conceit. He had declined the classics education they planned for him at Oxford because he preferred horses to books. Beyond that, their son had married to please himself, his choice being the daughter of the local vicar. She was not his equal even though her lineage was acceptable in most families. The Mansfields were not *most* families, as they would not hesitate to inform anyone impertinent enough to suggest they were. In their unbridled conceit, they had disowned their son, giving him little thought since.

Now, with no prior notice of her existence, here was a chit who claimed to be their granddaughter. Heaven knows she might be just anyone considering she grew up in an orphanage.

Lady Granville continued, "The countess does appear to be certain she is Jonathan's legitimate child. Regardless of Olivia's belief, we should have our solicitor check her out before we acknowledge her." The marchioness sat ramrod straight with the light from the chandelier shining on her graying brown hair, her dark eyes snapping at the thought someone might try to dupe them. They were not credulous enough to allow anyone to trick them.

Granville's harsh voice was even more grim than usual. "I intend to investigate the chit back to the day she was born. We must allow her to stay here while the solicitor investigates the matter. Our reputation will suffer if we turn her away even briefly in the event she has a *legitimate* right to be here." With that thought, he penned a note to Lady Olivia.

Two hours later, Louise stood inside the door of the Granville Manor drawing room, while the Countess of Shelburne introduced her to Lord and Lady Granville. Louise saw a tall, silver-haired man standing beside a straight-backed chair occupied by a woman whose gray hairs outnumbered the brown by a considerable number. Both showed grim faces, acknowledging the introduction with a bare movement of their heads.

These people rejected her mother and disowned her father. They did not appear to regret their actions either. Louise felt abandoned when the countess left without receiving an invitation to take tea. Louise called upon the stoic calm she had learned at the orphanage. Her chin raised, she endured their stares.

Louise knew what they saw. A young woman of above average height, her auburn hair arranged in subdued curls held back by a green ribbon. Her sprigged muslin gown with the fashionable high waist emphasized her slenderness. She held her arms at her sides, her feet standing together the way Matron had taught her.

"We will have tea while we talk." Motioning the young woman to sit in a straight-backed chair opposite her, the marchioness rang the bell. They did not speak until Foster had placed the tea tray on a table beside Lady Granville and quitted the room, closing the door behind him.

After a long moment of silence, the marquess cleared his throat. "I understand you lay claim to being our granddaughter."

"No, my lord, I make no claims of any kind." Outwardly calm, inwardly in turmoil, Louise prayed for guidance while she sipped her tea. The older couple stared first at each other, then at her.

"What? Why have you come here? Explain yourself," the marquess ordered.

"The countess noted my resemblance to my mother," Louise answered without expression. "Lady Olivia believes I should become acquainted with the people whom *she* says are my grandparents."

"Do you think you are our son's daughter?" her grandfather demanded.

Louise shrugged, letting go her visions of being wanted. She did not feel any kinship to these haughty people. "I have some recollection of my parents. I'm content being their child. Having other relatives is immaterial. I am capable of supporting myself."

"How can you support yourself? Scullery maid, I suppose. You lived in an orphanage. Can you even read? Write?" A pronounced sneer marked the older lady's face as she stared down her hawk-like nose at the young woman seated opposite her.

Louise leveled a gaze at her that many would recognize as identical to their son's when he chose to dispute his parents.

"You're mistaken about education in this orphanage, my lady. In addition to reading and writing, I received instruction in the Holy Bible, history, geography, mathematics, and the classics. I can speak fluently in French, Latin, and Greek. I had lessons on the piano for ten years, giving me the capability to teach others. I earned a comfortable living in London teaching students."

Louise had maintained an even voice. She now congratulated herself on not smirking when she noticed the amazement on the faces of these people who were treating her like scum.

"Latin? Greek? French? The classics? History? Mathematics? I do not believe you. Everyone knows females are capable of learning only the simplest things." When Granville's harsh voice came to a stop, his wife's voice filled the room with scorn.

"As for playing the piano, no female needs to play more than an air or two when called upon to entertain company. Females in The Family recognize their place. Even you must realize, only men are capable of teaching."

Louise endured their scorn until the room grew quiet. While they stared, she spoke for several minutes in a clear, even voice.

Lord Granville sat with opened mouth, while his lady spluttered, "What is she saying? She sounds like a heathen."

Granville searched for words. "She gave a brief account of Homer's *Iliad*, in both Latin and Greek." He fixed his sharp gaze on the young woman, forced to concede she did receive some education at the orphanage.

"Having received education far above your station does not mean you are our granddaughter, however. We require a thorough investigation by our solicitor before we acknowledge you as a *legitimate* member of The Family."

For the first time since early childhood, Louise allowed her temper full rein. "I am not interested in being acknowledged by you or anyone else as arrogant and stupid, yes, stupid! as are both of you. It is no wonder to me your son left home."

Ignoring their amazed expressions, Louise rose to her full five feet, six inches, her hazel eyes sending out green darts of fury. "I will appreciate the use of a carriage to take me to the closest stage stop. I will return to London on the instant."

"Sit down," the marquess thundered. "You listen to me, young woman. It is necessary to know if you are our legitimate granddaughter. Until we are sure of your legitimacy, we cannot know what action to take. You have no choice except to stay here. Do you understand? My word is final. I will not allow Society to scorn me again. Their attention was bad enough when my son left." Granville yelled through the closed door. "Foster! Send Brown in here."

To every argument Louise gave, her grandparents returned an implacable answer. She would stay there. The ungrateful chit did not know what was best for her. When a stooped, middle-aged man entered, the marquess instructed his secretary to escort Louise to London, wait until she packed her possessions. You will return her to Granville Manor immediately.

Despite her temper, Louise was level headed. Capitulation was necessary. In a stringent voice, she answered him.

"That will not be necessary. I will return only because the Countess of Shelburne believes I should be here. However, I must have time to explain my change in circumstances to my friends and students. I will return at the end of a sennight."

The marquess glared at her a moment. "Very well, we accept your plan. Brown will accompany you. Give him the particulars of your life, which he will convey to our solicitor."

The Marquess of Granville nodded his dismissal.

When the door closed behind them, Lady Granville cleared her throat. "She is Marie's image, although I could see our son's countenance in her face when she lost her temper."

"We could not miss her belligerent stare. We saw it too many times. We cannot deny her paternity. She might not be his legitimate daughter, though, which will make a difference in our actions."

"If she is legitimate, obviously she must stay here. What will we do if she is not?"

"I will decide that when the time comes. Why must this happen to us? Did not we endure enough when Jonathan deserted us?"

They sat in silence, listening to the carriage pull away.

Louise sat in the closed carriage with Gertrude, an elderly maid, and Mr. Brown, while the plodding horses pulled the carriage at snail's pace. After several moments of silence, Louise forced herself to speak in a level voice. These people were not at fault. They were only obeying orders. "Mr. Brown, are you ready to hear the details of my life?"

Pulling his notebook from a large case at his side, he prepared to write.

"My parents were John and Marie Tracy. At least that is what they called themselves," she corrected herself. "They owned a horse farm in Hampshire. We were very happy until they died of the influenza in 1800.

I was six years old. I lived in the orphanage until last spring." Louise stared into space, lost in memory.

Mr. Brown recalled her attention. "Was it a good orphanage? Did they mistreat you in any way? I understand ill-treatment is prevalent in such places."

"Oh, no," Louise assured him. "We were always treated with loving care."

She told him of the patronage of the lady they affectionately called Triple D: the Darling Duchess of Dorchester. "This is not an ordinary orphanage, you must understand. The girls receive education in book learning but also practical matters. The duchess finds proper work, depending on their aptitudes, for each of them when they reach eighteen."

"*Eighteen*?" Gertrude, her thinning, dull gray hair scraped back into an untidy knot, gasped in wonder. "Most girls go out to work by age ten, as my sisters and I did."

Under their interested gazes, Louise slowly relaxed, as she recounted the happiness she had known at the orphanage.

"The orphanage was not a bad place to live, quite the contrary. Both the duchess and the matron followed the teachings of Hannah More. They reared us according to her religious precepts, which assured we would never suffer mistreatment. This orphanage was better than any other place if one could not be at home with one's own family. Also, Rebecca Blackwell, the granddaughter of the Duke of Amesbury, and I were close friends, almost like sisters, which I doubt would have happened in the ordinary way."

"Tell us about your life in London," Gertrude urged.

"After Rebecca and I left the orphanage, we shared a flat in London with a chaperone named Mrs. Peters, whose family is well known to the Duchess of Dorchester. A few days ago, we learned from Lady

Olivia Shelburne that our mothers had been close friends from early childhood. In fact, our mothers and another friend had agreed to give their daughters their own first names except in a different order. I am Louise Rebecca Marie; Rebecca is Rebecca Marie Louise. The third girl is the granddaughter of Lady Olivia: Marie Louise Rebecca."

Mr. Brown appeared dazed by the names, but he persevered. "I understand that two of you lived in the orphanage. How did you meet the third girl?"

"After we moved to London, the duchess found employment for Rebecca in a solicitor's office. I taught piano lessons mostly to merchants' daughters. The Earl of Shelburne became enamored with Rebecca, whose features haunted him. He knew he had seen them some place but could not think where. He took us to his mother, Lady Olivia, who realized, because of our appearance, that our mothers were the friends of her own daughter."

Her companions remained silent while they waited to hear more.

A cloud settled on Louise's face. She had enjoyed the hustle and bustle of life in the metropolis. The thought of returning to the quiet life of the country did not please her. How could she bow to the wishes of those impossible old people after enjoying the luxury of independence? Maybe, just maybe, they would not believe the results of their investigation. Louise knew better. She reluctantly brought her attention back to Mr. Brown.

"Miss Louise, do you believe you are his lordship's granddaughter?" he inquired.

Louise realized Mr. Brown really wanted to know if she believed she was the Granvilles' *legitimate* granddaughter. Not wanting to upset her, he hesitated to ask the question outright.

"I am afraid so." Louise didn't bother to hide her regret. "You see, sir, the countess's daughter, Lady Becca Haverford, helped my parents elope. Their marriage vows are recorded at a chapel in Kensington."

Louise thought of her life in the musical terms of major key representing the happy times which greatly outnumbered the minor key, bad times. She grew somber reflecting that her life had turned to a minor key. Louise could not think how to begin living in a major key again. She would find a way. After all, had Matron not told the girls many times that a merry heart is better than medicine?

Chapter 2

New Life, New Lessons

> *I pray Granville's solicitor finds a flaw in Lady Becca's recollections. Perhaps I am not their granddaughter, legitimate or otherwise. Yet I fear my prayers are in vain.*

The first evening in her new—Louise hoped temporary—home seemed long. She retired to her bedchamber quite early to escape the stilted conversation. After brushing her hair the requisite hundred strokes, she wrote in the journal Mrs. Peters had pressed into her hand just before she left their Harley Street rooms. Louise described her tearful parting from her former chaperone and meeting the Granvilles before ending with the devout prayer she would not have to stay here.

How she wished she could talk to Rebecca! Regardless of her relationship with the Granvilles, her friendship with her childhood friend must change. Rebecca's betrothal to Lord Shelburne meant there would be no more whispered confidences after everyone else was asleep, which had been an ongoing secret between them.

The day after her return to Granville Manor, the marquess summoned Louise to the book-lined library, where he and Lady Granville awaited her. Through lips thinned almost to non-existence, he spoke the words she did not want to hear.

"Louise, it appears you are, in fact, our son's legitimate daughter. In that capacity, we welcome you to our home." Granville's half-closed eyelids hid the expression there. However, he did not trouble to hide the hostility in his voice.

Although she had known this must come, Louise's heart sank in despair before steeling herself to politeness. "Thank you, my lord."

"You know nothing of the respect due The Family, which we intend to rectify," he informed her. "It is imperative you realize our importance in the history of England, which would hardly exist were it not for The Family's support through the centuries. We will begin your lessons first thing tomorrow morning. In the meantime, you may familiarize yourself with the Manor. Also its immediate grounds, staying within view of the house at all times."

With a grim nod, the marchioness added, "First, you will call us 'Grandfather' and 'Grandmother' when speaking to us. At all other times, you will refer to us by our titles. Do you understand?"

"Yes," Louise forced out the hated word, the word which tied her to these people, "Grandmother."

"Next, you must forget your past including everybody connected with it. There is no person in your past who is worthy of you now. You begin your existence today. Do you understand?"

Louise stared at her in horror. How could she forget Rebecca, who was closer to her than these old people could ever be? How could she forget Matron, who had been a second mother to her? How did one forget eighteen years of life? She voiced these thoughts aloud.

"You will forget everything connected with those years. Now the subject is closed," the marchioness decreed in icy tones.

Her granddaughter's face froze into immobility, although her brain seethed with anger. "Do I understand that Lady Rebecca Blackwell, who is the granddaughter of a duke and the fiancée of an earl, is beneath my notice?"

"As far as her lineage is concerned, she is acceptable. Nevertheless, the life she has lived puts her beyond your recognition. Now the subject is closed."

"No, it is not closed, Lady Granville." Louise lifted her chin and met the gaze of each grandparent in turn. "Rebecca has been closer to me than a sister for twelve years. I shall not ignore her under any circumstances. The fact that the orphanage was my home for twelve years is your fault. Had you not allowed your unbridled conceit to drive your son away, my life would have been here. You may think, say, or do what you please. You cannot order my thoughts, my love, or my loyalty."

Without waiting for a reply from her stunned grandparents, she hurried from the room.

Louise must get away before they called her back. Paying no attention to the heavy, old-fashioned furniture, she rushed from the corridor across the drawing room to the wall of windows covered with drapes. She scrabbled among them until she found the window which opened to the outside. Standing on the flagstone terrace, Louise allowed her gaze to follow the sweep of rolling lawns to a pond reflecting the blue sky. If she could get across that expanse of green and beyond the pond into the stand of beech trees, she would be safe from discovery.

"Move," Louise ordered herself. Chewing her lip, her eyes darting from side to side, she lifted her skirts and ran across the lawn. She didn't pause until she was out of sight from the house. There, she leaned against a tree, fighting the tears stinging her eyes. Finally succumbing to them, she turned to face the tree, sliding her arms around its rough surface while her shoulders shook with silent sobs.

"May I help in any way?"

Louise whirled around at the sound of the concerned, masculine voice. In her misery, she had not heard the approach of a horse, yet there stood a large roan with a man astride.

"Go away."

"You're crying. Are you hurt? Did your horse throw you? I am Major George ...."

"I don't care who you are." Louise stomped her foot, glared upward into concerned eyes. "Leave me alone. I don't need help. I can manage my own life."

When he didn't leave, Louise demanded, "Are you deficient in understanding? Go away." She flapped her hands in dismissal. "I said, *go away.*"

The major gazed at her mutinous face for a moment longer. He wondered who she was, whether he would see her again. Major George Stafford, late of Wellington's army, vowed on the instant he would, even if he had to spend all his time on horseback searching the countryside. He never could resist auburn hair. He didn't bother to try when it adorned the head of a stunningly beautiful female. He recognized her—the auburn-haired beauty he had kissed in the home woods of Shelburne Park, the home of his close friend from childhood. He had thought often of the girl with the ready laughter. Now he found her on the Granville Manor grounds, this time in tears.

Early in his life, Stafford had learned few females were beautiful when they cried. This one was. No splotches of color stained her creamy complexion, no puffiness marred her luminous eyes. Even the fierce scowl failed to detract from her loveliness.

He glanced across his shoulder. She glared at him, her fists resting on her hips. Raising his hand in a farewell salute, he chuckled softly. She had a temper to match the fiery glints in her hair. Yes, he intended to see her again. How or where he knew not, but Major George Stafford would find a way.

Louise watched until the trees hid him from her view. With relief, she slumped backward against the tree trunk. The gentleman who had kissed her at Shelburne Park. He didn't kiss her this time. Why would he want to kiss a watering pot? Who would want to kiss a veritable shrew? He wouldn't ever want to kiss her again. Why was he here anyway, she fretted, could he not stay in one place?

The chirping of chaffinches high in the branches above her head penetrated Louise's misery. She began to think in her usual rational manner. She had to stay. That being apparent to the meanest intelligence, she would make the most of it. Maybe life wouldn't be terrible, Louise told herself, remembering the piano she had seen in the music room. She looked forward to exploring the library. Too, there would be riding horses on an estate this size.

She must face another problem. How could she ask favors after her earlier outburst? Louise gave furious thought to her dilemma and sighed in capitulation to the obvious—she must apologize. She would not give in to their demands, completely, Louise assured herself. No references to her past life or friends, since they insisted. She would cling to her memories until her grandparents no longer controlled her life. Somehow, she would get a letter out to Rebecca, who waited to hear from her. Giving up her independence, after enjoying it for even a short time, was terribly difficult, but she had no choice.

Louise retraced her steps toward the Manor. She was calm again, satisfied with her compromise. At the edge of the trees, she gazed at the home park spread out before her. The leaves were beginning to change color—the mix of hues appealed to her artistic senses. Below the deep blue of the sky, leaves of red, yellow, and green framed the house built of gray limestone. The air over Granville Manor differed from the pall of smoke which drifted over London. Nonetheless, she would rather be in the hullabaloo of the metropolis. With a determined air, Louise returned to the library to face the marquess.

She forced herself to speak in a level tone. "Grandfather, may I interrupt?"

Placing a finger on the page, he glanced up from the book he was reading. "Yes, what is it?"

Louise flinched at his rude tone but forced herself to speak. "I apologize for my outburst. I realize I need to exercise better control over my temper. I will strive to meet your requirements."

Granville's expression did not lighten, although he nodded in recognition of her apology.

Taking a deep breath, Louise continued. "I wonder if I might be permitted to ride each morning before we begin our lessons?"

"Impossible." Her grandfather glared at her, as if to dare her to continue.

She accepted the dare. "Why is it impossible, my lord? I assure you that you can trust me with even the finest horseflesh. Father tossed me onto my first pony before I could walk. Later, the Duchess of Dorchester supplied excellent riding horses for our use. I rode almost every day."

"Riding is impossible because we do not have riding horses." Granville smiled at her astonishment, obviously waiting for her temper to erupt.

Louise was too surprised to oblige him.

"No riding horses? I admit I know very little of a gentleman's country residence, but I have never heard of one which did not have a well-stocked stable."

"You have now. Besides, ladies in The Family ...."

Incredulity made her ignore the rest of his homily. "May I drive?"

Granville gave her an exasperated frown. "The only horses here are for the family carriage. We have a coachman to drive it. Besides, ladies in The Family ...." He lectured on, his words glancing off her consciousness. "Now if there is nothing else you wish to quibble about, I will return to my reading."

Louise stared at him for a moment, her face impassive. "My father loved horses. Is that the reason you got rid of them?"

Without waiting for a reply, she left the room. In her bedchamber, she stared out the window overlooking an enclosed garden. She could see her grandmother bending over a rose bush. She must offer her apology now. The longer she waited, the harder it would be.

Moments later, Louise stood a few steps behind Lady Granville. "Good afternoon, Grandmother. I've come to apologize for my rude words. I realize I must exercise more control over my temper. I will strive to meet your requirements."

The marchioness kept her gaze directed toward the blossoms she was clipping. "See that you do."

Louise seated herself on a wrought-iron bench close enough to converse if the older woman chose. She waited, breathing in the scent of roses. Rebecca would love it here. The roses, at least. Louise refrained from voicing the thought.

After several silent moments, Lady Granville offered what Louise chose to consider permission to talk of her past. "I suppose we cannot expect you never to mention your childhood. We do expect you not to dwell on your experiences. Therefore, we require you to stay away from those people you knew in the City."

"Yes, Grandmother."

The only sounds for several minutes were songbirds chirping high over their heads and the buzzing of insects among the plants. After ignoring Louise for several minutes, the marchioness spoke.

"Were there rose gardens at the orphanage?"

"Oh, yes, extensive gardens, one consisting only of roses. I was more comfortable with the common flowers like Michaelmas daisies." Louise paused a moment. "I see you have both here. Would you care for me to pinch the dead blossoms off the daisies?"

"You may if you like."

They worked in companionable silence for several minutes.

"You are a soothing sort of person when you're not in a temper," Lady Granville conceded.

"I am not a temperamental person. In recent days there have been so many upheavals in my life I feel out of kilter." Louise studied her grandmother's face, choosing her words with care. "In childhood, I learned playing the piano soothed me when I was out of sorts. I noticed one in the music room when I explored the house earlier today. Would it be permissible for me to play it? I promise I will not damage the instrument nor disturb anyone."

Lady Granville glared at her. "You may play a few airs after dinner when we have evening guests. Other than those occasions, you will be too busy to waste your time on such useless pursuits." She gathered her gardening tools and marched into the house.

Almost overcome by despair, Louise followed with lagging steps. How could she live without playing a piano? She needed the solace it brought as much as she needed air to breathe. Entering the house near the kitchen area, Louise saw the butler looking at her, an anxious expression in his dark eyes.

Foster had taken special note of Louise on her arrival and related the details to Mrs. Foster, the housekeeper. "She looks just like her mother." The uneasiness in his voice reflected in his wife's eyes. "She has her father's directness of speech, his way of looking one straight in the eye."

"So, there's nothing meek about her." Mrs. Foster's voice oozed satisfaction. "She will stand up to them, right enough."

"They got more than they bargained for." His grim smile faded. "I wonder, though, if she will have the stamina to last, or if she will run away like her father did."

"We will help her in any way we can, just like we did with Master Jonny. She won't be able to turn to anyone else in the household because no one else knew him like we did. There's no one else to help her anywhere around here either."

"They will expect Lady Louise to be perfect, just as they expected Master Jonny to be. He would never have left home if they had been more understanding, accepting him for what he was—a master horseman.

"Perhaps you will have an opportunity to talk with her, let her know how much we admired her father. I wonder if she inherited Master Jonny's enjoyment of macaroons."

Thus, Foster waited for Louise when she entered from the garden after her discouraging conversation with her grandmother.

"Lady Louise, Mrs. Foster and I have many happy memories of your father. Will you do us the honour of telling us how he got on after he left here?"

Louise's stormy countenance relaxed into a tentative smile. "You knew my father? You can tell me pleasant things about him?"

Foster's smile changed to genuine amusement, as he led her to the housekeeper's room where Mrs. Foster waited with a pot of tea and a plate of macaroons. This was the first time she'd had more than a glimpse of Louise. The girl's resemblance to Marie startled her even though Foster had warned her. She directed a smile toward the hesitant girl.

A cup of tea in hand, Louise sank into a comfortable, upholstered chair, releasing a sigh of pleasure. "What a heavenly scent. Macaroons are my favorite sweet biscuit."

"They were your father's favorite too," Mrs. Foster told her. "He would sit by the kitchen table, waiting for them to bake. Master Jonny burned his mouth more than once."

"I did too. When it was my turn to cook, I always made macaroons. I sneaked some off the pan the moment they came out of the oven. How the cook scolded!"

"You were taught to cook?"

Foster's incredulous words brought ripples of laughter from Louise. Controlling her mirth, she recounted how she not only had learned to cook but had learned other household chores required by the matron.

"No matter how much I pleaded, the matron was adamant. Mrs. Dysart insisted I would learn to cook. I soon realized the sooner I learned, the sooner she would stop the lessons."

"You can actually cook," Mrs. Foster marveled. "The granddaughter of a marquess can cook. I've never heard anything like it."

"I don't care to remember how many times the food was either undercooked or burned. I always managed to bake the macaroons properly, though." Louise sobered after a moment. "Can you tell me anything about my mother?"

Mrs. Foster gave her a sympathetic smile. "I am indeed sorry to say we hardly knew her family. The master didn't encourage us to attend services, you understand. After Marie left with Master Jonny, no one mentioned their names."

"The vicar moved his remaining family elsewhere soon afterward," Foster added. "We never heard where they went."

With reluctance, Louise rose to her feet. "I have enjoyed our visit, but I must go. May I come again?"

"You are always welcome here, my lady. Feel free to come anytime," the housekeeper assured her.

"You have given Mrs. Foster great pleasure by visiting her. We were both quite fond of your father. You are very like him." Foster escorted her back to the great hall, where she hurried up the stairs.

Back in her bedchamber, Louise searched the writing table for paper to write Rebecca. Finding none, she opened her journal. She pretended she was talking to Rebecca. After recording the good news of her visit to the kitchen, Louise wrote of her earlier encounter with the marquess.

> *Can you believe there are no riding horses here? Not even one. When I inquired about riding, my grandfather stated, "In The Family, ladies don't ride horses; they ride in carriages pulled by horses." When I asked if I could drive myself, he acted as if I had uttered an obscenity. However, his tirade showed one change in my status. When I first came here, I was "young woman." Since they have accepted me into The Family, I have become a "Lady."*

A tap on the door heralded an elderly maid to help her dress for dinner. Louise watched in astonishment while the sour-faced female dug through the mahogany armoire dismissing each gown after only a glance.

"This will have to do," she grunted.

Louise voiced her surprise over the choice of a rose silk she had worn for parties in their Harley Street rooms. "That gown is rather ornate for a family dinner. Is there a reason?"

"There are guests for dinner."

"Why was I not told?"

"Why would you? Guests are not your concern. You will wear this gown. Your hair needs attention. See to it." The maid swept out of the room as though she owned the place.

Louise stared at the closed door. Rebellion flared. After a moment, she turned to the dressing table.

Dinner was interminable. One course of bland food followed another. Louise pushed the food around on her plate. The visitors, every one of her grandparents' generation, ignored her efforts at conversation. She could not expect the guests to be different. Leaving the dining room, Louise followed when Lady Granville turned toward the music room instead of the drawing room, their usual after dinner place for tea.

"My granddaughter will play the piano for us while we wait for the gentlemen to join us." She stared into Louise's eyes, "A few airs."

Louise complied until Foster brought in the tea tray. She excused herself after serving the cups, however. Hurrying to her bedchamber, she reached for her journal in an effort to control her surging anger.

> *As for entertainment in this bucolic place, I doubt if my grandparents know anyone under the age of sixty. Tonight, they invited some old cronies to dinner. Grandmother requested me to "play a few airs" while they conversed. They were so loud I doubt they heard a note, which is just as well because the piano is out of tune. When they were not chattering, they sat staring at me. Although none dared inquire about my parents, I am sure they would question me if they found me alone. They would be incredulous to know that the son of the lofty Marquess of Granville was a horse trader. How they would laugh if they knew.*

After donning her night robe, Louise stood by the open window breathing in the scent of roses wafting upward on the quiet night air. In the distance, she heard a barking dog. Somewhere closer, the hoot of an owl. Louise had almost forgotten the soothing country night sounds during the months she lived in London. She went to bed in a quiescent frame of mind.

The Granvilles never mentioned her parents in her presence, so their conversation in the music room after the guests left would have surprised Louise.

"Did you notice her expression while she played the pianoforte?" Lady Granville voiced the question, receiving only a grunt in reply. "In repose she has an air of Jonathan about her."

"When his thoughts were on sick animals," the marquess concurred. "If only he had given as much attention to his studies, our lives would have been different."

"Jonathan's behavior was all Marie's fault. You should have sent the vicar on his way when she started to get her claws into our son."

Granville's face hardened, but he did not reply. Hindsight could not mend matters.

Lady Granville sighed. "I might be able to like Louise if she did not bear such a resemblance to her mother."

With that confession, she bade him an abrupt goodnight.

Chapter 3

The Family: Minor Key, Major Key

I spend a large portion of each day being lectured on The Family And Its Importance In The History Of England. Although I have given my grandparents ample evidence of my education, they persist in thinking I am deficient in comprehension. I am liable to commit mayhem if I hear "Do you understand" many more times. As for "Do you grasp the importance of that battle?" it is entirely possible I will light fire to those old journals just any day.

I will admit, though, that our family does have an interesting history. I could enjoy learning about those times, especially my early ancestors, under different circumstances. I'm confident that the orphanage's history tutors would have made learning these lessons much more interesting. Their voices never threatened to put me to sleep as the geography tutors had come close to doing on a regular basis.

Louise was finding some comfort writing in her journal, especially when memories of happier days in the orphanage schoolroom eased her unhappiness to a small degree. But, oh, how she missed Rebecca. The other girls, too, but especially her bestest friend. Louise smiled at her childish grammar. Rebecca could always calm her when life threatened to get the best of her.

The afternoon after the dinner party, Louise peeked out her sitting room window where her grandparents sat in the enclosed garden. Knowing this might be her only opportunity, she slipped into the library and filched a sheet of writing paper carrying the Granville crest. Returning to her room, Louise penned a note to Rebecca, explaining why she could not write again. In her haste, she dripped ink on the paper. She ended her message with, "I promise I will never forget you. Someday, somehow, we will be together again, my best, my *only* friend. I exist for that day. May it come quickly!"

Now how could she post the letter? Would Foster be willing to go against his master's wishes? Louise wouldn't know unless she asked. She would have to trust him not to report her actions.

After a quick glance into the garden where her grandparents remained, seemingly without having moved an inch, Louise raided her grandfather's desk again and affixed a glob of wax with his seal. When she entered the butler's pantry, Foster donned his jacket, asking how he could be of service.

Louise spoke in a rush. "Foster, I want you to do something which, without being told, I am aware his lordship would not approve. This will be the only time I ask something of this nature of you, I promise. I would not get you into trouble."

After studying her pleading face for a moment, he inquired what he could do for her.

"My grandparents have forbidden me to be in touch with anyone I knew before coming here to live. My dearest friend, Rebecca Blackwell, expects to correspond with me. Indeed, she hopes to visit here. I must tell her why correspondence is not possible while I remain with my grandparents."

"How may I help?"

Taking a deep breath, she said, "I want you to post this letter to Lady Rebecca without my grandparents' knowledge."

Foster studied the direction on the missive: Lady Rebecca Blackwell, Amesbury House, Berkeley Square, London. His long hesitation ended with the words, "Alright, my lady, I will post this missive. No others."

Louise let out her pent-up breath on a long sigh. "Thank you, Foster, I won't ask it of you again. I apologize in advance if I cause you a problem with his lordship."

With that taken care of, Louise could settle into her new life. The days at Granville Manor crept by while Louise adjusted. She would have quarreled with her grandparents on numerous occasions had she not vented her anger in her journal. They insisted she must be seen but not heard, as befits Young Ladies of The Family. Louise had excelled in history at the orphanage and would have enjoyed the mornings spent in the book-lined library if she could have asked questions. She tried.

"Grandfather, did The Family have connections with the Plantagenets? I always enjoyed reading about the Wars of the Roses."

"Quarrelsome bunch," he grunted, thus waving off an important part of English history as of no account. "Now listen."

Louise persisted. "Do you have anything in your papers about the little princes in the tower? I would like to know the truth about their fate. On some days I believe Richard III was the murderer certain people claim him to be. Yet, on other days I believe he was innocent."

Granville glared at her from beneath bushy eyebrows. "We are not discussing the Plantagenets, young lady, we are discussing the Granvilles. Now, we will continue with Hector, the second Marquess of Granville."

She swallowed a sigh but surrendered, as she knew she must. "Yes, Grandfather."

He eyed her a moment and then changed his mind without explanation. "You're dismissed for the rest of the day."

Louise did not need urging. She hurried to her bedchamber for bonnet and gloves. She had definite plans for the unexpected free time, the first her grandparents had allowed. They had ignored her questions about her maternal family, so she decided to get answers from somewhere else—the vicarage.

Louise approached the red-sandstone church through a stand of trees, which drooped as though weary of the wickedness of the people who walked among them. She gazed at the squat bell tower, where chimes rang three times a day. Louise had forgotten how delightful, how melodious church bells sound. In London, workaday noise prevented hearing the purity of the bells. Those chimes had drawn her thoughts to her maternal grandfather on the day she arrived at Granville Manor. He must have been vicar of this church, perhaps stood in this very spot. The records would give her some information about his death and that of her grandmother. They would have the record of her mother's birth too.

Louise lingered in the porch, admiring the angels carved in the walls before entering the quietness of the sanctuary. She made her way to the front, where similar angels adorned the sides of the small font. Had her mother been baptized there? Surely, she had. Louise ran her fingers around the top before slipping into the front pew with its built-up sides. As always when she was in God's house, His spirit calmed her until she was at peace.

Had her grandfather truly delivered sermons at that fine Jacobean pulpit? She tried to imagine him there. However, not knowing his appearance, Louise could not visualize him. Did he have auburn hair like hers? Or had she and her mother inherited it from the maternal side of the family? Which pew had her mother occupied all those years ago? Perhaps the center front one, where grandfather could keep a stern eye on her.

Louise smiled at the idea her mother might have been as lacking in proper attention as she, herself, had been as a child. Louise doubted she would ever learn the answers to her many questions. Gazing around, she took in the mullioned windows. There was only one of stained glass, portraying the nativity, which clearly indicated that, regardless of their wealth, the Mansfields through the centuries had considered themselves above noticing parish needs.

Louise uttered a silent prayer for her family, wherever they might be, before wandering out the side door to the cemetery where tiny flowers scattered among the tombstones lifted their faces to the dappled sunlight. There she saw a man who seemed familiar. He stood with his head bent next to a large tombstone. She hesitated, but yielded to curiosity—oh, the times Matron had chided her for doing that! When she approached, he raised his eyes to her. Louise regretted her impulse.

The gentleman who kissed her, the one who had seen her crying. The one she had spoken to in such a rude manner. Major George Somebody. She wanted to turn away despite the inward shiver of anticipation of seeing him. Quelling her opposing sensations, Louise forced herself to walk in his direction, her head held high, a slight smile on her lips.

"Good afternoon, Major." Matron had taught her never to shirk her responsibilities. Louise took a deep breath. Her words rushed out before she lost her nerve. "I apologize for my rudeness a few days ago. I was angry at myself for being so weak-willed as to cry over circumstances which I could not control. I should not have been rude to you."

His smile showed crinkles around his eyes. "That is alright, Miss …?"

Louise's hesitation was brief. Matron had also taught her not to speak to strange men. Too late to remember Mrs. Dysart's admonition. Louise had already spoken to him, to say nothing of returning his kiss. And wanting more. She might as well introduce herself. "I am Louise Tr—, uh, Mansfield."

The major tipped his hat. "I'm George Stafford, currently on leave from the army."

"Did you serve with Wellington? If you did, you might be acquainted with the gentleman who is betrothed to my dearest friend."

"Who would that be?"

"The Earl of Shelburne."

"Shelburne? Yes, I know him. In fact, he has been my closest friend since boyhood. He has not told me of his betrothal."

"Perhaps I spoke when I should not have. I would not want him to be in your black books. I shall amend my words. The betrothal is unofficial."

"Nevertheless, when I see him again, I shall take him to task for not confiding his intentions to leave bachelorhood behind." The major paused a moment in thought. "Does your friend have raven hair and dark blue eyes?"

His question surprised Louise. "Yes, she does. How could you know?"

"I was in London in early summer when Shelburne was making a cake of himself trying to find her. He was in raptures over a raven-haired female with haunting blue eyes. Those were his words. I had to come to the country before he found her. I have not talked with him since. I'm glad to know he found her." Peeping beneath the brim of her bonnet, he chuckled, "You're her auburn-haired friend he mentioned."

"At least you did not call it red, for which I am duly thankful."

Stafford's chuckles turned to laughter, which she joined.

"Major, I've enjoyed our conversation, but I must speak to the vicar now." Louise tilted her head. "I apologize again for my rudeness."

"I hope we meet again soon, Miss Mansfield. By the way, I never mistake auburn hair for plain red. After all, red heads have freckles. You don't." With a quick smile at her and a nod in the vicar's direction, he limped away.

The major must have suffered a battle injury. The thought passed through Louise's mind as she turned to greet the vicar. "Good morning, sir. May I introduce myself? I'm Louise Mansfield, granddaughter of the Marquess of Granville."

The vicar shook her outstretched hand. "Yes, we heard his granddaughter had arrived to live with him. I am pleased to welcome you to my parish."

"I want to learn something of my maternal family. Perhaps you can help me. My grandfather was vicar here twenty years ago. His name was Sanford. I don't know how long he served this parish."

"I have only been in this area for five years. The vicar I replaced was named Bowles. He rests over there." He waved his hand to the far side of the graveyard. "You are welcome to look at the record books if you like."

"Yes, I would like to see them," Louise assured him. Inside, the vicar showed her the shelf where old record books lay, then left her in solitude. She knew her mother had been born here some forty years ago. After a diligent search, Louise found the correct ledger. Sitting in the front pew, she ran her finger down the pages until she found the entry.

Marie Josephine Sanford was the name inscribed, perhaps by her own father. Louise passed one finger over the name, grieving for the mother she barely remembered. A deep yearning overwhelmed her until a familiar soothing presence enveloped her. This had occurred throughout her life when she most needed comfort. Rightly or wrongly, Louise had convinced herself the presence was that of her mother. Louise replaced the book on the shelf before returning outside.

Standing at the lych-gate, she glanced over the rows of tombstones. They reminded her of a congregation, some sitting tall and straight, others falling over in sleep. At least they did not snore. Louise chuckled at the irreverent thought. A breeze seemed to echo her laughter. For a short while, she wandered among the graves. A few monuments contained the name Sanford. She would never know if they were her family. Shaking off her melancholy, she turned her thoughts toward George Stafford as she left the cemetery.

He seemed a very pleasant person. A friend of Lord Shelburne, which surely made him a gentleman. He wore his fair hair cropped shorter than she was accustomed to seeing, but it was a becoming style. Were his eyes blue or gray? Those were such inadequate words to describe his twinkling orbs. Not the blue of the sky nor the gray of a cloudy day, somewhere in between. Ah, the blue of the London sky through a thin haze of smoke. Smoky blue eyes. With a wry smile, she wondered why she was poetic today. Perhaps yearning for her family caused it.

With that assessment, she reached the gates of Granville Manor.

When Stafford left the auburn-haired beauty speaking to the vicar, he limped homeward musing about her news. So, Shelburne is betrothed, caught in parson's mousetrap several years earlier than he had vowed. George chuckled. He would give that traitor to bachelorhood a thorough ribbing when next they met.

Stafford's thoughts turned to Louise Mansfield. Mansfield? She must belong to old Granville's family in some way. He'd have to listen to neighborhood gossip to learn the relationship, although he had avoided company since his return from Spain. He was tired of questions about his leg.

Where did Miss Mansfield get her glorious hair? That shade of red had not come from either the marquess or the marchioness. If only half of what he had heard about the Granvilles was true, the young lady would need the mercy of angels to survive in their household. A deep-rumble of laughter in Stafford's chest shook his frame. Gently bred notwithstanding, she had not swooned at his kiss nor been too flustered to send him on his way when he found her crying. Oh, yes, Louise Mansfield would survive—but would the Granvilles? It would be interesting to watch. Major George Stafford's life had suddenly become more interesting.

A sudden realization stopped him in his tracks.

He had forced a kiss on a lady of quality, which was a *faux pas* he never made under any circumstances. Relative of a marquess or not, Miss Mansfield could not be a lady of quality or she would not have returned his kiss. Her morals could not be sound either. She would have swooned at his feet. Still, the auburn-haired beauty intrigued him. Just the thought of her brought brightness in his mind, a lightness in his step, something he had not felt in many months.

Lost in his thoughts, Stafford could almost ignore the pain of walking.

During the long sessions in the library, the Granvilles took turns talking. God ignored Louise's devout prayer for them to become mute. Had Matron not cautioned against praying for selfish reasons? Louise swallowed a sigh and tried to focus her thoughts on The Family.

The morning after Louise visited the church, Lady Granville took it upon herself to instruct Louise on Proper Behavior As Befits A Member Of The Family. After an hour of "young ladies of The Family do …" and "young ladies of The Family do not …," Louise decided she had been patient long enough, had curbed her tongue long enough for even Matron to approve. "My lady, I received such instruction at the orphanage."

"I have already told you to call me Grandmother," the marchioness reminded her. "Pray tell me, just what would anyone at an *orphanage* know of proper behavior for people of our class?"

Louise hid her temper behind a sugary voice. "*Grandmother*, am I to understand the Duchess of

Dorchester, who traces her lineage to the Conqueror, is not an acceptable person to instruct young ladies in proper behavior?"

"Do not be absurd. Of course, she is. However, a person of her prestige—the daughter of one duke, the widow of another—would not concern herself with the daily operation of an orphanage. I doubt she ever saw the orphans."

"You are wrong in your assumption," Louise spoke in triumph. "She knew all of us by name, made a point of holding private conversation with each of us at least once a sennight. The duchess personally taught us proper behavior, even those who would one day become servants, because she believed everyone needs to know the niceties of life."

That bit of boasting earned a sniff from the marchioness. "Even scullery maids, I suppose?"

"The duchess feels it is beneath her girls to be scullery maids. She made sure we received proper training for higher positions, according to our capabilities. She taught us that all females are capable of being more than scullery maids if they have the privilege of education." How often had Louise heard the duchess say those very words to recalcitrant girls, herself included? How the duchess would laugh to hear Louise repeat them,

That conversation brought to a halt all further instruction on proper behavior. However, Louise was aware Lady Granville watched her closely.

Louise heard the expression "The Family" until she was ready to scream with vexation. Instead, she gritted her teeth until her jaws ached. In her journal she wrote of her last conversation with Rebecca at Shelburne Park.

I said I did not want to come to this
place. I was right. My argument people

who disown their child would not want a grandchild has proven to be all too true, Now, I wish I had gone back to our rooms in Harley Street and lost myself in London until the clamor had died. Yet, thinking again, had I done so, I would not have met Major George Stafford. Unbearable thought!

Louise closed the journal and crossed the room to the window. How many times had she found Rebecca doing the same thing during their months in Harley Street? Now she understood. Their reasons for unhappiness were different, but their reactions were the same. Louise glanced across the top of the enclosed garden to the colorful trees beyond. Above them, a few wisps of clouds drifted across the cerulean sky. Early autumn was beautiful in the country. Louise wondered what London is like in autumn. The parks must be a riot of color by this time. With a sigh, she shrugged off her homesickness for the Town she had come to love, promising herself that, one way or another, she would be there again someday.

Spying her grandmother in the garden, Louise hurried outside. She had been trying to find a peaceful moment to ask her grandparents about Major George Stafford. This seemed a good opportunity.

Strolling leisurely along the gravel paths, Louise sought an opening. She snapped the dead blossoms off some daisies, glancing at Lady Granville from the corner of her eye. Keeping her voice neutral, she asked about people in the neighborhood whose acquaintance she had not yet made.

"You have already met the only important ones," Lady Granville stated. "We do not associate with any others in the neighborhood."

"Am I to cut everyone else I might meet in the village or at church?"

"The question does not arise, because there is no reason for you to appear in the village. The Family does not attend church."

"Not go to church? Grandmother, I have always attended Sunday services, both in Hampshire and in London. May I not attend services here too?"

"Bah! You inherited that foolishness from your other grandfather. I don't hold with such fustian. Neither does your grandfather."

Louise jumped at this first voluntary mention of her maternal family. "Perhaps you are correct. However, I cannot be certain I inherited my belief from my maternal grandfather because I know almost nothing about him. Did my grandfather deliver his sermons well? Did he speak from his heart? Was he ...."

Lady Granville raised her hand for silence. "Considerable time has passed since I heard your grandfather deliver sermons. However, I remember them as being intelligent. He was educated at Oxford, quite a good scholar at one time."

"Oxford? I had not thought of higher education for him."

"Your grandfather would know more about Sanford's education than I." Grandmother stopped clipping the dahlias. "Perhaps I need to give more thought to attending Sunday services. We have not occupied our pew in many years. We probably should start again."

Louise flung her arms around the older woman, much to the surprise of both. "I would appreciate that. Thank you, Grandmother."

When Lady Granville went into the house, Louise remained in the garden. She could not say her grandmother had welcomed the embrace, but neither had she rejected it. Perhaps she would accept her granddaughter's presence someday. Life would be much easier if that happened.

The breeze again carried the joyful sound of the church bells, perhaps more joyful because her parents had heard these same chimes. Louise had always looked forward to them in Hampshire, had made a point of being either outside or near a window to hear them best. During the early months at the orphanage, the bells had brought comfort to the grieving child. Influenza had claimed the lives of her parents twelve years ago. Would she ever stop grieving for them? Missing their laughter? Perhaps being here, where they'd lived their early years, would help.

Louise hurried indoors. If the library were empty, she would smuggle a book up to her room. She had managed to do it a couple of times before without either of her grandparents' knowledge. However, this time was different.

"What are you doing?"

Louise whirled around at the harsh sound of her grandfather's voice. "I want something to read, sir."

"That shelf contains classics. You are not to read them."

"None of them, Grandfather? I feel sure you have many the orphanage library did not possess. Even if I've already read them, I would enjoy reading some in their original language."

"Ladies in The Family do not read the classics."

"Why is that? You're aware that I read them at the orphanage."

"It is common knowledge ladies are not capable of having a true understanding of the workings of ancient minds. Reading their works is a waste of time. The fact you read them indicates your instructors were lacking in sense. Have you read all The Family diaries?"

"No sir." Louise persisted. "Lady Olivia told me you are an authority on the classics. She believed I inherited my love for them from you. I've never had the opportunity to discuss classics with a person who was truly knowledgeable. Discussing them with you would give me great pleasure."

Louise was not above flattery when it suited her purposes. Now for instance. Her grandfather was not immune to her honeyed words.

"Humph!" Granville gazed into her anxious eyes. A ghost of a smile touched his austere face as he waved her to a chair. He questioned her for an hour on Virgil's *Aeneid* to Homer's *Iliad* and *Odyssey* to John Milton's *Paradise Lost* before dismissing her to dress for dinner. When she left the library, Louise was careful not to smirk her satisfaction. She directed a saucy wink at Foster who grinned, albeit out of Granville's range of view.

From the day they met her, the Granvilles had discussed their granddaughter each night after she had retired to her bedchamber. On this night, both overcame embarrassment to reveal their thoughts which differed greatly from their usual conversation.

"Louise is a sweet child when she is not in a temper," Lady Granville remarked. "She managed to convince me we should attend Sunday services again."

The marquess chuckled. "She wheedled me into a discussion of *The Odyssey*, which she had only read in English. The chit carried a Greek copy of it away with her. I had intended to teach her a lesson, instead she taught me one. Our granddaughter has a high level of intelligence."

They sat in silence a moment before the marquess spoke. "Although Louise is not Jonathan, not even a male to carry on the name, perhaps she will do. She has a good grasp of the classics." Granville believed that said everything necessary.

The Granvilles were content as they parted for the night.

Chapter 4

A New Friend

The following morning, Louise entered the library with a smile on her face. "Good morning, Grandfather. Which marquess will we discuss today? Or could I suggest Homer instead? Or even John Milton?"

Granville raised an admonishing finger. "First, a short while on The Family. Thereafter, perhaps, one of the classics."

Louise could not say she had enjoyed their first hour, but she was in a more amiable frame of mind than usual, the result of their discussion of *The Odyssey*. Interesting though their family history had become, she would rather discuss the classics if she could just keep her grandfather on that subject for at least part of each session.

Foster approached Louise when she left the library. "Miss Louise, would you like some tea?"

"May I have it in the housekeeper's room with Mrs. Foster?"

Soon ensconced in her favorite chair in the house, Louise munched macaroons. Mrs. Foster seemed uncomfortable, a puzzled expression on her face. "Is there something amiss, Mrs. Foster?"

The housekeeper rushed into speech. "It's only that Foster and I wonder why you haven't yet visited Nanny Buckner."

"Who is Nanny Buckner?"

Mrs. Foster's eyes widened at the innocent question. "Do you mean the master has not told you about Master Jonny's old nanny?"

"My father's nanny is alive? Oh, I would love to see her." Louise hesitated. "Are you sure she would care to see me? She might resent my mother, too, for taking her Jonny away."

They didn't have to inquire who resented her mother. They knew. They reassured her with the suggestion she visit Nanny after luncheon, if she was free.

Thus, a couple of hours later, Louise knocked on the door of an old cottage on the edge of the estate. Old, Louise noted, but as well kept as the rest of the estate with what appeared to be a newly thatched roof.

The door opened to reveal a woman as wrinkled as an apple after long storage. Leaning forward, she stared at the countenance before her, straining to see. The sun glinted on Louise's auburn hair. The old woman's eyes lit up, and her mouth spread in a toothless smile of delight. "Come in, child. Foster said your name is Louise."

"Yes, it is." Inside the tiny cottage, Louise stood in some anxiety, awhile Nanny peered at her for longer than was comfortable. Her temper raised, Louise raised her chin, staring the old woman straight in the eye. Much to her surprise, that impertinence brought a cackle.

"Just like your father when he thought I was going to punish him." Nanny waved toward a well-worn chair. "Sit down, child. I wondered if you would come visit me."

Louise relaxed at the cordial tone. "I didn't know of your existence until this morning when Mrs. Foster told me."

"I'm not surprised your grandparents failed to mention me. They never forgave me for telling them a few home truths when my Jonny left. I gave them an earful they probably haven't forgotten."

"I'm not surprised he left if they preached at him the way they do at me about The Family." Louise's voice was faint with hope when she continued. "Did you know my mother? They refused to talk about her to me. I asked Mr. and Mrs. Foster, but they could not tell me much."

"Oh, yes, I knew Marie Sanford. Determined little creature. My Jonny was too, so they were well suited. Although you look like Marie, I wager you got your temper from your father. My Jonny was a rare handful when he was roused, which was all too often. In his own way, he was as autocratic as his father. That's the worst I can say of my Jonny."

"I remember them a little bit. I don't recall any evidence of temper in either of them. Perhaps my memories are what I want them to be."

"Take comfort in them, child. Whether they be real or only imagined, they are real to you. Nothing else matters."

"I believe so."

Nanny studied the girl's posture for a moment. "I wonder if you sit a horse as well as my Jonny did."

"I have no way of knowing but I do enjoy riding. Do you realize my grandfather does not have riding horses? No driving teams, either. At the orphanage, we had bloodstock available to us every day. In London Lord Shelburne supplied us with good mounts." Louise shook her head in wonder. "I really do miss riding."

"There used to be some good horse flesh here. My Jonny was forever in the stables, much to his lordship's displeasure. Biggers, the head groom, never hesitated to call on Jonny when anything went wrong with one of the horses. My Jonny had a way with all animals on the estate, forever setting broken bones or mending wings."

Louise raised her eyebrows but refrained from speaking when chuckles issued from the wizened old woman seated opposite her.

"That's how he met your mama. They were about nine or ten at the time. Marie had hurt her arm falling from a tree. Jonny braced her arm with a stick and wrapped it with his shirt. He told me she might have a broken wing. Marie bore up under his ministrations without protest."

Louise's laughter filled the room. "Can you tell me anything about my mother's family? Where they are now, perhaps?"

"I'm sorry, no. His lordship changed vicars after Jonny and Marie eloped. I don't remember where your grandfather went. I did hear later the entire family was wiped out in an influenza epidemic."

"That's how my parents died. Perhaps in the same epidemic. I was six years old at the time."

They were quiet for several minutes, each lost in her thoughts. Louise brought her attention back to the present.

"Tell me more about my father." For the next hour she laughed over the childhood antics of the big man who used to swing her high in his arms, his ready laughter ringing out as she waved her arms. In return, Louise told Nanny what she could remember of the life of the grownup Jonny. In this way, she received an additional measure of peace. Nanny grew quiet, her gaze fixed on something Louise couldn't see.

Louise waited a few moments before interrupting the old lady's thoughts. "I am told I have considerable talent playing the piano. Was either of my parents musical?"

"Marie was, although she never had a lesson. Vicar said he couldn't afford such nonsense. She would listen to someone else play a tune, and soon she was playing it too." Nanny's quiet laugh held a hint of smugness. "I'll wager her ladyship doesn't approve of your musical ability."

"My grandmother doesn't approve of anything about me," Louise replied with indignation. "But I must be fair to them. Both of my grandparents are relaxing their attitude toward me. I do not believe they resent me to the degree that they did when I first came. They got the piano tuned, yet are not quite reconciled to my playing anything except a few tunes when company comes."

"You're my Jonny's daughter. I wager you manage to play what you choose when they don't hear it."

"Foster is my ally," Louise confessed with a grin. "I play in the early mornings. He reminds me of the time, so I stop before my grandparents leave their rooms."

Nanny nodded her approval but appeared to tire. Louise left with promises to come again when the Granvilles' schedule allowed.

This had been a marvelous afternoon. Louise walked toward the Manor, her feet shuffling in the dry leaves as they did when she was a small child. Inhaling the scent, she allowed her gaze to wander over the glorious color of trees in their autumn finery. The red of maples, the russet of spreading oaks swept upwards to the blue sky where a few fluffy clouds played a game of tag. The sheer joy of living swept over Louise. Lifting her skirts, she danced through the fallen leaves, singing a lilting tune.

A masculine pair of hands joined hers. Startled into missing a step, Louise gazed into Major Stafford's twinkling eyes. Correcting her stumble, she matched her steps to his. They laughed as they danced with abandon until Louise realized the circumstances and stepped away from him. With a heated face, she swept her glance upward until it met his. What must he think of her?

The major leaned against a tree, his face pale. "There is no reason to be embarrassed, Miss

Mansfield. Your singing and dancing are what this kind of day brings forth."

"This is a marvelous afternoon, is it not? I have just visited my father's old nanny, who told me about my parents when they lived here."

"You're old Granville's granddaughter? At least, that's the village gossip. If I knew he had a son, I've forgotten it."

"I imagine many people have forgotten my father's existence. His parents disowned him when he eloped with the vicar's daughter."

"How did you come to live with your grandparents, if you don't mind telling me? The village gossip has several versions, my lady."

"I would rather be plain Miss, if you please, or even if you don't," she said with a grin. "Changing my name from Tracy to Mansfield was difficult enough without being burdened with a title even if it is only honourary."

"You will grow accustomed to having a title."

They strolled toward the Manor while Louise told him about the orphanage. She touched lightly on living in the City.

"We hoped to find Rebecca's family, but I never thought about searching for mine. There have been times in recent days in which I wished I had not found them." Louise laughed. "That's enough about me. Now tell me about you. Forgive my inquisitiveness. I cannot help noticing you have a slight limp. Were you wounded in battle?"

"I took a ball in my leg during the Siege of Badajoz in the spring. The ball missed my knee, for which I am thankful. My horse fell on me when he too was shot, which worsened the situation. Although healing is slow, I will have a complete recovery, the surgeon assures me. I can only bide my time to see if he knows what he is talking about."

"I truly am sorry, Major Stafford. According to the newspaper account, many of our troops fell in that battle."

"I am luckier than most of my men because I'm one of the few in my company who survived the winter and spring battles."

Louise hesitated to question him, as she watched the play of emotions across his face. "Do you intend to return to Spain?"

"My father wants me to sell out, learn to manage the estate. I'm heir to his barony, you see. He wants me to get on with my life here." The major shrugged. "I prefer the military, even the hardships. The question is moot for the near future, though, because the sawbones has not released me from his care. I fear he never will."

"I believe God has a purpose in everything that happens," Louise told him in quiet conviction. "He brought you home for a reason. If He wants you to return to Spain, you will."

Louise stopped at the edge of the home woods. Embarrassment flooded her again. She wanted to invite him to meet her grandparents, even as she realized they would not approve of him because a barony was much too low in the hierarchy for them to notice.

Stafford solved the predicament for her. "The doctor said I am to walk without stopping for part of each day, so I will leave you here. By the time I get back to Fieldstone, I will have completed my required exercise for today."

"You walk every day? I've seen you on a beautiful roan twice."

"Riding is better for executing errands for the estate, which I was doing those days. I need to become accustomed to long hours in the saddle again too, so I do both most days."

Louise wanted to ask if he walked in this direction every day but decided it would be too familiar. Instead, she smiled at him when they said their good-byes. Louise knew he watched her walk away and schooled herself not to turn around. Would she see him tomorrow? Would visiting Nanny tomorrow at the same time be too obvious? She had never laughed so much with any gentleman, yet he could be serious too. Laughter was more important than anyone's idea of decorum.

That evening Louise excused herself as early as was permissible. Her journal awaited. She had much to write.

> *Today I visited with my father's old nanny where I learned so much about both him and my mother. They had been attracted to each other since childhood. That never changed because I can remember their love for each other.*

Louise sat with a smile, lost in the few memories of her parents. She returned to the journal with the thought she could almost consider Nanny's stories as memories.

> *After leaving Nanny's tiny cottage, I danced from sheer joy. Alone at first but with Major Stafford when he fell into step with me. I hadn't realized he was near. I fear the dancing caused his leg*

to ache, but we laughed together. I laughed a lot today, first with Nanny and later with the major. I do so enjoy having an occasion to laugh!

Louise didn't return to Nanny's cottage as soon as she wished.

The following morning, Louise woke to the sound of thunder rumbling in the distance. She stood by the window watching the lightning play across the sky while the storm drew nearer. The rain continued throughout the morning sessions in the library. Neither of them could go outside on such a day, causing Lord Granville to extend the sessions into the afternoon. The sudden claps of thunder disrupted Louise's ability to concentrate. When a particularly loud crash sounded, she gave up all pretense of listening and ran to the window.

"Oh, Grandfather, do come. Lightning struck a tree on the edge of the lawn."

"Not the big beech, I hope." Granville moved faster than normal to look over her shoulder at the damage on the lawn. "No, that is an elm, which I should have removed a year ago because of disease. I never got around to having it done. Nature is forcing me to take better care of the estate."

"Granville Manor is a beautiful estate, Grandfather. You obviously have never neglected any part of it," she assured him.

Granville patted her shoulder. "I believe we have studied enough for today. I need to spend some time with ledgers in the estate office. You're free the rest of the day."

The storm passed in late evening, leaving silence in its wake. Unable to sleep, Louise opened the door into the corridor. The household was quiet. She wandered along the carpeted hallway to the front of the house. There, she stared out over the front lawn, where the moon formed a halo over the old beech. On an impulse she hurried down the stairs and opened the door, hoping no one would hear the bolt moving.

Louise had forgotten how fresh everything smelled after a rainstorm in the country. She stood on the flagstone terrace a few moments before she gave in to another impulse. Soon she was dancing where the old beech spread its moon-dappled cloak over the lawn. She wondered if the major would enjoy dancing in the moonlight. He probably would. Perhaps someday she would ask him. Louise returned indoors, wiping her bare feet on the mat. What would her grandmother have to say about this behavior from a Young Lady in The Family? Louise didn't want to know.

Unable to sleep, Louise opened her journal.

> *At long last, I'm beginning to feel I live instead of simply exist. Meeting Nanny Buckner helps. The atmosphere around my grandparents is easier than it was. Perhaps I am about to get out of the minor key at last.*

Chapter 5

Her Major Key Continues

Even though Louise was awake late the evening before, she rose at her usual time the morning after her moonlight dance and made her way to the music room for an hour at the piano. She played a Beethoven sonata, leading into a Mozart concerto-rondo. She started a Bach fugue when she became aware she was not alone. Her fingers stopped in midair. Glancing toward the door, she met her grandmother's eyes.

"You play quite well, child," the old lady admitted in an almost grudging tone.

Louise swallowed her astonishment. "Thank you, Grandmother. The duchess provided an excellent music master. She allowed me to practice every day after I finished my other lessons and completed my chores."

"Times change. In my younger day we called the instrument a pianoforte. I've noticed you call it by the shorter word."

"The shorter word seems natural to me, although the duchess always referred to the instrument by the longer word. The music master at the orphanage said it is not the precise same instrument, although they have most of the same features. The piano has a broader range of notes."

"I haven't heard the piano enough to know the difference, although I did notice the sound varies in loudness."

"The duchess allowed me to play her harpsichord so I could hear the difference. The harpsichord sound did not vary. The music master said that is the major improvement from the harpsichord to the pianoforte, just as the range of notes is the distinction between it and the piano." Louise wondered if she was talking too much because her grandmother didn't respond for several seconds.

"Listening to you reminds me of how much I wanted to play the harpsichord when I was your age. The sounds coming out of such an unprepossessing object fascinated me. I had not brought that to mind in years."

Louise almost held her breath while her grandmother reminisced.

"My father considered such nonsense to be a waste of time—refused permission for me to learn. He was like most men of his generation, I suppose. He insisted I confine my time to household chores, the only fitting thing for a female to do."

"I am sorry, Grandmother. You have lovely long fingers. You could have played with ease."

"I never quite forgave him for denying me that pleasure. I have treated you the same way, have I not?" Grandmother hurried on before Louise could form a reply. "Memories are scars. They never quite go away. They dictate our behavior even when we're not aware. I've learned there is a very fine line between the good and the bad memories. There are times when even the good ones hurt."

She seemed to realize she was becoming maudlin. Rising to her feet, she said, "Feel free to play anytime you choose, Louise. We expect guests to dinner. Perhaps you will play for them like you have this morning?"

Louise gave her a quick hug. Again. Hugs might become a habit, Louise thought with pleasure. They left the music room together, surprising Foster who had come to warn Louise of the time. She winked at him and followed her grandmother into the breakfast parlor.

Her life was indeed returning to a major key.

Louise hoped her day would continue in the same pleasant way, even though she had to survive The Family lectures. They had reached modern history, which was more interesting. Perhaps the end of the morning sessions was in sight.

Soon after luncheon, Louise donned her jean half boots for a visit with Nanny Buckner. She did not admit it even to herself, but she kept a sharp eye out for the major. Louise tried to hide her delight when he joined her soon after she entered the home woods but feared her smile betrayed her.

"Good afternoon, Lady Louise. May I walk with you?" Stafford gave her a dazzling smile, which she answered with one of her own.

"Yes indeed, Major, despite your use of my title."

"I feel I should use your correct title even when we're alone because, without thought, I might address you informally in public. We would suffer censure—you for allowing the familiarity and I for being rude."

"I wouldn't want either to happen." Louise took a deep breath. "I'm going to visit Nanny Buckner to see how she survived the storm last night. Did you have any damage at Fieldstone?"

"Not to speak of, no. Just some limbs down. What about the Manor?"

"Lightning struck an old, diseased elm tree, which Grandfather said should come down anyway. The groundskeeper is already busy cutting the wood into logs for the fireplaces."

They indulged in desultory conversation during their stroll toward Nanny's cottage. When the wizened old woman opened the door to Louise's knock, she stared at the major. "Who is this handsome creature, child? I don't believe I know him."

Louise hid a smile at her obvious flirting. Do women ever get beyond that age-old pastime? Probably not nor should they! "This is Major George Stafford, Nanny."

"Stafford, from Fieldstone, I warrant, although I thought you were helping Wellington beat old Boney. Come in, do." Nanny bustled about preparing tea, casting darting glances at the gentleman.

"I was in Spain until one of Boney's bullets felled me, Mrs. Buckner."

"Call me Nanny," she urged. "Everybody does."

He flashed a smile. "You make delicious scones, Nanny. May I have another?"

"Get on with you, Major Stafford," she chortled. "You know the way to an old woman's heart."

Nanny's pleasure in a gentleman's company was evident. She probably rarely saw people living so far from others as she did, especially men. Possibly only Mr. and Mrs. Foster. When the visit was over, she urged them to come again. "Anytime, Major, even if you're alone. I'll always have scones for you."

As Louise and the major ambled back toward the Manor, she realized they were comfortable together. She had never been in close association with many gentlemen—only those few clerks she had met during her months in the City. They were not gentlemen in the eyes of Society, of course, but Louise had never been quite at ease with them because she didn't feel they had much in common with her. She hated to think she was snobbish. Perhaps her breeding was showing even before she knew of it. Heavens, was she more Mansfield than she chose to believe? Or want? Louise wished she could talk to Rebecca about this disturbing thought, or to Mrs. Peters. *Someday, please, God. Sooner rather than later.*

Louise returned her attention to the major's words.

"I've never seen you on a horse. Do you not ride? I do not suppose the orphanage had horses available for the girls, but you might have learned while you lived in Town."

"I've ridden all my life, Major. My father tossed me onto my first pony before I could walk. At the orphanage, we had good bloodstock for those of us who wanted to ride. Not a horse for each girl, you understand. We had to take turns. I rode almost every day even if only for a few minutes. I also had ample opportunity to ride in Town."

"Why do you not ride here?"

Louise cast him a sidelong glance. Should she tell the major about her family circumstances? For some reason, she hesitated to share the differences she had with her grandparents, so chose her words with care.

"My grandfather resented my father's interest in horses. He sold off their stable when my father left home."

"I suppose that's understandable if your father lost large sums on racing wagers, but still, I'm surprised he doesn't ride around the estate at least."

"Oh, no, gambling was not the problem. My father simply enjoyed being with horses. Nanny said he was quite knowledgeable in their care."

"I don't understand his lordship's resentment. Knowledge of all animals is needed on an estate, especially one the size of Granville Manor."

"Grandfather wanted him to have a classics education. My father refused. Grandfather has not said, but I imagine he was disgusted to learn his heir had a profitable horse-trading business at the time he died."

"Horse trading?" Stafford didn't say that was not an ideal occupation for an aristocrat. Raised eyebrows showed his surprise.

"Yes. He obtained them in Ireland and sold them in Hampshire."

"Hmmm, does Lord Granville resent your being here?"

"They both did at first," Louise confessed. "In the last few days, though, they've accepted my presence. I hope, after they know me better, they will have kinder thoughts about my parents."

"I don't see how they can help doing so," the major said holding her gaze until she turned away.

"Goodness, I did not realize we had come this far." They were at the top of a small knoll overlooking the Manor. "I must get back to the house before someone starts searching for me."

"I need to make my way back to Fieldstone. Walking is more enjoyable since I met you."

Stafford continued before Louise could answer. "Do you attend Sunday services in the village?"

"Not yet. My grandmother has indicated it is time to occupy their pew again."

"Perhaps I shall see you this Sunday. I look forward to it."

Louise nodded and strolled away. She could see he would have to push for an introduction to the Granvilles in some public place. Otherwise, her only meetings with the major would be on their clandestine walks. This was better than nothing, but clandestine meetings were not in accordance with Matron's teachings.

Although the dinner guests that evening again ignored Louise, she accepted their lack of attention with equanimity. She did wonder if they would chatter while she played the piano. They did at the beginning, but soon grew quiet. They even applauded her efforts when she stopped after a glance at the clock. Louise accepted their exclamations, hiding her gloating thoughts. They could never again think of her as a nonentity.

Lady Granville retired immediately after the guests departed, leaving Lord Granville and Louise in the music room where they now spent most evenings. Her grandfather was in a mellow mood. Louise decided this was a good time to ask about her maternal grandfather.

"Sir, Grandmother said you could tell me about my other grandfather. I had not realized how highly educated he was until she told me."

After a long pause, staring at her from beneath his bushy eyebrows, Granville answered her. "Yes, we were at Oxford together, although we did not see each other on a regular basis. I read the classics. He read theology." His lips twitched. "He read classics, too, on his own after I gave him the living. We used to have some lively debates in his early years here. I even read up on theology, but could never hold up my end of our debates on that."

"Perhaps I inherited my love for the classics from both my grandfathers," she said. When he nodded, Louise decided to risk another question. "Was his lineage so bad?"

At length, Granville took a deep breath. "Not bad at all, child. I have never wanted to admit his lineage was impeccable but on a lower level than ours."

They remained quiet for several moments, he deep in memories, she content to wait for whatever else he wanted to say. "I was too rough on Jonathan. I have realized for many years, although I refused to admit my failure, even to myself. He hurt me when he rejected everything I stood for, all I hoped to pass on to him. My son could never understand the importance of The Family. Your coming has eased some of the hurt, but it is not quite the same as having him."

"I am pleased, Grandfather," Louise dropped a light kiss on his forehead before leaving him to his thoughts.

In her bedchamber, Louise picked up her journal. She rarely wrote her thoughts since her relationship with her grandparents had improved. Goodness, could that mean she only wanted to complain to Rebecca? She hoped she was not so shallow. They'd shared every aspect of their lives all these years. Louise hated to lose their closeness.

> *I wonder how much of Grandfather was in my father. I do wish I could remember him better because I might be able to ease Grandfather's hurt if we could talk about him. I only remember his happiness, especially his love of horses. Grandfather does not want to hear about either of those.*
>
> *My life is better than when I first came. I wonder if I will ever go back to London. Perhaps I will bring up the possibility to Grandmother soon. I would love to see Rebecca. But Major Stafford must remain at Fieldstone. I would miss him and our walks. I would miss visiting Nanny too.*

The following morning, Louise entered the library to find her grandparents already there. Suppressed excitement filled the air, so she greeted them with restraint. She wondered why they had not joined her for breakfast. Quizzing the Granvilles was out of the question. "Good morning, Grandmother, Grandfather. Where are we on the family tree this morning?"

"Good morning, Louise. Ah, I believe we will forego our usual session this morning. There is something outside we want to show you instead." They led the way out the long window.

Lord Granville showed traces of embarrassment. Lady Granville smiled with pleasure. Whatever they wanted her to see must be something nice, Louise mused, as they stepped aside to give her a view.

Louise gasped. "Is she for me?" With tears in her eyes, she turned toward her grandparents. "May I at least ride her?"

"Yes, she's yours," her grandfather said.

With her hand extended, Louise approached the chestnut mare talking in low tones. The mare whinnied in reply, tossing her glossy mane. Louise laughed with delight, while she ran her hands over the mare's sloping shoulders and admired the small head, the deep chest. Built for speed, that was easy to see. "She is lovely. Does she have a name?"

"The breeder's papers identify her as Petersham Juno Monthaven of Meadowlea," her grandmother remarked.

"That's a mouthful—I shall call her Juno. How do you like your new name, my proud beauty?" Louise received a nicker in reply. The horse searched her hand. "Sorry, Juno, no sugar. I will have some next time."

"Do you have a riding habit, Louise?" At her nod, Granville told her to get dressed. "Juno would like some exercise too."

Louise needed no urging. Within fifteen minutes she was downstairs again. She led Juno to the mounting block and settled into the saddle. Louise was eager to be off but realized she must prove to her grandfather she could indeed handle a horse, which promised some spirit.

He watched while Louise put the mare through her paces in the paddock. Satisfied, Granville indicated she was free to ride. "Your groom's name is Baker. You will not ride without him in attendance, do you understand?"

"Yes, Grandfather." Turning to Baker, mounted on the ugliest rawboned bay Louise had ever seen, she asked if he was ready. When Baker tipped his hat in answer, she took off at a slow trot that soon lengthened into a canter. When they reached a long straight stretch, she threw caution to the wind, urging the mare into a full gallop. She glanced back once to see if Baker was keeping up. His mount in action made his ugliness disappear.

Baker was right with her when she pulled to a stop. He gazed at her in admiration. "My lady, I've never seen a female ride so well, nor many men for that matter."

Turning Juno homeward, Louise laughed with sheer exuberance. "Thank you, Baker. I had excellent instructors at the orphanage."

They returned to the stables in silence. When Louise handed the reins to the groom, he delved into his pocket bringing forth a sugar cube for Juno. With a final caress on the mare's nose, Louise went in to dress for luncheon.

She could hardly wait to tell the major about Juno. However, her grandmother had plans of her own.

"Louise, would you care to help me in the garden this afternoon? I could teach you to prune roses, if you do not already know how." She tried to hide her eagerness under a nonchalant tone of voice.

Swallowing her disappointment, Louise admitted she did not know how to prune roses, but it was high time she learned.

Thus, Louise spent the balmy afternoon hours watching and listening. As she concentrated, she began to understand her grandmother's love for roses.

She would love Rebecca too, Louise was sure, if they ever met. They had roses in common, even if nothing else.

Lady Granville changed the subject, although she continued to work with the shrubs. "I became interested in flowers only after Jonathan left us. This enclosed garden was my escape, my place to brood over the misbehavior of my son. Or what I considered Jonathan's misbehavior," she amended. She glanced sideways at Louise. "Since you came to live with us, I have come to realize I stopped condemning him many years ago. I am not quite sure when I forgave him for going his own way. I only know that I did, even though I have never admitted it, even to myself, until this moment."

Louise hardly knew how to answer. Her grandmother's confession would have been difficult for a woman of her superiority. "If it means anything, they were happy together. At least, I remember a lot of laughter in our home. I adored both my parents. I have the confidence of knowing they returned my love in full measure."

They finished pruning in companionable silence.

Over dinner, Louise spoke of church attendance. "At what hour does the service begin tomorrow, Grandmother?"

"Ten o'clock, I believe. I will order the carriage for half an hour earlier."

"Grandfather, will you accompany us?" Louise assumed her most cajoling voice.

"Humph! I suppose I had better." His sudden laughter filled the room. "The roof might cave in when this old reprobate walks inside."

Indeed, they did create something of a stir when the Granville crested carriage rolled to a stop at the church steps.

Dressed to the nines, Louise accompanied her distinguished grandparents into the porch, sparing only a glance for the bystanders. When they settled into the family pew, she whispered, "You were wrong, Grandfather. The roof is intact."

Louise heard his chuckle as the organ began playing the opening hymn. She kept her gaze fixed on the vicar, although she didn't have any real choice in the matter, given that they occupied an enclosed pew. After the benediction, she followed the Granvilles down the aisle. When they passed the second pew, a slight movement caught her eye. She met the major's eyes for a moment before continuing her measured steps.

In the porch, he caught up with them. Stafford stood so close the vicar had no choice other than to introduce him to the Granvilles.

"Major George Stafford? Are you the baron's son from Fieldstone? I believe I heard you were serving with Wellington."

"Yes, my lord, the baron is my father. I returned from Spain a few months ago due to a minor mishap to my leg." He glanced at Louise who was standing quietly by her grandmother's side.

Granville glared from beneath his bushy eyebrows until Lady Granville touched his arm reminding him of his manners. "Major, may I introduce Lady Granville? This is our granddaughter, Lady Louise Mansfield. Lady Louise, this person is Major George Stafford of the neighboring property, Fieldstone."

Stafford bowed over Lady Granville's hand. Turning to Louise with a twinkle lurking in his eyes, he said, "It is a pleasure to make your acquaintance, Lady Louise."

"Likewise, Major Stafford," she answered with a slight smile.

"Major Stafford, we must take our leave of you." Lord Granville ushered his ladies into the carriage without acknowledging other people standing near enough to warrant at least a nod.

On the ride back to the Manor, Louise kept her voice neutral when she asked about the major. "Do you know Major Stafford's family, Grandfather? I do not believe anyone of that name has been among the guests since I came."

"Stafford is a mere baron," he grunted. "Not worth our notice."

Louise cringed at the arrogance in his voice. They had softened in their attitude toward their son since she came, but their family pride was intact. In despair, Louise realized they would not permit her to see the major again. If they knew, which at some point they must, because she intended to pursue their friendship. She would have found her grandparents' conversation later that evening quite interesting.

"Granville, has it occurred to you there is no one suitable for Louise to marry? Am I correct that we do not have even a suitable distant relation?"

"There is our Cousin Gertrude's son, Jasper Winningham, who is at least of Louise's generation, although he is some years older. We have not heard anything of that branch of the family in several years, have we?"

Lady Granville shook her head. "What we last heard was not creditable. I recall Jasper was involved with a tavern owner's wench."

Granville nodded in confirmation. "As I recall, his father sent him to Italy to get him away from her."

"He will not do for our granddaughter. Considering the ages of the rest of your male relatives, I am afraid he will become your heir. We must find someone suitable for her to marry. Sons to carry on our lineage are mandatory."

"I realized the urgency today when Stafford cast his eyes in her direction. That connection certainly will not do. What do you suggest?"

"Perhaps we should take her to London for the autumn? There are several weeks left of *ton* activities before people return to the country for yuletide. We are out of touch with Society, but we stand a better chance of finding an acceptable match there than anywhere else."

Granville cringed at the thought. "Town will place her in proximity to people we want her to forget. However, it will at least remove her from Stafford's vicinity."

At breakfast, they announced their plans to a quietly exultant Louise. She was returning to London. She was eager to tell the major. She remembered she had not told him about Juno. They would have much to discuss this afternoon on their walk.

Louise didn't have to wait until afternoon. The doorbell started ringing in late morning, the usual time for at home calls, except they did not have any in the usual way of things.

Lord Granville raised his eyebrows when Foster entered the room, interrupting his monologue on The Family. "Yes?"

"Excuse the interruption, my lord. Several morning visitors have arrived. Lady Granville requests your presence in the drawing room."

"Visitors, Foster? Who is visiting us? Never mind, we must join Lady Granville. Come, Louise."

Dared she hope the major was one of the visitors? Louise scanned the drawing room, which was filled with faces she recognized from the worship service the previous day. Hiding her disappointment when she failed to see him, Louise passed the teacups, smiling at each person. Her heart lurched when Foster again opened the door to announce another visitor.

"My lord and ladies, Major George Stafford."

Louise restrained herself until he had greeted all the older people. She managed a demure smile when he seated himself in a chair next to hers, stretching out his injured leg.

"Good morning, Major," she murmured. "I am pleased you called."

"I admit I was not sure I would be welcome."

Louise spoke for his ears alone. "Grandfather gave me a chestnut mare all my own. Was that not marvelous of him? She's the first horse I could ever claim as mine alone."

"His generosity is marvelous, indeed, considering why he disowned his son," Stafford concurred. "Perhaps we can ride together one day soon."

"There is something else too. You will never guess what we will do next week."

"I was never good at guessing games. Tell me."

"We're going to London! Will you be there?"

"I had not planned to go. However, my plans have undergone a sudden change. Can you give me the directions to the Granville townhouse?"

"I know their house is in Chesley Square, although I don't know where that is, except certainly not in the vicinity of Harley Street where we had rooms."

"I will find Granville House," he assured her with a twinkle.

The major took his leave soon after Lady Granville interrupted their tête-à-tête.

That night, Louise stood by the window of her bedchamber sniffing the night air. Nights were getting cooler, there was less flower scent on the air, yet the stars seemed brighter than usual. After a quick dance around the room, Louise crawled between the sheets. She would be back in her beloved London next week. Major Stafford would be there too. She wondered what Rebecca would think of him.

Chapter 6

Happy But Unhappy

Two teams of Welsh bred grays pulled the cumbersome traveling carriage on its slow trek to London, while Louise ground her teeth in frustration. For several hours, she had wanted to tell the coachman to spring 'em. She smothered a giggle as she thought of the furor that would cause. Instead, she watched for the pall of smoke that always hung over London.

The Granvilles had reprimanded Louise several times on her tendency to stare out the windows. She had forced herself to calmness by thinking back to her first arrival in London. There had been many changes in the months since, but her memories were as sharp as if her arrival were only yesterday.

Vendors, beggars, and clerks on foot had jostled for space on the cobbled streets midst the drays, the sporting vehicles, the carriages of the affluent. Highbred horses had taken exception to barking mongrels running around their feet. Only the strong grip of their riders controlled their mounts' sidling movements. How she had longed to have such horses readily available but had known those days were past.

And the noise. Louise had thought the orphanage was noisy with all those children. Their clamor did not compare to the City, however, the bells in particular. Hawkers used them to draw attention to their wares. The Punch and Judy man rang one to draw a crowd— most often dirty, ragged urchins who didn't have the required penny. They stood on the outer edge of the crowd to listen. As then, Louise's blood quickened with excitement. Oh, how she longed to join the bustle of Town life.

While she wandered around Mayfair during her months in the City, Louise had not seen Chesley Square. Now, she approached the square with curiosity turning to disappointment. Chesley looked much like any other square in Mayfair. Louise had somehow thought the Marquess of Granville with his long family history would have managed to be different. She hid her disappointment when the ancient carriage stopped in front of a door exactly like its neighbors.

In one of the many lectures her grandparents had given on The Family, Louise learned that her paternal family had occupied this house since its construction some six hundred years earlier. She could only hope succeeding generations had updated the house.

Against her inclinations, Louise managed not to gape at the entrance hall with its medieval armor and a variety of tapestries depicting great battles of bygone eras. She wondered if one of them represented the Wars of the Roses. She knew better than to ask. With her steps echoing on the marbled floor, Louise climbed the stairs to the rooms that would be her home for several weeks.

Dark, heavy furniture filled her bedchamber and sitting room. Dull burgundy drapery added to the gloom, with equally dark fabric covering the few chairs. No trinkets livened the dresser top. No colorful pillows or cushions adorned either the bed or the chairs. A very minor key place. Louise decided on the instant to spend as little time as possible occupying these rooms.

Louise wanted to send a note to Rebecca but refrained from upsetting her grandparents the instant they arrived. She was sure to see her dearest friend without significant delay. As far as Louise knew, their former companion, Amelia Peters, still lived in the rooms on Harley Street, now chaperoning other girls who had come from the orphanage. That had been the

Duchess of Dorchester's plan, at any rate. Louise had to figure a way to visit Mrs. Peters, which must wait until she had a maid she could trust. She could not trust one already employed by The Family. There was not a doubt in Louise's mind on one point—her grandparents would never approve, probably even forbid, their granddaughter to visit her old friends anywhere outside Mayfair.

For now, she had plenty to do. Refurbishing her wardrobe before Major Stafford arrived in Town was at the top of the list. Louise didn't quite understand why she felt poorly dressed in his presence, when she did not feel the same way with anyone else. Nonetheless, she did. She wanted him to see her dressed in the height of fashion.

The days passed in a blur of shopping expeditions to the most exclusive modistes Lady Granville could find. Louise had suppressed a groan when the marchioness accompanied her on the first forage in Bond Street. Hiding a shudder, she eyed her grandmother's old-fashioned clothing. Would her own gowns be the same? Louise drew a quiet breath of relief when Lady Granville surprised her by admitting to Madame Bouchet that she was out of touch with styles for young ladies and needed guidance. The modiste used the word "elegant" to describe Louise, which turned the trick in her favor.

Lady Granville did put up some resistance when Madame Bouchet suggested white muslin was not right for Louise's creamy complexion.

"Grandmother, I am somewhat older than the other girls making their come-out. Perhaps my age will excuse me from wearing the usual styles required for the younger girls." Louise almost held her breath while Lady Granville considered her words. Louise released another soundless sigh of relief when her grandmother accepted the suggestions of ivory, pale jonquil, and other pastel colours. Louise would have preferred deeper shades but accepted the necessity of the lighter hues.

When the daily shopping expeditions ended, Louise approached Lady Granville with a question.

"Grandmother, should I not have my own maid now that we're in Town? Your Simpson has taken good care of me," she assured the older lady. "However, she might now have too many calls on her time to assist me."

"Yes, I rather imagine she will, what with both of us doing the pretty during these weeks. I do not believe anyone else on the staff will suffice. I shall contact the agencies tomorrow."

Sending up a silent prayer, Louise made her awaited request. "May we choose one from the orphanage?" Seeing her grandmother's quick frown, she added, "I realize you want me to grow away from that time in my life. Just once, though, I would like you to meet the matron and see where I lived throughout most of my life. You will see I had good care there. We might find an acceptable maid at the same time. I know the girls there received excellent training in their most suitable abilities."

Her grandmother considered for a moment, a finger tapping her lower lip, a consistent habit when she was in deep thought, Louise had noticed. "Yes, I believe a visit to the orphanage is a sound idea. I have complete confidence in the duchess, even if not in the matron at this point. Just remember that I must approve anyone you choose."

Louise gave her a quick hug as an impish grin stretched across her face. "Do you expect to convince Grandfather that he should offer his protection by accompanying us to Hampshire?"

Lady Granville smiled. "You do realize you are fast wrapping us around your little finger?"

Louise gurgled in response. "I admit I'm trying." In her mind she added, 'However, I don't believe I will ever accomplish that herculean task.'

She had a pleasant two days in Hampshire, renewing old acquaintances and meeting new children. Louise forgot all her lessons in decorum when she flung herself in Matron's arms for a tight embrace. Her eyes filled with tears. Her lips trembled as she whispered in the ear of her substitute mother. "I have missed you beyond anything imaginable."

Turning to her grandparents, she introduced Mrs. Dysart who had kept her in line throughout childhood.

The matron sank into a curtsy. "I'm pleased Louise has found her family. I confess she was one of my favorite children, although she was a rare handful at times."

"She still is," Lady Granville replied, albeit with a smile.

Louise showed rather more propriety when she curtsied to the duchess. She introduced the distinguished couple whom she called grandparents. She did not always get along with them, but she admitted to a feeling of pride when they met the Duchess of Dorchester. Louise gaped with surprise when her reticent grandfather bowed over the bejeweled hand of the duchess and called her Elizabeth. A glance at Grandmother revealed a calm face, but a flash of something in her eyes.

After tea, the marquess broached the possibility of hiring a lady's maid for their granddaughter. "Have you someone you can recommend?"

Louise sustained a noncommittal mien, although her eyes sent a plea when she met the glance of the duchess.

"Yes, I believe Agnes Balder would suit. She received training as a dresser in my own household. She is also adept with hairstyles and quick to learn new duties. She can go to London with you, if you wish."

With agreement reached, the conversation turned toward the past, while the duchess excused Louise to re-visit places from her childhood.

Louise began with the music room, where she rippled a few arpeggios on the piano. From there, she wandered through the rose garden thinking of Rebecca, who had loved it better than any other part of the orphanage. Louise wondered how soon she could see her closest friend. She recalled Agnes Balder from her own years here. Lady Granville's choice for a maid pleased Louise. In the stables, she whispered loving words in her favorite mount's ears while smoothing down his luxurious mane.

Louise knew her grandparents were questioning the duchess about Louise's life at the orphanage. She was not concerned. Louise restrained herself later when saying good-bye to the duchess until her Grace stretched out her arms. Louise was at home again.

On the return trip to London, Louise questioned her grandparents. "You never told me you were acquainted with the duchess."

"Of course, we knew Elizabeth. We know all the aristocracy," her grandmother informed her. "She was a flighty young thing. I'm thankful to see she appears to have settled down."

From the corner of her eye, Louise saw a smile cross Lord Granville's face when he turned it toward the window. Just how intimately had the young Lord Granville known the flighty Elizabeth? Louise knew better than to ask.

Moments after they returned to Chesley Square, several boxes arrived from Madame Bouchet. Louise had never dreamed of owning so many gowns. Morning gowns, afternoon gowns, ball gowns, walking gowns, carriage gowns, riding habits—she would have to change five or six times a day to wear all of them.

Agnes assured her that would indeed be the case. She was a few months younger than her new mistress and had stood in awe of this elegant creature when she, too, was at the orphanage.

Louise remembered Agnes's prosaic attitude and now rejoiced that the duchess had understood her silent plea. She asked, "Agnes, can I trust you to deliver a note for me, without anyone in this house knowing?"

"Oh, yes, my lady, to be sure you can." Agnes glanced toward the door, speaking in a whisper.

Louise laughed. "The message is only to Rebecca Black—do you remember her?" At the maid's nod, Louise continued, "Her real name is Blackwell. You must remember to call her Lady Rebecca because she is the granddaughter of a duke. I also need a note delivered to Mrs. Peters in Harley Street. Agnes, they are dearer to me than anyone. I ache to see them."

"Never mind, everything will come right in time, you will see." With a philosophical nod of her mouse-brown hair, Agnes began straightening the sitting room, while Louise wrote out directions for her to deliver the notes.

Louise had not put her grandparents' strictness to the test in London. She had developed a smoother relationship with them while in the country. Would that ease continue in Town? She learned the answer on the morning after they returned from Hampshire.

Louise would have loved to walk in Hyde Park, yet she knew her grandmother would not permit that. Instead, she chose a quieter park with the hope her grandmother would agree. "Since we are not going shopping this morning, Grandmother, I believe I will take a walk in Green Park. Agnes will accompany me."

"No." Lady Granville stared down her nose. "Young ladies in The Family do not walk in public parks. How could you even contemplate such a thing?"

With a silent groan, Louise attempted to cajole her grandmother. "I realize ladies in The Family would not walk in *Hyde Park*. I would never dream of going there. Green Park is much quieter. I thought it might be acceptable."

"No."

"What about Ranelagh Gardens?" Louise persisted. "They are quiet too."

"You may not walk in any public park. Do you understand?" Her ladyship's icy voice filled the morning room.

Louise strove for control. "Grandmother, I need some exercise."

"You may obtain all the exercise you need in our own garden. Be sure to remain on the graveled path." She turned back to her writing table with a nod of dismissal.

Louise had to get out of the house before her temper erupted. She changed her slippers for a pair of jean half boots. Wearing a chip straw bonnet with a wide brim, she marched round and round on the gravel path of the small garden behind Granville House, her mind in turmoil. Her stride grew shorter as her thoughts grew calmer.

She was back in London. She would not allow disagreements with her obstinate grandparents to destroy her happiness. There were things she could do besides walk in the parks. She would borrow books from Hookham's Circulating Library. She would purchase sheet music from the Exeter Exchange. She might even visit the menagerie. No, the animal odor might cling to her clothing. That certainly would upset her grandparents.

Louise learned that making plans and carrying them out were two different things. Back to her bedchamber, she rang for her maid. "Get your bonnet, Agnes; we're going shopping in a place like none you have ever seen. You will surely be agape with wonder."

"Considering I have never seen any shopping place, I'm sure you're right." The maid's wry comment floated behind her as she quitted the room.

Moments later, Lord Granville's strident voice stopped Louise in her tracks. "Young lady, where are you going?"

Louise wondered with resignation why he did not call her by her name. She stood at the front door, which Foster held open.

"We are going to Hookham's Library and to the Exeter Exchange, Grandfather." Louise kept her tone soft in direct contrast to his overloud voice. "We will return in an hour."

"Why would a lady of The Family go to such places?" His incredulous demand caused Louise to stare in amazement. She managed a civil answer.

"We are going to Hookham's to borrow some books." She stopped herself just in time. It would not do to tell him she intended to purchase sheet music. She remembered the evening at the Manor when she had commented she would purchase new sheet music in London. He had informed her that she did not appear to need any. She told the first deliberate falsehood that she could remember. "At the Exchange, I want to purchase ribbons for the children at the orphanage."

She would make the purchase so it would not be a lie. She soon learned her mistake.

"You will do no such thing. I forbid it," the marquess thundered at her. "Books at Hookham's are trash. Ladies of The Family do *not* read trash. You insisted upon reading the classics. There are plenty of them here, so read them. If you are tired of them, you will find some improving sermons on the shelves."

Granville shook a finger at her. "Let those brats at the orphanage buy their own ribbons. I will remind you that you have no money of your own. I do not intend for mine to be wasted on females who probably are no better than they should be." He strode from the hall, daring her to disobey him when he turned his back.

Louise felt almost faint by the time her grandfather finished his rant. She watched him leave the hall and then, without a word, turned toward the stairs, Agnes at her heels.

Foster closed the door. "My lady, please try to understand. His lordship's digestive system has been troubling him ever since he arrived from the country. London water has never agreed with him when he first gets here on one of his rare visits."

Louise nodded and hurried up the stairs to her bedchamber. There, she paced the floor, muttering to herself, calling down the wrath of the angels on her grandfather. How dared he embarrass her in front of the servants? Her grandparents had not changed, Louise realized with resignation. They accepted her only while she conformed to their ideas.

Agnes tried to comfort her, suggesting tea.

Before it arrived, a footman tapped on the door. "My lady, visitors have arrived. Lady Granville requests your presence in the drawing room."

Louise pasted a smile on her face before entering the drawing room. The smile became genuine when she spied Major Stafford across the room. She greeted her grandmother's cronies, as she handed round the teacups. Louise served the major last and took a chair near him.

"Good afternoon, Major. It is a pleasure to see you here."

"It's a pleasure to be here. Are you enjoying yourself in London?"

Remembering she had told him of her difficulties with her grandparents in the country, she shrugged. "If ever I am allowed to get outside the back garden, perhaps I shall tell you how I enjoy being back in London."

He grinned his appreciation and asked if she was keeping all the modistes busy. When Louise replied, he congratulated her on her purchases. "You appeared to be in something of a dither when you came through the door. More disagreements with the Granvilles?"

"It's just the usual Family arrogance, which I should be accustomed to by now. I suppose I expected it to end when we came to London. I have learned better."

"Perhaps they will loosen their restrictions once you start attending evening festivities."

Louise answered in a low tone. "Whether they do or not, I have made definite plans to meet Rebecca Blackwell at our old flat. I will not miss that excursion, even if it means I must leave through a window."

"Be careful not to break your neck, otherwise think of all the fun you would miss."

Louise felt better after his teasing. She even managed not to upset her grandparents over the next couple of days.

The long-awaited day came. Louise made her escape to Harley Street. Her grandparents were out, so it was not necessary to climb through a window, she thought with a chuckle. She regretted using a closed hackney because she would have liked to see more of the area where she once lived. Louise whiled away the time by telling Agnes something of her earlier stay in London. "You will like Mrs. Peters, Agnes, but you must not heed her horse cant."

"Horse cant, my lady?"

"Yes. You see, she was married for many years to a horse fancier. When she gets excited, she reverts to the language he used, which embarrasses her no end. Rebecca and I became accustomed to it."

"I will ignore it," Agnes promised, as the hackney stopped in front of a well-maintained building in Harley Street.

"Jamison, it is good to see you again." Louise smiled at the doorman, who greeted her with a deep bow.

"Miss Louise, if I may be impertinent, I would like to say I have missed your smiling face. This building just isn't the same without you and Miss Rebecca."

"Thank you, Jamison. I have missed you too." At the entrance to their rooms, Louise greeted the butler. "Good afternoon, Morton. I hope you and Mrs. Morton are well."

"Yes, we are, Miss Louise. May I say you appear in blooming health?" He ushered her through the inner door.

"Should they not call you Lady instead of Miss?" Agnes asked in a whisper.

"To be proper they should. I didn't know of my title when I lived here, so I am Miss to these people. In truth, I prefer to ignore my title."

When Louise entered the familiar drawing room, the misery of the intervening weeks since she was last here faded into nothingness. What fun they'd had furnishing the rooms last spring. A myriad of memories flitted across her mind, as she greeted her companion with a big hug. "Amelia, I declare I don't know how I have managed without you all these weeks."

Mrs. Peters' eyes were moist as she studied the face before her. "I've missed you, too, dear."

"Rebecca is not here? She is coming, though, is she not?"

"Calm yourself, dear, she's coming. You're as frisky as a foal that has just discovered its legs."

"Oh, I have missed your horse cant." Louise turned toward her maid, standing by the door. "This is Agnes Balder, who learned at the orphanage to be a lady's maid. She keeps me in order."

Rebecca's voice preceded her when she erupted into the room, her arms outstretched toward Louise after a quick glance around the room. While the girls clung together, Amelia directed the maid to the kitchen to order tea. A smile settled on Amelia's face as she watched her former charges.

Louise wiped away her tears. "I don't know how I've managed to survive without you, Rebecca. These weeks have been horrible beyond words. I pretended I was talking to you while I wrote in my journal."

"I must admit your letter surprised me. Only my grandparents' strictures kept me from storming the castle, in a manner of speaking. I am tempted to tell the Granvilles what I think of them. I didn't believe anyone could or would keep us apart."

Louise smoothed away the other's ferocious scowl with a quick hug. "I'm here now. No one can keep me away from you ever again."

"How did you persuade them to bring you to Town?"

A soft chuckle accompanied the answer. "I believe they've tolerated me as long as they can. Now they want to find me a husband."

Their conversation turned to Louise's activities since arriving in Town. Rebecca must hear every detail of the visit to the orphanage. She reciprocated with a minute account of her social life.

"Have you met any fops, Rebecca? Or dandies?"

"Oh, yes. Also, court-cards and wags. Just wait until your first ball. You'll see all of them. They're a common sight in Society."

"That will be this evening. I can hardly wait. Heavens, has it been two hours already? I must return to Chesley Square before Grandmother misses me. Are you going to the Haverfords' ball? You are? Stupendous! This is my first big party. Grandmother is in an even bigger dither than I am."

With that, Louise rushed to the door calling for Agnes.

Chapter 7

Her First Ball

Louise stared at the stranger who returned her gaze from the mirror. Pierre had performed an amazing work of art with her hair. Gone was the length she had worn since childhood. Her now shorter auburn hair was a mass of curls around her face, softening the contours of her high cheekbones. The cream-coloured silk gown, edged with matching rosettes around the low square neck, fell from its high waist straight to the matching dancing slippers emphasizing her height. Louise felt the need for some jewelry, but the cream-coloured silk flowers in her hair would have to do.

In alt, Louise had to force herself to remain calm, while she waited for Lady Granville's approval. She sat on the edge of a chair and allowed herself to think of the major. Would he be at the Haverford ball? Louise wanted to see his reaction to her new coiffure.

Her grandmother's knock brought Louise to her feet. She gazed with admiration at the older lady. The sight stunned her. Lady Granville's gown was an awesome expanse of purple brocade, which extended upward at the back, creating a high, stiff collar. Louise had never seen that style. Had she realized it, nor had anyone else seen the style in forty years.

"Grandmother, you are beautiful."

Lady Granville's austere face softened into a smile. She inspected her granddaughter from head to toe before handing to her a small oblong box.

With considerable curiosity, Louise raised the lid, a gasp escaping her gaping mouth at the sight of a double strand of perfectly matched, creamy pearls. "Am I to wear this?"

"They belonged to my grandmother. Now they have come down to you," was the gruff reply. "They suit you better than me. Turn around, so I can fasten them."

Turning from the mirror, Louise gave her grandmother a quick hug. "I am happy you trust me with a family heirloom. I am sure I do not show them to the advantage you did when you wore them."

Hiding her pleasure with a grunt, the marchioness turned toward the door. "It's time to go. We must not keep your grandfather waiting."

Half an hour later, Louise mounted the stairs at Haverford House, where Marie greeted her. "I am glad you came to our ball, Louise. I've spent considerable time with Rebecca and love her already. I know I will love you too when we have become acquainted."

Louise chuckled at the exuberance. This was the first time she had seen the petite, blue-eyed Marie since they met at Shelburne Park—the day of infinite surprise when Louise learned she had some family. "I want to know you better too," she assured the third girl who shared her names.

When Rebecca arrived, Lady Becca Haverford excused Marie to join her new friends.

"Since you girls know few people, I will find you partners for some of the dances. Shelburne will dance with both of you, naturally. Still, you must not expect partners for many dances." Marie smiled in a condescending way. "I know everyone here, so I will stand up for every dance."

Louise and Rebecca exchanged amused smiles. Rebecca had already attended several parties. She would have no difficulty obtaining dance partners. Louise could be confident of only one dance partner— Major Stafford, if he could perform the steps despite his limp. Otherwise, she feared she would spend the entire evening sitting on one of the gilt chairs lining the wall.

Louise felt like a fish out of water when she entered the ballroom, which was aglow with several candelabras. She welcomed Lord Shelburne's appearance with considerable relief.

"Good evening, ladies." He turned toward the marchioness. "My lady, may I find a suitable partner for Lady Louise?"

"You're very kind, my lord. I will appreciate your doing so." She watched his maneuvers sorting out dance partners for a moment before joining the other chaperones lining the wall.

Shelburne sent his niece, Marie, off to dance with the first young buck who caught his eye. He snagged his friend, Sir Justin Morrison, to escort Louise. With a smile, he took Rebecca by the arm, leading her into the dance. Unofficial or not, Louise knew that both he and Rebecca considered their betrothal a fact. Shelburne would not willingly find other dance partners for his love.

Louise managed not to stare at the ivory-paneled walls interspersed with long windows draped in soft shades of green and gold. Throughout the evening, more than one of her dance partners vowed the room set off her beauty to perfection. With dimples on constant parade, Louise accepted all compliments without remembering the names of even one admirer.

A couple of hours later, Louise and Rebecca sent smiles of gratitude toward the young men, who volunteered to get lemonade for them. The girls sat near Lady Granville to catch their breath after a strenuous Scottish reel. Louise wafted her fan to cool her heated face. "I've stood up for every dance, what about you?"

"I have too. I am happy to sit out this one. I wonder if Marie noticed we danced every dance. She didn't find us even one partner."

"Marie has been much too busy with her own admirers. She is quite lovely. I would have expected her to make a match in the Spring Season." Louise's voice held only admiration for the way Marie kept her coterie of young men dangling.

The young lady in question arrived beside her friends at the same time their escorts delivered the lemonade. Mr. Wood and Mr. Seton flushed when the diminutive charmer pouted at her empty hand held in front of their faces. Both gentlemen thrust their own glasses toward her. With a giggle, Marie debated which to accept. Lady Becca solved her daughter's dilemma when she joined them and relieved Mr. Seton of his glass, with the suggestion the gentlemen obtain more beverages for themselves.

"I can see you girls are enjoying yourselves. Have you noticed how many of my friends are staring at the three of you? I knew you would set the *ton* on its ear when you appeared together."

Indeed, the *ton* was abuzz with speculation about the newcomers who resembled two young ladies of a generation earlier. The scandalous double elopement, aided by a third girl, had been a seven-day wonder. Now, their daughters had turned up. They bid fair to being more beautiful than their mothers had been. There was one perplexing thing—their names. Each had a face resembling her mother, but their names were the same as other members of the threesome who had set the *ton* on its collective ear some twenty years before.

Becca turned toward her namesake. "I saw you talking to Lady Catherine Callandar earlier, my dear. Did you enjoy the chat? She can be difficult since her memory isn't what it once was."

"Is she the lady wearing the purple turban?" At the affirmative nod, Rebecca said, "Try though I did, I don't believe I convinced her I am not my mother. She called me the wrong name the entire time I sat with her, even introduced me by Mother's name to the lady wearing crimson plumes in her hair."

Louise interjected, "I haven't talked to those ladies, but do you see the elderly gentleman just coming out of the card room? He is convinced I am my mother. A couple of his remarks made me wonder how well he knew her."

"He pursued Marie—your mother—not my daughter. How confusing these names are, but such fun we had all those years ago dreaming up the scheme. Anyway, he believed the daughter of a vicar would be the perfect stepmother for his numerous offspring, completely ignoring the fact she was very little older than his oldest daughter."

Becca grinned. "I personally counseled her to avoid him like the plague. His sons were little hellions, completely out of control. I know, because their land is very near our country home. He never found a wife who would take on their upbringing. His housekeepers left on a regular basis. As each son reached an appropriate age, he stuck them in the army."

She glanced around the room and lowered her voice even more. "Heavens, just listen to me, gossiping like an old biddy."

Louise glanced at her grandmother. It would not do for that lady to hear this conversation. The arrival of dance partners ended the chatter. Receiving a nod of approval from her grandmother, Louise accepted the arm of a blushing young gentleman for the country set, just beginning.

Later in the evening, Louise stood alone while her dance partner went in search of a glass of lemonade. She had felt someone staring at her throughout the last dance and now glanced around the ballroom. Her eyes locked with a pair of smoky blue eyes set in a cheerful countenance below fair hair cut in what she now knew was a Bedford crop.

Major Stafford had arrived. Catching her eye, he directed a bow toward her.

Louise had looked for him all evening—had almost despaired of his coming. His evening clothes hugged his broad shoulders like a glove. He seemed almost a stranger. In confusion, Louise turned away. Before she could accept lemonade from Simon Abernathy, the marchioness appeared before her.

"Come, it is time we leave." Without waiting for a reply, she started toward the door.

Louise glanced at her cavalier in bewilderment, noting the sardonic expression on his face, his hands still holding the glasses of lemonade. She had wanted to ask him if he knew the Abernathies in Oxfordshire, whom she had visited during the summer. Her question would have to wait for another time. Louise followed her grandmother.

In the carriage, Louise attempted to discuss the ball with her grandmother, who ordered her to be quiet. "I will talk to you at home. I hope you have an acceptable explanation for your disgraceful behavior."

Louise sat in stunned silence, reviewing her actions throughout the evening. When they arrived at Granville House, she followed the marchioness into a small sitting room on the first floor.

"Explain yourself."

"Grandmother, I have no idea what I have done wrong. All the way home, I tried to remember anything disgraceful I did. I cannot think of a thing. I didn't dance more than twice with any gentleman. I sat out the waltz. I smiled and chatted to everyone who spoke. I didn't drink champagne. I returned to your side after every dance."

"Not the last one. Who introduced that loose fish to you anyway? I did not. Surely Shelburne knows better. You not only danced with a gazetted fortune hunter, you stayed with him after the dance. You even allowed him to leave you standing alone while he went for beverages. No respectable girl would even speak to him."

Louise pulled her mental faculties together. "Are you speaking of Mr. Simon Abernathy? You were talking at the end of the last dance. Your friend, Lady Hardwick kindly ...."

"Lady Hardwick is no friend of mine—she will do anything to spite me."

"Grandmother, she told me she has been a close friend of yours since childhood, that you came out together. She said you had remained friends until you and Grandfather retired to Granville Manor. How could I know otherwise?"

Lady Granville didn't answer, simply nodded her dismissal, but Louise persisted.

"If Mr. Abernathy is such a terrible person, why is he received by the Haverfords? I saw him dancing with several young ladies."

"The Family does not receive Simon Abernathy. The marquess and I have agreed we must allow you to have this time in London. Nevertheless, we draw the line at associating with Abernathy. You will not speak to him again. Do you understand?"

"Yes, I understand. I suggest you make a list of who is acceptable to The Family, if anyone is, so I will not err again." Louise rushed from the room, slamming the door behind her.

After she dismissed her maid, Louise crawled between the sheets, where she stared into the darkness of the canopy overhead. Is this how her entire time in London would be, never knowing who was an acceptable acquaintance or dance partner? Louise had known she must return to her chaperone's side after every dance. Had not her grandmother lectured her on that point during the carriage ride? While it was true that she had not returned precisely to Lady Granville's side, she was within that lady's view when Mr. Abernathy went to obtain lemonade. Louise had done nothing which would excuse Lady Granville for humiliating her by such an abrupt departure. What had Major Stafford thought?

The major stared in astonishment when Louise Mansfield disappeared through the door. He was late arriving at the Haverford's townhouse because he had allowed himself to linger over dinner with some friends. He had planned to dance with Louise despite his limp, regardless of what others thought of his awkwardness. Now, he would have to wait for another opportunity. There would be other occasions.

Stafford wondered why Lady Granville left in such a hurry. It appeared her granddaughter had done something to upset her. The major couldn't think what that could be. True, she had danced with a known fortune hunter—heiresses could hardly avoid them in Society. Louise Mansfield would dance with plenty of others. Perhaps he should just give her a hint when next they met. That meeting occurred the following day.

Foster ushered him into the drawing room at Granville House at one o'clock. If the major hoped to be the first caller to arrive, he was disappointed. Babbling voices filled the room. He had to weave through a crowd to reach his hostess. Lady Granville sat in regal splendor behind the tea tray, a fierce scowl on her face. Stafford gathered his courage to greet her with a smile, while he accepted a cup of tea.

"Good afternoon, Lady Granville. It appears your granddaughter has become an instant success, the new toast of the *ton*, in fact."

"Bunch of toadeaters with empty pockets," she muttered. "Not one of them up to scratch."

"She's a beautiful young lady, Ma'am. I'm confident your granddaughter would attract an instant crowd regardless of her expected wealth."

The marchioness stared at him. "If you believe that, you have an empty cockloft."

She didn't say "also empty pockets," but Stafford received her message. He curbed a smile at her use of cant, even as he bowed and moved toward Louise. The major studied her strained countenance for a moment before insinuating himself into the crowd of dandies surrounding her. The fawning pups took one look at the newcomer and then faded away.

"I see you're entertaining the pick of the collective litter, roaming among the *beau monde*."

"Pick of the litter, Major? Not according to my grandmother."

He didn't know how to answer her bitterness. Lady Granville had obviously read her a homily. Stafford didn't want to add to her discomfort, yet Lady Louise must understand the lure of her expectations as the heir to a vast fortune. He amended his thought. Being a female, Lady Louise was not heir to the marquisate, though she could expect a more than adequate dowry. He considered his words with care.

"I suppose your grandparents do seem rigid in their standards, quite old-fashioned in fact. Nonetheless, they must shield you from undesirable men to protect your future."

"Undesirable by what standards, Major? Is a gentleman undesirable because he is not as rich as Croseus or a blueblood of rank above a duke?" Louise gave him a scathing look. "If either is the criteria for judging people, I should not be here. After all, my father was a penniless horse trader."

Her blunt statement silenced him for a moment. "Your father was what he chose to be. He did not gamble away his fortune, which many of these men did."

"Many did, perhaps, but not all. Although she introduced all except one of them to me, Grandmother condemned everyone I danced with last evening. Every one of them, mind you. How do you explain that away, Major?"

Before he could reply, Louise turned her attention toward a hollow-eyed young gentleman who began spouting nonsense about the shell-like ears peeping from beneath her glorious halo of curls. With a disgusted glare at the cork-brained youth, Major Stafford quitted the room.

Driving away from Chesley Square, Stafford's thoughts were on the bitter girl he left behind. He resisted even admitting his attraction to her, yet he was not sure what caused the resistance. Lady Louise Mansfield was beautiful, witty, not the least bit missish. Ah, was that the problem? Girls making their come-out were supposed to be missish, were they not? Lowering their eyelids or peeking from behind a fan? Did her lack of missishness translate into forwardness? Stafford shook his head. He would have to spend more time in her presence to figure out what his feelings really were.

He smiled at the thought of being with the auburn-haired beauty.

Over the succeeding days and evenings, Louise kept a steady rein on her temper during Lady Granville's strictures. She was careful to dance only with the gentlemen her grandmother introduced, returning precisely to her side. Lady Granville still condemned them.

One such incident occurred after Louise returned from an afternoon visit with Rebecca Blackwell. Louise had taken her frustrations to her long-time friend, who listened while Louise paced the floor.

"I am confined to the point I cannot call my soul my own. They don't approve of any of my dance partners, even though Grandmother introduces them. They ordered me not to walk in any public park. They refuse to allow me to attend a concert, yet they know how much I love music. Grandmother loves music, too, just not in a public forum. She did accompany me to Lady Edgeware's musicale last night but dragged me out at intermission."

Rebecca stared at her in wonder. "Was the music so bad?"

"She said Paganini playing his violin is heathenish," Louise explained. "Paganini, mind you. One of the greatest violinists of our time."

"Louise, this restlessness is not like you. Please sit here beside me. We must discuss this matter."

"I have never felt so criticized or condemned in my entire life," Louise said as she joined Rebecca on the sofa. "Why can they not appreciate me for what I am instead of criticizing me for what I am not? The Triple D never made me feel worthless. She is a high stickler too."

"I agree our Darling Duchess of Dorchester is all we believe the aristocracy should be. However, she is out of the common way. We must not judge others by her." A rueful smile crossed Rebecca's face. "Just listen to me prattle on. I am truly sorry you have such difficulties with your grandparents."

"I truly wish I had never learned of my family connections." Louise's voice trailed away to nothing, a tender smile crossing her face. "That is not quite true. I doubt I would otherwise have met George. I could not bear that." Louise glanced at Rebecca when she realized she had used the major's given name.

Her friend gazed at her with surprise. "Who is George?"

"Major George Stafford, a gentleman I met several times while I was in the country. Here in Town too. He is a friend of Lord Shelburne, have you not met him?"

With a quick hug, Rebecca replied, "Yes, I have. He is Shelburne's best friend. He must be acceptable to your grandparents."

"You cannot be serious. His family estate marches with Granville Manor. My grandparents only brought me to London to get me away from him."

Rebecca answered with surprise. "His family has a lesser title, but their fortune is more than respectable. There is nothing disreputable about their lineage, and I understand that he distinguished himself in several battles. Wellington even mentioned him in dispatches on more than one occasion according to the news sheets. That should count for something with Lord Granville."

"Nothing counts with either of my grandparents except family name." Louise took a deep breath—her determined gaze on Rebecca's face. "I have decided to go back to Harley Street. I believe Major Stafford would seek me out there."

"I'm sure he would if he is truly interested in you," Rebecca assured her. "Do you not see? The Granvilles would force you to return because you are a minor. They would probably take you back to the country."

"Oh no, I cannot tolerate living there under their restrictions. Never to see you? Those few weeks we were apart were the longest of my life. I shan't go through such misery again."

"Louise, ask yourself what Matron used to ask us. 'What choices do you have'?"

They were quiet while Louise came to terms with what she knew she must do. With a heartfelt sigh, she admitted the obvious. "I shall strive to obey their wishes. They don't make obedience easy."

When Louise left Rebecca's sitting room, she was in no better frame of mind than when she had arrived. Entering the Granville's landau, she ordered the coachman to drive through Hyde Park. She ignored his surprised glance as he put the horses in motion. Louise relaxed during the drive, returning to Chesley Square calmer than when she left earlier. The calmness lasted until she made the mistake of telling her grandmother that several people in the park sent their regards. She was not prepared for the result.

Lady Granville stared with astonishment at her granddaughter. "Hyde Park? What were you doing there? Ladies in the Family do not disport themselves in Hyde Park."

This statement produced a protest. "I was not walking or riding in Hyde Park, Grandmother. I was seated sedately in an open carriage driven by our own coachman, properly chaperoned by my maid."

Before the marchioness could speak, Louise explained her actions. "Grandfather said ladies of The Family don't ride horses, they ride in carriages pulled by horses. That is what I was doing."

The marchioness was adamant. "Ladies of The Family simply do not display themselves in any fashion in Hyde Park, where they might be observed by the rabble."

Louise reached the point of standing with polite attention, her lashes lowered to hide the hurt, while her grandmother ranted. When Lady Granville grew silent, Louise walked out the door without responding.

Had Louise not reached the point of rebellion for its own sake, perhaps she would not have rushed headlong into another escapade guaranteed to upset her grandparents and set the *ton* on its ear.

Chapter 8

Oh, The Upheaval!

Late the following morning, Louise strode along the graveled path of the garden behind Granville House. Her feet ached already. She should have worn half boots.

"Why must Grandmother pinch at me over every little thing I do?" she muttered in a savage tone. "I'm tired of being confined like a schoolroom chit. I dare say I am the only person in the *ton* who cannot appear in Hyde Park at the fashionable hour. Grandmother's strictures are ridiculous."

This thought came as she stood in front of a gate leading out into the mews. Succumbing to an impulse, Louise slipped through the opening. Seeing no one around, she scurried toward the street turning away from Granville House. A few minutes of walking brought her to a busy thoroughfare. Waiting for an opportunity to cross the road, Louise spied her old friend, Toby Williams, whom she had known when she lived in Harley Street. Waving, she caught his attention and waited while he maneuvered his whiskey to her side of the road.

"Good morning, Mr. Williams."

"A good morning to you, Miss Tracy," he answered, tipping his hat. "Oh, pardon me, you are not Miss Tracy now, are you?"

A slight grimace crossed her face. "Not any more, I regret to say. I would rather have my old name."

"Here now, we cannot talk with you standing in the road. I must not keep my horse standing either. Perhaps I can drive you to your destination if you will direct me."

"Oh, I am only getting some air," Louise answered with aplomb, ignoring the fact she should have a maid or footman with her. "I would enjoy a drive."

Grasping the reins in one hand, Toby helped her into the carriage with the other. "Where shall we go?"

"Let us just go where the mood takes us, shall we?" Louise asked with an impish grin. She had not felt this carefree since she learned her true identity.

Returning her grin, Toby urged the horse forward with a light touch of his whip. When they reached a corner, he turned onto a quieter street where they could more easily converse.

Louise explained her present circumstances, avoiding mention of titles. They soon were in conversation about mutual friends. Neither noticed the passage of time nor where they were going as they relived the few months they had been acquainted earlier in the year. Oh, the parties they'd had in the Harley Street rooms!

Returning to an awareness of the present, Louise glanced around. "I don't recognize this street. Where are we?"

"St. James Street," Toby Williams replied.

"Oh." Louise looked about her before asking in a subdued voice, "Am I correct that this is the street where the gentlemen's clubs are located?"

"That's right," he assured her. "We passed Boodles'. White's is just ahead of us. We might see Brummell standing in the bow window, which was added this year."

Dear me, Louise thought in panic. I have truly outdone myself this time. Perhaps no one will recognize me. I'm here. I will enjoy myself. She nodded at some gentlemen, who tipped their hats to her. Nevertheless, Louise breathed easier when the carriage turned onto King Street.

"Do you go to Almack's, Miss Tr, uh, Mansfield?" Mr. Williams inquired.

"Not yet," she replied.

"You might not be aware the assembly room is just there." He nodded toward an undistinguished building, which had little to recommend it to any observer.

"How plain it is," Louise exclaimed in surprise. "I had thought it would be more ornate."

The knowledge she was in a place she should avoid caused her heart to thud. Grasping her usual poise, Louise said she should perhaps return to Chesley Square. When they reached the corner closest to Granville House, she avoided his surprised glance when she asked him to stop.

She slipped along the road to the mews and into the garden by the back gate. There she gasped in horror when she saw her grandmother working with the flowers. Edging backward toward the gate, Louise's one thought was to get around to the front door where Foster would let her in without any fuss. It was not to be.

"Louise, what are you doing here? I thought you were in your room. Where is your maid? Explain yourself."

Louise cringed while Lady Granville hurled harsh words toward her. Keeping her face expressionless, she replied, "I went for a stroll."

"Who gave you permission to leave the premises? Without your maid or a footman too."

"No one."

"Tell me where you went, who you saw, you shameless girl."

No matter what else might be said of her, honesty was a natural part of Louise's character. She prized it in others, so honesty was the only answer now. Therefore, she gave a succinct account of her morning's activities, all the time speaking in a level tone but hiding a quaking heart.

"You have been driving about the City with a stranger without even a groom beside you?"

"While it is true no groom accompanied me, I was not riding with a stranger. Mr. Williams is an old friend, a respectable gentleman."

"He is not gentleman—he's a Cit."

"His behavior is what a gentleman's behavior should be but too often is not."

"I want to hear no more of your impertinence, do you understand me? If word of this gets around, you will never get vouchers to Almack's. Come, we must apprise the marquess of your behavior at once." Tossing her gloves onto a bench, she marched into the house.

Louise followed and stood at attention in the library during her grandfather's thundering tirade. "You reprehensible chit, how much more wanton behavior must we expect from you? Your shocking behavior is a disgrace to The Family. You will go to your rooms where you will remain until we decide what to do with you."

Without uttering a word, Louise left the room. In her sitting room, she ignored her maid, who took one look at her face before hurrying away. Half an hour later, Lady Granville entered.

"We have reached a decision," she announced. "You will stay at home this evening. Your grandfather goes to his club. I go to Lady Melville's card party. If there's any gossip about you, we will decide what to do about you."

Louise inclined her head but refrained from speaking until, with relief, she heard the door close after her grandmother's exit. Louise received supper on a tray. Her actions of the morning kept her mind in a whirl. How could she be so thoughtless as to indulge her temper in such a way? What would the major think if he heard about it? Perhaps no one had recognized her. How could they avoid recognizing her? The bonnet she had worn boasted only a narrow brim. Louise released a deep sigh. There was nothing else for it— she would have to pay the consequences of her behavior.

Thus, she was able to bear with equanimity her grandmother's blistering scold the following morning over breakfast. Louise was the talk of the *beau monde* because numerous personages had seen her driving around Town unaccompanied.

"Your grandfather feels that perhaps, just perhaps, the *ton* will excuse your behavior based on your upbringing at the orphanage. Nevertheless, you will have to face the questions and innuendoes hurled at your head."

With breakfast over, Lady Granville glared at Louise. "You will go to your room until summoned. It is too much to hope we will not have visitors."

Louise remained at the table for several minutes after her grandmother left the room. "Foster, I need to talk with Lady Rebecca. May I ask you to have a message delivered to her and then show her to my sitting room when she arrives?"

He answered the plea in her voice. "Alright, my lady, I will do as you ask."

Louise pushed back her chair. "I shall write the note. You are a good friend, Foster. I don't know how I would go on without you."

At her writing table, Louise scrawled a few words on a sheet of stationery. "I'm in disgrace again. I need you, my bestest of friends."

Half an hour later, a scratch on her door heralded Rebecca's arrival. Without a word, Louise pulled her into the room and clung to her, neither noticing when Agnes closed the door.

Rebecca pulled away from Louise but held her hand as she led the trembling girl to a chair. "Now, my dear, tell me how I can help."

"You must have heard the gossip last night. My grandparents said my name was on every lip."

"I did hear something about a drive," Rebecca admitted after a moment. "Perhaps you should give me the details."

Louise moaned. "I never do anything right in my grandparents' eyes. Yesterday I rebelled without giving the consequences a thought. I went for a walk without escort. When I met Toby Williams nearby, I asked him to take me for a drive."

After hearing a gasp, Louise turned her face away rather than see Rebecca's dismay. When she finished the tale, she waited for whatever was to come.

"What did the Granvilles say?" Rebecca asked after a long pause.

"They believe the *ton* will excuse my behavior because of my upbringing in an orphanage, which is unfair. You know the duchess schooled us in proper behavior. I cannot—will not—allow criticism to touch the orphanage."

"What will you do?"

With a defiant toss of her auburn curls, Louise answered, "I shall tell anyone impertinent enough to comment that I knew better, that my actions were thoughtless, not the result of my upbringing."

"I believe it highly unlikely that your reason will satisfy your grandparents, but I believe both the matron and the duchess would approve. You know you have my support in whatever you do."

"Yes, I do know, although I don't know why you bear with my bird-witted behavior the way you do."

"Because we're 'bestest friends,' or have you forgotten you declared we would be on the day I most needed a friend?"

With a quick hug, Louise assured her she had not forgotten that long ago day when Rebecca arrived at the orphanage. Now, they walked arm-in-arm to the door.

Rebecca's visit helped Louise cast off her megrims for a short while. Throughout the day, she received several homilies by her grandparents and endured the stares from the morning callers who kept the doorknocker busy. Louise managed to restrain her temper while enduring twitting by one old harridan who was the only visitor with the audacity to reprove her. She made up for the rest of the old biddies.

Louise's worst moment had been when Major Stafford arrived in late afternoon. His expression was grim, his smokey blue eyes accusing as he bowed over her hand.

"My lady, I trust I find you well?"

"Yes, Major. You?"

"I believe disquieted is a better word to describe my feelings at the moment."

Louise controlled her expression. "Why are you disquieted, sir?"

"I have heard some disturbing comments about you," he replied. "How could you be so ill-advised as to drive down St. James Street? Do you not know better? Surely your grandmother informed you, even if those people at the orphanage didn't."

"Yes, I do know better because I received thorough instruction from the Duchess of Dorchester. I met an old friend and became so lost in conversation I did not notice where we were. By the time I realized it, we were already on St. James Street. We did turn off at the first possible moment."

Stafford leaned down to hear her whispered explanation. His expression softened to a small degree. "That's what comes from associating with the lower classes, Lady Louise. They do not know the rules of polite Society."

Louise bit her tongue on the words she wanted to hurl at his head. He was right, because Toby Williams had not known to avoid the area. Nonetheless, she resented having her friends called lower class.

"You will know to be more careful of your acquaintances in the future." With a nod, Stafford left the room.

Louise fumed in silence throughout the remainder of the long day and the evening, excusing herself when Foster removed the tea tray.

To regain a degree of calmness, Louise stood at the window of her bedchamber, staring out at the evening sky.

The movement of scattered clouds dancing across the heavens gave her a measure of peace. Louise thought of the major, but knew with bitterness he was not acceptable to The Family. They considered him in the same low class as the major considered Toby Williams. She didn't question why she wanted to be with Stafford, even though she acknowledged they had no future. After her latest escapade, he would not care to pursue their acquaintance beyond the ordinary. Nevertheless, Louise determined she would accept every possible opportunity to be with him, even though she had to be devious at times.

The Covington ball, which took place a couple of evenings after her cork-brained drive with Toby Williams, presented Louise with one such opportunity. She welcomed it.

From the corner of her eye, she saw the major arrive, while she endured a *contredanse* with one of her grandfather's cronies. When the dance ended, she turned in the direction of the major. Her escort perforce had to follow. "Good evening, Major."

"It is a pleasure to see you this evening, Lady Louise. May I have this dance, please?"

Without sparing a glance at her dance card or a thought for her grandmother, Louise ignored the older man's spluttering and accepted the major's arm. He had not ignored her. With a sigh of relief, she floated through the movements as though in a dream, a contented smile on her face each time they met in the dance. If his limp interfered with his enjoyment, Louise was not aware of it. She was unable later to recall anything about the evening after their one dance.

Until, her grandmother called down the wrath of the angels on her head.

"You are a disgrace to our name, dancing with Stafford. I have never witnessed such an idiotic expression displayed on your countenance for the *ton* to see. Stafford is so far beneath The Family that we brought you to London to get you away from him." Her catalog of misdemeanors stopped. In her excitement, Lady Granville had forgotten Louise was not supposed to know why they had brought her to Town.

"I know you did, Grandmother. Your actions were obvious even to the meanest intelligence. I am not stupid, even though both you and Grandfather choose to believe I am."

"You will not throw yourself away on a mere baron. I forbid it. Do you understand me?"

Louise ignored the question. "Major Stafford's lineage is beyond question, his fortune is respectable, he is a close friend of the Earl of Shelburne. Therefore, he should be acceptable."

"What do you know about his lineage or his friends or his fortune?"

"I made it my business to find out because you consider those things important." In truth, she had asked Rebecca to find out what she could about the major by some judicious questioning of Shelburne.

When the tirade continued, Louise walked out of the room. She did not answer the maid's chatter while Agnes prepared her for bed.

Nonetheless, she stared out her window, fighting tears over her grandparents' obsession with lineage and wealth.

The strain between Lady Granville and Louise was obvious, which led to whispers in the ballroom. When the gossip reached White's later in the evening, the marquess realized he must intervene. He spoke to his marchioness after Louise had retired.

"The club was buzzing tonight about you and Louise."

"Despicable though it is, I can certainly understand people are talking about her, but why would they talk about me?"

In the face of her belligerence, Granville chose his words with care. In truth, the comments he had heard about himself dismayed him. He had given serious thought to the situation, while he waited for the ladies to return home from their evening activities.

"I am afraid it is the same situation we went through with Jonathan. People believe we are unreasonable in our expectations, that we place too much emphasis on our lineage."

"We have good reason to have high expectations," the marchioness declared. "How else can we maintain the purity of our family lines?"

Granville ran his hands through his thick silver hair. "We have searched our family trees trying to find her a suitable match. We must lower our standards some. There simply is no one with a comparable bloodline."

Lady Granville grimaced. "When we think about it, we must admit our bloodline has already been tainted by the red-haired chit who trapped our misguided son. How he could allow her to persuade him into an elopement is beyond me. He should have married his cousin, as we wished."

The marquess agreed. "There is nothing we can do about that now."

They discussed the matter a few minutes longer reaching an agreement to draw the line at rakes and fortune hunters, regardless of their lineage, but to relax their requirements otherwise. Perhaps they could find an eligible earl at the very least if they persevered in their efforts. They certainly would not go any lower.

With this decision, Granville hoped the strain between the ladies of his house would ease.

While the Granvilles discussed their recalcitrant granddaughter, the major lounged in an oversized leather chair, his injured limb propped on an ottoman. He had returned to his Jermyn Street rooms after his dance with Louise Mansfield. The dance had been too much strain. He was paying for it now, yet he would not have missed the opportunity of dancing with her.

Staring into space, the major allowed his mind to dwell on Louise's many qualities. Her simple acknowledgment that she knew better than to appear on St. James Street had surprised him. Most chits would have used any excuse possible to avoid being thought in the wrong. Not Louise Mansfield, Stafford thought with satisfaction. Her ready acceptance of her misbehavior indicated an innate honesty almost unknown in ladies of the *ton*. Or any other ladies he had ever encountered. The Hampshire orphanage had a lot to commend it if all the girls turned out as well.

Chapter 9

From Minor Key to Major Key

*My life has returned to a major key,
beginning at breakfast this morning. I
can only hope the détente will last.*

Louise chewed the end of the quill she was using for a journal entry, her first in several days. With Rebecca nearby to share her thoughts, Louise did not feel the necessity to resort to pen and paper. She thought back to the breakfast parlor conversation. She was aware that she interrupted her grandparents' conversation when she entered. She bid them a good morning and filled a plate with toast and buttered eggs from the sideboard before joining them at the table.

Lord Granville cleared his throat. "Louise, we have something to say to you."

Louise lifted her eyes to his face, retaining a bland expression even though she cringed inside. "Yes, Grandfather."

"We have come to realize several changes have taken place since we were in Town. We recognize we have been unduly strict with you." When Granville poured himself another cup of tea, his wife spoke.

"We realize it is acceptable for ladies of quality to attend public events. Therefore, we will take steps today to hire an opera box for the remainder of the time we're here, if such is available."

Louise lifted shining eyes to her grandmother. "Oh, thank you, Ma'am. I learned just yesterday that a renowned pianist will perform the works of Mozart beginning at the end of this week. I will enjoy hearing him play. I am sure you will too," Louise added.

Her grandfather drew her attention back to him. "We also accept that it is proper to, ah, disport yourself in Hyde Park during the fashionable hour. I have sent a groom to Granville Manor with instructions to bring Juno to Town."

Louise rewarded him with a dazzling smile. Her words tumbled over each other in her eagerness. "Thank you, Grandfather. I have truly missed riding. When will she arrive?"

"The groom should return in two days."

Louise didn't know why they had changed their minds, but she welcomed whatever degree of freedom she would now have. She must tell Rebecca on the instant. Therefore after breakfast, she ordered the landau to carry her to Amesbury House.

"Rebecca, you will never guess what has happened." Louise had barely waited until the maid closed the door, leaving the girls alone.

"I won't try," replied Rebecca with a grin, "Tell me. What has happened to put you in alt?"

"My grandparents have decided to relax their restrictions to some extent. We are to have a box at the opera if Grandfather can obtain one. He has sent for Juno too."

Their conversation stopped when the footman entered with a tea tray but resumed after the door closed behind him.

"I wonder what brought about the change," Rebecca mused, as she handed her guest a cup of tea. "I heard some comments that you and Lady Granville do not appear to be on good terms."

Louise placed the teacup on a small table at her elbow. "I must admit we have created something of a spectacle a few times. Always over my misbehavior. My grandparents did admit they had been too strict. Perhaps that is why they have relaxed their views.

Regardless, I intend to enjoy myself while their lenience lasts."

"Shall we take advantage of your newfound freedom by visiting Amelia Peters? I've been too busy to see her in several days."

"I have seen her only the one time since my return to Town." Louise thought for a moment. "I must do some shopping this afternoon because my gloves are in deplorable condition. So, tomorrow afternoon?"

After visiting the glover, Louise went to Hookham's Library where she spent two hours happily browsing the shelves. She hoped to find a new novel by the lady who wrote *Sense and Sensibility*. The clerk advised she had not published one so far that year.

"I would like to know 'the Lady's' name. She might be someone we know."

"If she is indeed a lady, revealing her name would ruin her in Society," the clerk said. "Maria Edgeworth does not have that problem. Perhaps you would care to read her new novel instead. I understand *Vivian* is her best effort to date."

"She doesn't measure up to 'the Lady.' I do enjoy her books, though, so I will take *Vivian*." Louise tucked the book under her arm and motioned for her maid to find the coachman.

The following afternoon, Louise took up Rebecca in the Granville landau for their drive to Harley Street. "I really do miss living in this part of the City. I almost wish I were back here. Mayfair is a different world, is it not?"

Rebecca agreed. Her employment with a solicitor in the City had not damaged her in Shelburne's eyes because he had never considered her lowborn, even though she had to earn her living. "I do not want to return to Mr. Wright's office to work, yet I must admit I would not trade those months for anything. Can you imagine never having known our dear Amelia?"

"And her horse cant." Louise burst into laughter, which lasted until Jamison opened the door of the Harley Street building.

"It's good to see you ladies again."

"Thank you, Jamison," They answered in unison, then hurried up the broad stairs to their former rooms. The butler was on the lookout for them and opened the door before they could knock.

"Good afternoon, Morton. Is this not a *stupendous* day?" Louise inquired, directing a wicked grin toward Rebecca, who shook a playful finger at her.

He stood back for them to enter the drawing room before hurrying to the kitchen for a tea tray. By the time he returned, the girls had finished greeting their former chaperone.

Mrs. Peters motioned them to chairs across from her seat behind the tea tray.

The girls chattered over the teacups.

"How is Mr. Rogers, Amelia? Is he still enamored of you?" Louise teased her. A dull red stain rose above Amelia's collar, moving upward to her hairline. Louise exchanged a glance with Rebecca before turning back to Amelia. "I do believe you are blushing. Have you something to tell us?"

Mrs. Peters' teacup rattled in its saucer when she set it down. "As a matter of fact, I do. Mr. Rogers has asked me to marry him. I said yes."

They rushed to give her another hug, exclaiming their good wishes.

"When is the wedding to be? Will you invite us? Will you go on living here? Chaperone other girls?"

"Louise, one question at a time," admonished Rebecca. "Although I must admit I want to hear the answers to all those questions too."

"We have not set the wedding date because I wanted to talk to you girls first." Amelia bit her lip before asking, "Will you stand up with me? Both of you?" Before they could respond, she hurried into speech again. "I will understand if you don't care to attend my wedding, but you're both special to me. I would never have met him if it were not for you."

"Certainly, we will stand up with you," Louise exclaimed. "I believe we would have been offended if you had not asked us. Do you agree, Rebecca?"

"I would not miss this wedding for the world."

They happily discussed wedding plans, the girls agreeing they would make a point of being free on any afternoon Amelia chose.

"Which rooms will you live in, these or his above here?"

"Both." When her guests exchanged surprised glances, Amelia chuckled. "I wrote to Elizabeth Dorchester—you remember she owns this building. She sent an architect, who assured us he can put in a staircase down here and close off the upstairs entrance to Mr. Roger's rooms. He will convert the upstairs kitchen into another room."

"The combined flats are a marvelous solution if you want to continue living in the City," Rebecca congratulated her.

"We talked about getting a house a little distance out but came to realize we both prefer the commotion of City life."

"I can understand your decision," Louise assured her. "I was surprised at how much I missed the City, even the dust and noise, while I was in the country for those few weeks. It was too quiet to sleep."

After their laughter faded away, Rebecca rose to her feet. "I really have enjoyed this visit. Now I must get changed for a ride with Shelburne."

With warm good-byes all around, the girls left Harley Street.

When Rebecca alighted from the carriage, she glanced at Louise. "I wish you could ride with us."

Louise smiled her thanks. "I'll ride with you when Juno arrives."

Marriage, not riding, was the subject of Louise's thoughts. Both Rebecca and Amelia were looking forward to being married soon. She didn't even have a real prospect. Her thoughts slid to Major Stafford before she gave herself a mental shake. Even with her grandparents' new attitude, Louise doubted they would find him acceptable.

Thoughts of her grandparents brought another question. Would they permit her to attend Amelia's wedding? Louise decided she would not mention the wedding until Amelia set a definite date before deciding whether to tell her grandparents. In the meantime, she had the Creighton ball to enjoy this evening. Perhaps the major would be there.

Arriving at the Creighton townhouse, Louise assumed a calmness she did not feel. Lady Granville had told her that she must apologize to Almack's patronesses for showing herself on St. James Street if she hoped to receive vouchers.

"Oh, Grandmother, must I indeed? Just the thought of approaching them scares me out of my wits."

Lady Granville was adamant but relented enough to make a suggestion. "Maria Sefton is friendly enough. Emily Cowper is the nicest of them. The most approachable too. Mrs. Drummond-Burrell is the highest stickler, followed by Sarah, Lady Jersey, who has her moods. You may hope Lady Cowper is at the Creighton's soirée this evening."

"Grandmother, how do you know about the various attributes of the ladies? Earlier, you said you have been out of Society for many years. They must be strangers to you."

Lady Granville gazed at her in surprise. "I made it my business to learn about them. How could I do otherwise? After all, I am sponsoring you. I have many friends who know everything happening in the *ton*."

Now, climbing the wide staircase to the first floor to meet her hostess, Louise took a deep breath. She would apologize if it killed her. Now that she had more freedom, Louise intended to enjoy it to the hilt, which included attendance at Almack's Assembly Rooms. If an apology was necessary, so be it. There was nothing she could not do should the need arise, she assured herself.

After greeting Lady Creighton, Louise glanced around the ballroom. With dismay, she found herself the cynosure of many eyes. She turned to her grandmother. "Is Lady Cowper here? I do not believe I have ever seen her. I want to get my apology over with so I can enjoy the rest of the evening."

"If she does not accept your apology? What will you do?"

"I will stay in a major key, Grandmother." Louise chuckled when she noted her grandmother's stare. "I mean to say, I will remain optimistic."

With a slight smile, Lady Granville led the way across the room to an attractive woman with a pleasant face. "Good evening, Lady Cowper. May I introduce my granddaughter to you? Louise has something to tell you."

Lady Cowper's expression turned cold. Louisa gathered her courage. "Lady Cowper, I owe you and the other patronesses an abject apology. I know better than to drive on St. James Street. I simply did not notice. It was such a pleasure to see an old friend that I neglected to notice our whereabouts."

Louise gazed toward the older woman who was viewing her with hard eyes. "Lady Cowper, I do most sincerely apologize for my thoughtless behavior. I shall not be so careless again."

There was a hush in their immediate vicinity, while the bystanders waited for Lady Cowper to give the heedless young woman a well-deserved set-down. They waited in vain.

Lady Cowper studied the anxious face in front of her and apparently approved what she saw. She nodded. "I suppose your behavior is understandable under the circumstances, but do not allow lack of attention to happen again. I cannot speak for the other patronesses, but if your behavior remains circumspect throughout autumn, we might—just might—consider you for vouchers for the Season next spring."

Louise produced a smile and a curtsy. "Thank you for your graciousness, Lady Cowper. I realize your kindness is more than I deserve."

With a brief nod to Lady Cowper, Louise followed her grandmother to the chairs lined against the wall. She maintained a determined smile, when, in fact, Louise was seething. She had apologized, had she not? Very prettily, too, in her considered opinion. How dare that old harridan withhold vouchers? Next spring, indeed, perhaps not even then. She might not even want vouchers in the spring. She took a deep breath to calm herself, when a young man whom she had not previously met approached.

"Good evening, Lady Granville, Lady Louise," Lord Ingraham greeted them. "May I have permission to dance with your granddaughter, my lady?" Receiving Lady Granville's gracious nod, he extended his arm toward Louise.

Summoning some inane chatter to her rescue, Louise presented a picture of smiling happiness to the room throughout the evening. She returned to the vicinity of her grandmother's chair after each dance. When a gentleman invited her to dance, she first looked to Lady Granville for permission. She was in a quandary when she received a frown instead of a nod when a gentleman of rather dissolute appearance approached her. The lines of dissipation in his face gave witness to his drinking habits. Alcoholic fumes preceded him. She cudgeled her mind for a response.

"I am afraid I must say no to your kind offer." Louise glanced at the card attached to her wrist. "I believe this dance is already promised."

He challenged her. Glancing around, he sneered. "I don't see any line forming."

"You are looking in the wrong direction, Hurley." Major Stafford elbowed him aside. Offering his arm to Louise, he said "I apologize for being a moment late."

Taking his arm, Louise flashed him a brilliant smile. "You are forgiven, Major." In truth, she had about given up all hope he would put in an appearance. They chatted when the movement of the country dance permitted it. Then he escorted her to her grandmother.

"Good evening, Lady Granville," he greeted her. "I trust I see you well?"

"Good evening, Major Stafford."

After a few moments of stilted conversation, the major excused himself and went to the card room.

The evening was suddenly flat for Louise. Turning to her grandmother, she said, "The hour grows late. I'm ready to leave whenever you are."

The following morning held two surprises for Louise, one of which was pleasant. Her grandfather greeted her at the breakfast table with a sly smile. "Have you been to the stables this morning, Louise?"

She stared at him in amazement. He knew she never went to the stables during the morning hours. "Oh! Has Juno arrived already? I must see her on the instant."

"You may see her, but she needs to rest today." When he saw her disappointment, Granville relented. "Perhaps you can ride her this afternoon."

Louise finished her breakfast and stopped by the kitchen for a sugar lump before rushing to the stables to welcome the mare. Assured by the groom that Juno had traveled without mishap, Louise returned to the house with barely enough time to change to a fresh gown before morning visitors began arriving. Her second surprise occurred there.

Among the visitors were Lady Amberly with her daughter, Jane, who appeared to be just out of the schoolroom. Louise felt ancient in her presence, yet made every effort to engage her in conversation.

"I believe I saw you at the Creighton's ball last evening, Lady Jane." A frown crossed the girl's features. "Is something wrong? Am I mistaken about seeing you there?"

"No, you are not mistaken, Lady Louise. I was indeed there. You ought to be ashamed of yourself," she announced in a ringing voice.

Louise closed her gaping mouth. "What can you mean, my lady? Why should I be ashamed?" She racked her brain trying to think of anything shameful she had done. Her grandmother had not found anything amiss in her behavior.

"You danced with Major Stafford," Lady Jane accused her.

"Yes, I did. He asked me to dance. I promise you. Is there some reason I should not have accepted?"

The younger girl stared at her. "The Major is a *cripple*. You should have more concern for him."

"He has a slight limp ...."

"He is a gallant gentleman. Such a hero. He received his injury in battle, fighting for his country, fighting for me, as it were. Is that not the most romantic thing?" A dreamy smile crossed the young girl's face.

Louise controlled her mirth. "I am aware he was injured in battle. However, I had not viewed the situation in the same way as you. Am I to understand you would decline if he asked you to dance?"

"Yes, of course, I would," Lady Jane answered. "I would suggest we sit out the dance. I would listen while he told me about his wounds. I would tell him how much I appreciate his care of me."

Fortunately for Louise's composure, Lady Amberly called for her daughter to leave. Lady Jane followed her out, a beatific smile on her face.

A few moments later, Major Stafford returned to Louise's side. She controlled herself until he greeted Lady Granville. However, when he seated himself next to her on a sofa, she asked, "Did you know you are a very romantic person?"

One elegant eyebrow rose. "I am not aware of that, no," Stafford answered. "What has given you such an idea? I cannot think of anything I've done to deserve such an accolade."

"The injury you received while protecting your country. In doing so, you also protected a certain young lady. She raked me over the coals for being so inconsiderate as to dance with you."

"Oh? Just what were you supposed to do if not dance with me when I asked you?"

"Sit on the sidelines while you tell me about your terrible wounds." Louise widened her mock solemn eyes. "Oh, yes, I owe you an apology for not thanking you for taking such good care of me while you were in the Peninsula."

The major's lips twitched. "That was remiss of you to be sure. Am I to know who this young lady is?"

"Lady Jane Amberly."

"Ah, yes, she of the dreamy face. Had I known she would spend all her time at balls making sheep's eyes at me, I'm not sure I would have protected her."

"Shame!"

The major interrupted their laughter to ask, "Will you ride in the park with me this afternoon? You never have. I can supply a mount for you."

"Neither with you nor with anyone else, Major," Louise responded. "My grandparents have relaxed their restrictions somewhat. I am now allowed to 'disport myself' in Hyde Park. My grandfather had Juno brought to Town, but she should rest today. I would enjoy driving with you this afternoon though." Louise caught her grandmother's eye. "I believe Grandmother desires my attention."

"I will take my leave now, but I will return this afternoon." With a smile for her, followed by a slight bow toward Lady Granville, he took his leave.

Chapter 10

Lady Jane Intervenes

Louise chose a jonquil muslin gown with a matching parasol and reticule for her drive with the major. She fidgeted with excitement but forced herself not to wait for him on the steps, which, without doubt, would upset her grandmother. Her lips set in a tight line, Lady Granville had refrained from speech when Louise told her of the proposed drive.

"My lady, Major Stafford is here." A footman spoke through the bedchamber door.

Louise hurried down the stairs. "Good afternoon, Major."

"A good afternoon to you too, Lady Louise."

Louise admired the major's handling of the ribbons in the heavy afternoon traffic. When they entered the park, they perforce drove at snail's pace, pulling to a stop several times to greet people who hailed them. Nearing the midpoint of the loop, Louise turned laughing eyes toward the major. "I believe we are about to be stopped by your most ardent admirer."

A grimace crossed his face when he followed her glance to their left. "I do believe you're right." Stafford tipped his hat. "Good afternoon, Lady Jane."

She turned adoring eyes toward him. "Major Stafford, it is good to see you this afternoon. Are you sure you ought to be handling the reins yourself? Horses are so unpredictable."

"Thank you for your concern. I assure you I will have no difficulty." He glanced toward her companion with raised eyebrows.

"Oh, do forgive me, sir. May I introduce my cousin, Herman Amberly? Herman, this is Major George

Stafford. He served in the Peninsula, you must know," Lady Jane breathed with shining eyes. With belated manners, she said, "and Lady Louise Mansfield."

"Amberly," the major acknowledged. "I don't believe I have seen you in Town before."

The moon-faced young man turned almost vacant eyes toward him. "No, sir." He turned back to Lady Jane who rushed into speech.

"Major, do please be careful with your health. We must protect our heroes. Do you not agree, my lady?" She turned an admonitory stare at Louise.

"Oh, indeed, I do, Lady Jane." Controlling her mirth, Louise added, "Major, perhaps I should take the reins for the rest of our drive."

Before he could reply, Lady Jane berated her. "You should not have allowed him outside in the first place."

Louise turned laughing eyes toward her escort. "Perhaps we should proceed on our drive, Major, before your health is damaged beyond repair."

With a tip of his hat, he put the horses in motion. "Wretch! Go ahead—laugh. My turn will come when a love-struck cub starts writing odes to your earlobes or something equally foolish."

They returned to Chesley Square in merry conversation. There, the major inquired her plans for this evening.

"I believe we are promised to the Holgarths for dinner with some sort of entertainment provided by the guests."

Stafford gazed at her in mock horror. "I am pleased I was not invited. I don't care to hear any harp playing until I reach the hereafter."

Turning soulful eyes toward him, she murmured, "I am wounded to the core of my being, sir."

The major's mouth dropped open. "Don't tell me you play the harp."

"No, I only play the piano," Louise answered with a heartfelt sigh. "I think harp players are so divine, so angelic. Not quite of this world when they play."

Stafford stared at her in horror until she burst into laughter.

"Baggage! I draw the line at listening to harps, but I look forward to hearing you play the piano someday. For now, will you ride with me in the morning?"

"Oh, yes, I look forward to trying Juno's paces again. How early can we start?"

The major shouted with laughter, unmindful of the stares of passersby. "Shall we at least wait for daylight?"

Louise flushed with embarrassment. "What I meant was, what is the proper time for morning rides in Hyde Park?"

The major clasped her hand. "Forgive me for teasing you. I could not resist. Shall I meet you at Juno's stable at eight o'clock? Hyde Park is less crowded at that hour than later in the morning."

"I will be there," Louise assured him.

Louise allowed herself a smile while she chose her gown for the evening. Harp players were angelic? She had never even seen anyone play a harp, but oh, the expression on Stafford's face when she said it. Teasing him was fun. Louise looked forward to their morning ride. First, she must get through an evening of amateur performances. Truth to tell, she was not looking forward to the entertainment any more than the major would.

Louise enjoyed dinner despite Herman Amberly sitting on her left. She tried to converse with him, yet was unable to find any topic of conversation which drew more than a brief reply. She hated to think he was lacking in his wits but was ready to believe he was by the time they finished dinner. Her discomfort truly began then.

In the drawing room, Lady Jane took her to task over driving with Major Stafford. Did she not know fresh air was bad for invalids? "You truly must give more consideration to Major Stafford's health."

"I believe Major Stafford's physician would have warned him to stay indoors if it were necessary for his good health," Louise answered. "Furthermore, you must give the major credit for having sufficient intelligence not to harm himself."

"It is not a question of intelligence," Lady Jane instructed her in stern tones. "Men are intelligent in many matters but are unconcerned about their health. For that reason, we ladies must protect them from themselves."

Louise found herself speechless after Lady Jane's absurd statement.

Unfortunately, the younger lady had not finished. "Lady Louise, I insist you stay away from Major Stafford. Leave his health to those of us who know what is best for him."

During this pompous speech, Herman Amberly joined them and now sat glaring at Louise. He made his first voluntary statement of the evening. "Don't upset Jane," he ordered her. "I don't allow anyone to upset Jane."

Lady Jane smiled. "Herman always supports me. Do you not, Herman?"

It was fortunate for Louise's temper that Mrs. Holgarth announced the entertainment would begin. The presentations met Louise's expectation of mediocrity. The first was Lady Jane, honoring them at the harp. Louise soon changed her mind about harp players. Angelic? Could she have said such a thing even in jest? Heaven could not hold that noise.

Louise was duly thankful Lady Jane was the only person present who aspired to heaven's notice on the harp. The singing and the poetry recitations were no better. Thankfully, no one attempted Shakespeare's work. She closed her eyes in pain while a young miss plowed her way through something on the piano. Louise thought she recognized a Beethoven sonata, but there were so many mistakes she was not sure. Her former, much younger, students could do better. She turned to her grandmother in consternation.

"Grandmother, I cannot play tonight."

Lady Granville stared at her. "Why ever not? You play much better than anyone here. Hearing you will be a real treat for them."

"The problem is these girls might never have the confidence to perform again." Louise told herself that might not be a bad thing.

An arrested expression crossed Lady Granville's face. "You're quite right, Louise. I admire your thoughtfulness. You must perform, though, because it would be an insult to Mrs. Holgarth if you did not. What do you suggest?"

Louise mulled it over, while a shy young lady trilled her way through an Irish ballad. "Perhaps I could volunteer to play some light airs while everyone sings. Will that serve?"

"Your suggestion is perfect, my dear. I will be sure you play at a gathering of some description at our house. I want our friends to know how talented you are."

Thus, Louise made it through the most boring evening she had experienced since coming to Town. She heaved a sigh of relief that it was over when she climbed into bed later. Louise wondered if she should tell the major about this evening on their ride the following morning.

The sound of drapes scraping along their rods awakened Louise.

"Good morning, my lady." Agnes placed a cup of chocolate on the bedside table. "Which habit shall I lay out for you?"

Louise raised herself against the pillows. "The green one, I believe, Agnes." She hurriedly dressed, arriving at the stables with five minutes to spare. The major was already there.

He greeted her with raised eyebrows. "I must admit I was not sure you would be up this early after your thrilling entertainment of last evening."

Louise sent him a saucy grin over her shoulder and greeted Juno with a carrot, talking to her while Juno munched. Louise nodded to Baker, who was standing by ready to toss her into the saddle.

The restless horses required their riders' strict attention as they threaded their way through the early morning traffic of farm carts, stray dogs, and other early riders.

Once in Hyde Park, Louise released her firm hold on the reins. A quick glance indicated there was no one about this early. She urged Juno into a longer stride, galloping down the long avenue. She did not make the mistake of thinking she would leave the major or the groom behind. She and the major galloped side by side to the end of the avenue with Baker on their heels. Breathing deeply, Louise said, "That was exhilarating. I have really missed my early morning rides."

"I like coming to the park this early when there aren't many people around," Stafford agreed. "Even a little later in the morning, we could not enjoy the freedom of a gallop."

A dimple played around her mouth. "Are you telling me it is not proper for ladies to ride *ventre à terre* through the park, Major?"

"I can see it was not necessary to be mealy-mouthed."

Her laughter filled the air. "I can assure you the Duchess of Dorchester was not 'mealy-mouthed' when she instructed us at the orphanage. She did not limit her strictures to the park either. According to her, the only time it is proper for ladies to allow their mounts more than a sedate walk is during a hunt. I daresay she heard about the races which Rebecca and I enjoyed on the property, but she never admonished us about them."

"You haven't told me about your entertainment last evening," Stafford quizzed her while they rode around the loop. "Did I miss anything thrilling?"

"Major, you missed a real treat," Louise assured him. "Lady Jane dedicated her efforts on the harp to a certain military hero whom she blushingly declined to name."

Stafford pulled his mount to a sudden stop, causing his mount to rear up scattering leaves. Louise held Juno under control. Bringing his horse under control again, he said, "Do you mean to say Lady Jane played a military march on a *harp*?"

"And a stirring rendition it was," Louise informed him with aplomb.

"You are gammoning me, surely you are." The major studied her countenance for a moment. "No, I can see you are not. You almost make me regret not being there. Almost, you understand, not quite. I hope

I don't hear about this from anyone else. I'm not sure I could take the ribbing my friends would offer."

Near the gate, the major's gaze sharpened a moment before turning to Louise. "You are being observed quite closely," he nodded forward to their left. "Is he someone you know?"

She glanced in the direction he indicated. A slender gentleman sat astride a horse that appeared much too large for him. "I don't believe I've met him, Major, yet something about him seems familiar. You know many more people than I. Do you recognize him?"

When they approached him on the avenue, the gentleman bowed toward Louise, a slight smile on his face. She nodded briefly. Stafford touched his hat with the tip of his crop before they continued their ride.

Louise met Stafford's glinting eyes. "If his shirt points were any higher, they would surely poke out his eyes. I must admit the curl dangling on his forehead is quite romantic though. Do you not agree?"

Stafford snorted. "He's a dandy of the first stare, alright, a Byron emulator." He gave her a disgusted glare but joined her soft laughter, as they discussed the latest poetic rage of London.

Louise grew somber when they neared Chesley Square. She glanced at the major when he inquired if something bothered her. "Not exactly. I'm not sure how my grandparents will react to a request. I must approach them this morning, otherwise it will be too late. I admit to shaking in my boots at their possible, no probable, reaction."

"Is there any way I can be of service?" he asked with quick sympathy.

"You will remember that Rebecca Blackwell and I lived in London for several months early this year. Our chaperone was a widow named Amelia Peters, whose family was known to the duchess. Mrs. Peters told us some days ago she's getting married to a gentleman we also know from our time in the City. She wants us to stand up with her. I'm not sure my grandparents will permit me to attend. I must be there for her. I truly want to stand with her, yet I don't want to upset my grandparents."

"I see your dilemma. Will it be easier if they know I will escort you to the wedding chapel and back?" He answered his own question. "No. That might be the one thing which would make them refuse."

On an impulse, Louise reached out her hand toward him. "I would be pleased to have your escort, Major, were it possible."

"I would be pleased to escort you. To your friend's wedding, or anywhere else," he replied. Nodding to Baker, the major rode away.

Louise changed from her riding habit into a pale green morning gown before joining her grandparents in the breakfast parlor. After filling her breakfast plate, she took a deep breath. "Grandfather, Grandmother, when I visited my former chaperone in Harley Street a few days ago, she told me she is wedding a gentleman with whom I am also acquainted. She asked Rebecca and me to stand up with her."

The Granvilles glanced at each other for a long moment of silent communication. "Where is this ceremony to take place?" he asked. "And when?"

"The ceremony will be held at St. Mark's, which is where we attended services. Mrs. Peters sent word late yesterday that the wedding will take place this Sunday afternoon." She turned pleading eyes to her grandmother. "It would mean a great deal to me—to her also—if I could take part."

Lady Granville forced the grim expression from her face. "Yes, I believe you may participate. Have you an escort in mind?"

"I would like for both of you to meet this lady. Will you consider accompanying me?" Louise held her breath while her grandparents again communicated in silence. If they would accompany her—see for themselves how proper Mrs. Peters is—they might be more understanding of her life during those months she lived in Harley Street.

"Yes, we will," Lord Granville answered. "It is only right that we meet the female who took care of you after you left the protection of the orphanage."

Thus it came about that the current Marquess and Marchioness of Granville of an old and storied family attended the wedding of Mrs. Amelia Peters, the indigent widow of a horse fancier, to Mr. Nathaniel Rogers, a tailor's assistant.

The newlyweds overcame their surprise at such condescension and invited them to attend a small reception at their Harley Street lodgings.

There, the Granvilles were able to fit another piece of their granddaughter's life into perspective. Her grandmother later admitted to Louise the gentility of her friends had surprised them. "Although the rooms are somewhat small, they are well furnished."

"That is due to the Duchess of Dorchester's generosity. The same applies to the domestic help. I am not sure I told you the duchess owns the building. The duchess has Amelia in permanent employ to chaperone other girls."

"Elizabeth made good choices in the chaperone. The household domestic staff too," Lady Granville admitted. "She always did have a sound head on her shoulders."

Louise was eager to tell the major of the amiability the Granvilles had displayed toward her old friends. This must augur well for her friendship with him.

They met the following day at a Venetian breakfast, hosted by Lady Garland in honour of her two simpering daughters. Although, why people called it breakfast at three o'clock in the afternoon was more than Louise could fathom. The food did not correspond with the usual breakfast food, plentiful though it was.

After Stafford had done his duty by talking with the hostess, he bowed toward Lady Jane Amberly with her cousin at her side and made his way across the room to Louise. He clasped her hand a moment. "I haven't talked to you since our morning ride. How have you been?"

"I have been very well, I assure you, Major, in particular since my grandparents not only gave me permission to attend Amelia's wedding but actually went with me."

"They are unbending, are they not?"

"Yes. They even permitted me to come here today with only my maid as chaperone. This is a definite improvement over my first weeks in Town."

Before they could talk further, the exquisite young dandy they had seen in the park approached them with mincing steps. "Well met, Cousin," he drawled with a smirk when her mouth popped open. "Jasper Winningham at your service."

"Cousin, sir? I am not aware I have any cousins. Perhaps you are mistaken in my identity." Seeing him up close, Louise realized he was older than she first thought. Too old to be dressed in the fashion he chose, that of gentlemen newly out of school who had not yet learned better.

"No, Cousin, I'm not mistaken," he assured her. "You're Louise Mansfield, the long-lost granddaughter of the Marquess of Granville. I am distantly related to him on my mother's side."

Louise was speechless. This creature with his ridiculous padded shoulders and wasp-waisted coat bore some relationship to the proud Marquess of Granville? She tried to imagine her grandfather's reaction to this dandy and swallowed an impulse to laugh.

Taking a steadying breath, she commented, "I have had reason to study the family tree in recent weeks, but my grandfather has not mentioned you to me, Mr. Winningham. Have you seen him in recent times?"

"No, I've just returned after residing several years in Italy."

Louise nodded. "Oh, gentlemen, please excuse my rudeness. Mr. Winningham, allow me to introduce Major George Stafford, currently on leave from service in the Peninsula."

"We saw you in the park some days ago, Mr. Winningham," the major said. "Have you not notified Lord Granville you are again on your home shores?"

Winningham tugged at his cravat. "Uh, no, I have been busy with my tailor and various other details. I do expect to pay them a visit tomorrow." He turned away leaving them staring after him.

"I cannot quite imagine him being related to the Marquess of Granville. His heir, in fact. So, why hasn't Granville kept him in England? Nagged him into producing more heirs for the family dynasty? Although I didn't see anything about Winningham to persuade Granville to encourage him."

Louise agreed. "I hope to be present when they meet face to face."

"I believe we are to be seated at the same table, Major Stafford." Lady Jane interrupted their *tête-à-tête* without apology. Slipping her hand through his arm, she cast a smug glance at Louise as she led the major toward a small table.

Stafford cast an anguished glance toward Louise. "I am sure Lady Louise will want to join us," he said. Thereupon, he disengaged his arm, offering it instead to Louise, who hid a smile.

"If she insists." Lady Jane directed a ferocious frown toward Louise, who smiled but did not reply when the major seated her next to him. Lady Jane stared in surprise at the heaping plate set before the major. "My dear sir, you do not intend to eat so much food? It cannot be good for your delicate health. Perhaps I should order some broth from the kitchen. You must avoid the champagne at all costs. Barley water is what you need."

Before Lady Jane could follow through with her intentions, the major attacked the heap of food before him. He ignored her sputtering and made a good meal. He talked primarily with Louise, although he did direct a few remarks toward his tormentor.

Lady Jane sat with a heavy scowl on her face. She was unsuccessful in her efforts to catch Louise's eye. At length, she broke into their conversation. "My lady, you must add your voice to mine. An invalid should not eat such foods. I am aware of your unusual life, but surely you learned rudimentary health needs in the orphanage. I am surprised you allowed him to come to this breakfast."

Her criticism of Louise Mansfield was too much for the major. Stafford turned a stern visage toward her, which would have warned many a subaltern to retreat.

"Lady Jane, please understand this. I am not an invalid. I had a minor leg injury, now almost healed. Nothing I eat or drink will have any effect on the injury. Furthermore, Lady Louise is not responsible for anything I do."

Herman Amberly aimed a scowl at Louise. "You are upsetting Jane."

Louise gazed at him. "I fail to understand you, sir. I have not spoken any words to Lady Jane that could be upsetting."

"Don't upset her," he warned again.

Louise turned to the major. "I believe it is time for me to leave. Will you excuse me, please?"

"I will escort you to your carriage, my lady." Placing his napkin on the table, he spoke to Lady Jane. "Perhaps you should explain to your cousin that Lady Louise does not control my actions. If anyone is upsetting you, it is I. However, I don't care for your interference in my life." Stafford executed a slight bow, then hurried after Louise.

Major Stafford handed Louise into her carriage, where her maid waited. "I hope neither Lady Jane nor her cousin upset you."

Louise shook her head. "They don't bother me. I should think you would give her a sharp set-down."

"I just did," Stafford assured her.

The moment Louise entered the door at Chesley Square, she asked Foster where she would find her grandparents.

"In the library, I believe."

With a smile, she opened the library door. "Grandfather, Grandmother, guess who I met this afternoon."

Chapter 11

Uninvited Picnic Guest

"You should have seen their faces when I told them Jasper Winningham was in Town." Louise met Rebecca's amused eyes across their teacups. The afternoon of the next day, Louise had called upon her old friend to tell her of the latest happenings in the Mansfield family. "They would not have been more surprised if I had told them the duns were at the door."

"I gather he is not quite up to their standards?"

Louise almost choked on a sip of tea. "Wait until you see him. He is a dandy of the first order. He looked like a bird of paradise in the somber environs of Granville House this morning. Grandmother avoided staring at the fuchsia trousers worn with a puce coat."

Rebecca's eyes widened. "You must be joking! He truly wore that combination?"

"Yes. To complete the insult to fashion sense, he wore a bright red waistcoat with broad white stripes. He did not seem to notice Grandmother's pained expression while he rattled off compliments."

"How did Lord Granville react to this sudden resurrection of a long-lost cousin?"

"Grandfather made it clear Mr. Winningham is not welcome, later instructing me to have nothing to do with 'that dissolute fop.' Those are Grandfather's words, although I agree with him." Louise paused a moment. "I felt rather sorry for my cousin. I know how it feels to be unwelcome."

"Things are better for you now, though, are they not?"

"Much better." Louise's countenance lightened. "Someday I will show you my journal of those early weeks at Granville Manor. When I wrote in it, I pretended I was talking to you, just like I have always done with my problems."

Rebecca clasped Louise's hand. "I'm sorry I could not be with you."

"I know you would have been if circumstances had allowed. Now, that's enough about me. You never told me how your grandparents accepted you. I have been too self-centered to ask. Did you have any problems?"

"Not a one. Both graciously accepted me as their grandchild immediately, never questioned my legitimacy." A mischievous grin crossed her face. "I cannot say the same for some of the Carlton cousins, though, especially those of my generation. Some said I was an impostor. My resemblance to my mother put a stop to that ridiculous notion. A cousin who cherished hopes of inheriting my grandparents' fortune questioned my legitimacy. My parents' marriage lines ended his speculation."

"Have you learned anything of your paternal family?"

"Both those grandparents are deceased, and my father was an only child. If I have any paternal family, the kinship is quite distant. I do have my maternal family, which is more than I ever expected to have during those years at the orphanage."

"You have Lord Shelburne too."

"Yes," Rebecca replied with a softened voice, "I have Edward. He is truly all that matters."

"Is your betrothal official?"

"Our betrothal has not yet been puffed off in the newspapers, but my grandparents accept our engagement as fact. I consider it official."

"I dare say Shelburne does too," Louise assured her. "Are you going to the Saunderson ball this evening?"

"To be sure I am. Andrew Saunderson is certain to be in attendance at his mother's ball. Watching the schoolroom misses and their doting mamas trying to attract his attention amuses me no end." Rebecca slanted a glance toward Louise from beneath her lowered eyelashes. "Do you find him attractive?"

"Oh, yes, he is certainly attractive. I understand his wealth rivals that of Golden Ball; however, he's too solemn—seldom has a word to say for himself. I prefer someone who laughs with me."

"Like Major Stafford, perhaps?" Rebecca teased.

"Yes, just like Major Stafford."

On this light note, Louise took her leave with plans to meet in the evening.

Louise sat beside Lady Granville in the Saunderson ballroom, waving a fan as she surveyed the crowd. She had gone down three country dances with amiable young men, including Lord Saunderson. Louise wondered when Major Stafford would put in an appearance. She glanced toward her grandmother, when Simon Abernathy bowed over her hand.

"Good evening, Lady Granville. I trust all is well with you. May I have the pleasure of dancing with your granddaughter?"

Louise almost held her breath while Lady Granville opened and closed her mouth without speaking, finally nodding her permission.

"Are you enjoying the Season, my lady?"

"Better than I was, Mr. Abernathy," she admitted with a twinkle. "I am pleased my grandmother permitted me to dance with you because I want to ask you a question."

The steps of the dance separated them for a few moments. When they again touched hands, he said, "Ask away, Lady Louise. I am at your service."

Her eyes widened at the intimacy of his smile. Flustered, she dropped her gaze for a moment. Berating herself for being missish, she looked him in the eyes. "In the summer, Lord Shelburne, Rebecca Blackwell, and I had occasion to visit a family by name of Abernathy in Oxfordshire. Are they perhaps relations of yours?"

"Michael Abernathy is my brother, although he does not boast about the connection," he answered with a laugh, as the dance again parted them.

"Why not, sir?" Louise asked the moment she again stood beside Abernathy.

"Oh, I am the black sheep of the family. You don't want to hear about it. Suffice to say Michael inherited our father's industriousness, while I inherited our mother's indolence."

Louise glanced at his modish splendor. "You apparently find ways and means to clothe yourself in the first stare of elegance, at least. You are certainly accepted in Society, so in my view you cannot be all bad."

There was a distinct twinkle in his eyes, but he did not contradict her. Instead, they talked of the latest *on-dits* throughout the remainder of the dance. Then he returned her to Lady Granville's side.

Louise wondered about the tiny smile that played around his mouth when he bowed toward the marchioness before strolling away. Knowing him better might be diverting. If she dared.

Lady Granville eyed her. "You seemed to find a deal to say to him."

"Rebecca and I visited a family of the same name in Oxfordshire late in the summer. I asked if they are relations of his. It turns out Mr. Michael Abernathy is his brother."

Her grandmother frowned. "I do not know Mr. Michael Abernathy. How did you come to make his acquaintance?"

Louise related the story of Rebecca befriending a small girl, which led to a fortnight stay at the country residence of the child's parents. "They are quite nice people, Grandmother, with a very handsome property. I believe you would like them."

"Perhaps. Nevertheless, you already know I do not care for this member of the family."

"Yes, Grandmother, I do remember. I appreciate your allowing me to dance with him because I wanted to ask him about the other Abernathies." Louise wondered how many more times she would have to hear her grandmother's strictures about Simon Abernathy.

"I hope that is the end of your conversation with him," Lady Granville stated, then nodded toward Lord Saunderson. "Now, there is a gentleman you might care to cultivate. He's heir to an earldom—the catch of the Season. Several Seasons. Attracting his attention would be quite a feather in your cap."

"Yes, Grandmother," Louise answered. "Oh, look, here is Rebecca Blackwell."

Rebecca curtsied to Lady Granville before taking the chair next to Louise, who relayed the information about Mr. Simon Abernathy.

Louise struggled through another country dance with Lord Saunderson, during which she was able to elicit exactly six words from him in his dry monotone, "Yes, my lady" and "No, my lady." When he returned her to Lady Granville's side, Louise sighed with relief. Grandmother would not expect her to dance with Saunderson again that evening.

When Major Stafford arrived midway of the evening, he asked Lady Granville's permission to lead Louise in the supper dance. A grudging nod gave her permission.

Louise and the major shared a supper table with Rebecca and Shelburne. Louise used the opportunity to quiz the latter. "Lord Shelburne, did you know that Mr. Simon Abernathy is the brother of Mr. Michael Abernathy of Oxfordshire?"

"No, a relationship between them never occurred to me."

"I cannot recall hearing of Michael Abernathy," the major looked askance at Louise, who related the story.

The major chose his words with care. "His branch of the family sounds delightful. It is a pity I cannot say the same for Simon Abernathy."

"I like him," Louise remarked without emphasis.

The major exchanged a glance with Shelburne, who remarked, "I find him a pleasant enough person, but his methods of attracting heiresses render him suspect in the eyes of Society."

"He returns to Town in funds after being missing for months. Many people wonder how he comes by the money," Stafford added.

"I'm not acquainted with him, but I've seen him," Rebecca said. "He's accepted everywhere,"

"Not quite everywhere," Shelburne reminded her. "If I remember correctly, your grandparents did not invite him to your ball."

"Simon Abernathy was at the Haverford ball," Louise pointed out. "I met him there."

"The music is starting," Rebecca interrupted what was turning into an unpleasant conversation. "Shall we return to the ballroom?"

While the girls danced the first set with other partners, Shelburne stood with Stafford on the sidelines. He noticed the major's eyes as he watched Louise moving through a cotillion.

"You appear to be quite taken with Louise Mansfield, George. Do you have hopes in that direction?"

"I have given some thought to the possibility," George admitted after a moment. "However, the Granvilles are looking higher—much higher—for their granddaughter."

"Logical," Shelburne commented. "You know they're family proud. Granville will not take lightly the business of finding her a husband."

"You would think they had learned their lesson with their son."

"I agree. How does all this affect your going back to the Peninsula?"

A shrug was the major's only answer. "I'm coming around to thinking my father might be right after all. Perhaps it is time for me to sell out. My leg has not healed anyway. I suppose I will make my decision when the sawbones releases me for duty, if he ever does. Sometimes I wonder if the wretched limb will ever get back to normal."

Shelburne nodded his understanding. "Care to join me for a few hands in the card room?"

"Not this evening." The major watched Shelburne saunter away and then turned in the opposite direction into the path of a heavyset man. He glanced into the dissolute face of Lord Hurley. "I beg your pardon."

"Watch where you're going, Stafford," Hurley muttered, pushing on by him.

Louise observed the incident. When the major joined her in the gilt chairs lining the wall, she asked if he had a previous acquaintance with Lord Hurley. "For you must know, Major, I sensed once before that he is not a particular friend of yours."

"No, I do not believe anyone would consider us friends. We had some run-ins at school, which he has not forgotten."

"You were in school together?" she asked in astonishment. "He appears years older than you."

The major chose his words with care. "Hurley has not always been as careful of his life pursuits as he perhaps could have been."

"In other words, he is a reprobate."

A hint of amusement touched his mouth. "That is one word used to describe him, yes. Would you consider it a dare if I pointed out to you that your grandparents would not approve of him?"

"Goodness, what you must think of me, Major. I assure you I don't court their displeasure." Louise dimpled up at him. "However, I do have a mind of my own in the choice of my friends."

A glance assured him Lady Granville was listening to a dowager on her other side. "I won't preach at you, but it never hurts to be guided by other opinions to some extent. I don't mean just family lineage. Your grandparents are high in the instep on that subject, but don't discount all their advice based on one attitude."

Louise nodded. Their gazes held until Lady Granville noticed them. She promptly declared it was time to leave.

The next several days passed in a flurry of outdoor activities while the *beau monde* enjoyed the lingering warmth of autumn. After the morning coolness passed, the days were sunny, much too nice to remain indoors.

Major Stafford approached Lady Granville with the prospects of a picnic on the heath.

"What, pray tell, is on the heath that would encourage any one of sense to go there?" She raised haughty eyebrows.

"Ah, perhaps nothing on the heath, my lady; however, it presents an opportunity to leave the heavy air of London for a few hours."

"Who do you propose will make up this party?"

He enumerated a few names. "The Duchess of Amesbury has given Lady Rebecca permission to go, with Shelburne as her escort; Lady Becca Haverford has agreed to be a chaperone, bringing her daughter. Mr. Robert Desmond will accompany them. Also, Lady Amberly is bringing Lady Jane with her cousin." He paused before adding his *pièce de résistance*. "Lord Saunderson has also expressed an interest in joining us."

Her expression softened. "Tell me about the travel plans."

"Several of us will ride, but Lady Becca and Lady Amberly will take their carriages. They will take up any ladies who care to join them."

"The food? I do not believe you maintain a household in London."

"I arranged with Fortnum and Mason's to prepare several baskets. Lady Becca has volunteered the services of her servants."

The marchioness nodded. "I can see no problem with your plan. I will allow Louise to participate." She permitted a brief smile to cross her face. "I would prefer she accompany Lady Becca in her carriage, but I realize that would spoil her pleasure."

"My lady, I assure you we will take the best possible care of Lady Louise." With a bow, Stafford left the room before she could change her mind. Now, to find Louise, who, he believed, was at Hookham's this morning.

An exuberant group stopped in Chesley Square the following afternoon. Lady Becca paid pretty deference to Lady Granville, thanking her for allowing Lady Louise to join them. "This is such a pleasant day for a ride in the country. Are you sure you will not join us? There is space in my carriage. I would enjoy becoming better acquainted with you."

"I appreciate the invitation, although I must decline the honour. My idea of pleasure doesn't coincide with yours." A wry smile accompanied her words.

With a laugh, the party left the square. They paid close attention to traffic until they were clear of the City but then allowed the horses to lengthen their stride. Soon, those on horseback outdistanced the slower moving carriages.

Louise and the major rode side by side with Rebecca and Shelburne close behind, ignoring the remainder of the party, which divided itself between riding in or accompanying the two coaches.

The wagon carrying the servants with the food had gone earlier to the appointed location on the heath. When the carriages arrived, Major Stafford's group already sat on rugs under a huge oak tree.

"We were about to start eating without you," Shelburne informed Lady Becca with the bluntness permissible between siblings. "Did you get lost?"

Becca accepted his assistance leaving the carriage. "Don't be absurd, Shelburne. We enjoyed a nice, leisurely drive out here, which is what I understood was the purpose of this excursion."

"Don't let him to tease you, Lady Becca," Stafford intervened.

Soon the entire party relaxed on a variety of rugs, heaping plates of food and tall glasses of lemonade, satisfying their inner cravings.

Relaxing against a broad tree trunk, Louise dozed until Lady Jane rudely brought her back to her surroundings. Louise had been quick to note she had avoided Major Stafford, although she had directed fuming glances at Louise throughout the picnic. Now, Louise sighed with regret when the harsh voice sounded in her ear.

"I vow you have not paid heed to anything I have said, have you? Are you determined to kill Major Stafford? Do you not realize this jaunt today could be the death of him?"

"Lady Jane, I must protest. I don't care for your constant nagging about him because I have no control over the major's actions."

"You pretend you do not, yet I know better. He practically sits in your pocket. In truth, you exert considerable influence over him. You should use your influence in a more constructive way."

Louise managed to keep her voice low, although she wanted to scream. "Lady Jane, you have become an absolute bore on the subject of Major Stafford's health. He is in a better position to know what he can and cannot do than either you or I. I don't care to hear any more about it. Do you understand me? Not one word."

Herman Amberly glared at Louise. "Don't upset Jane. I have told you before not to upset her. You paid me no heed. I am telling you once more. Do not upset Lady Jane."

Louise decided enough was enough. Rising to her feet, she said, "Mr. Amberly, I must protest your continued inference that I am in some way upsetting Lady Jane. All she needs to do is stay away from me if

I am bothering her in any way." Louise stalked away, heedless of their glaring faces.

She slowed her pace to a reasonable level after a few moments of fuming. Louise glanced over her shoulder to see how far she was from the others. The major was close on her heels, so she waited for him to join her. They strolled along in silence for a few minutes before turning back toward the rest of the party.

"Are you calm enough now to tell me what sent you off at a gallop?"

"I hoped no one had noticed. It was nothing, really. Lady Jane refuses to understand I am not responsible for your health. Mr. Amberly persists in accusing me of upsetting her." Louise shrugged. "Let us talk of something else."

She had barely stopped speaking when they heard a crack and felt the wind when something whizzed between their heads.

"What was that?" Louise looked around while the major hurried her to the shelter of a small copse.

"Someone shot at us," the major answered, peering toward the trees where he believed the culprit was hiding.

Louise could hear the excited exclamations from the party.

Shelburne ran to them. "That sounded like gun fire, George. Are you both alright?"

"I'm a little surprised, my lord." Louise maintained a light tone, despite her fright. "I must admit I had not thought I would have to dodge bullets this afternoon."

"Nor I." The major's voice was grim. "Highwaymen are rarely active on the heath in these modern times. At least, not in broad daylight."

They made their way back to their party, who bombarded them with questions they were unable to answer.

At length, Louise stated the shooter could only have been a poacher. "After all, why would anyone fire at us?"

When Stafford and Shelburne returned from their search of the area, Lady Becca commented, "I believe we should start back to London now. Do you agree, Shelburne?"

"Yes, I do. Is everyone here?"

"I believe … no, here comes Saunderson and Amberly."

Excited chatter broke out again when the young men joined the rest of the group. Saunderson managed to ask if Lady Louise were injured. Amberly stared around until he fell into step beside Louise on their return to the carriages.

"Don't upset Lady Jane again."

Since talking to him did no good, Louise turned away.

A subdued party returned to Chesley. Lady Becca and the major escorted Louise inside.

The Granvilles glanced up in surprise at the intrusion when Foster announced them.

"Lord Granville, my lady," the major began. "I must confess I have not met my responsibility to care of your granddaughter." When Louise started to interrupt, he waved her to silence. "The simple fact is, someone fired a gun on the heath. The shot passed very close to her. Too close for comfort."

This time Louise would not be denied. "Major Stafford was not at fault in any way, I promise you. It was a stray shot, probably from a poacher's gun, not intended for me at all. The shot was as close to the major as it was to me."

"I was not comfortable with the idea of Louise going on the heath," Lady Granville said. "I should have forbidden her participation."

"You could not have known there would be trouble," Lord Granville answered her. He turned to the major. "I assume you searched for the culprit?"

"Yes, my lord. Shelburne and I did but could find no trace of anyone. I apologize again for my carelessness. I would never lead Lady Louise into danger."

"I do not believe carelessness played any part in this occurrence," Lady Becca said. "There was an unforeseen incident with no way to guard against it."

"I suppose you are right. Nonetheless, I do believe Louise should confine her outings to the immediate vicinity in the future." Lady Granville gave her granddaughter a firm look receiving a nod in reply.

Lady Becca dropped into a respectful curtsy, gave Louise a quick hug, and left the room. Major Stafford lingered a moment, then sketched a bow to the Granvilles, and followed Lady Becca.

Louise remained in the room, waiting for their condemnation of her carelessness or at the very least a demand for a more detailed explanation. None came.

Lord Granville cleared his throat. "I am pleased you were not harmed, child."

After Louise answered him with a small smile, she turned to her grandmother for whatever else was to come.

Lady Granville nodded. "What are your plans for this evening? We must all put in an appearance, so the *ton* can stop the speculation it is no doubt already indulging."

With a short laugh, Louise mentioned a dinner party, a musicale, two balls, and the theater. They chose the two balls as being the places the most people would see them.

In his lodgings the major also was contemplating evening activities. He didn't like to admit how shaken he was over the afternoon occurrence. He broke into a sweat when he thought of how close to death he had been. He hoped he had not survived the Peninsula battles only to meet his death at home. Stafford shivered when he remembered Louise's frightened face. To think he could have been the cause of her death. It didn't help matters any that he had strained his injured leg when he rushed Louise into the sheltering copse. He used both hands to lift the aching limb onto a low stool. He would rest until he must dress for dinner with Shelburne. Leaning his head on the tall chair back, he closed his eyes as the pain eased.

"Major Stafford?"

The voice of his batman roused the major, who shook off the effects of a dream in which someone was chasing Louise with a gun. "Yes, Miller, I'm awake. What is it?"

"Lord Shelburne is here, sir."

The major groaned. He had slept through his dinner engagement. "Show him in."

"Evening, George. Since you didn't come to the club, I came to see if you're alright." Shelburne took the proffered chair.

"I apologize, Edward. I dozed off when this wretched leg stopped aching."

Shelburne commiserated. "I saw the Granvilles at a ball earlier. Did they give you a rough time over the shooting incident?"

"No, surprisingly, they did not. I wonder what they said to Louise though."

"They appeared to be on amicable terms at least."

"She could have been killed. My fault. Why in heaven's name did I suggest such a foolhardy thing as a picnic on the heath?" Stafford ran his fingers through his already disheveled hair.

"An accident, George. You could not have foreseen someone would have a gun on the heath." Edward soothed his old friend as best he could. After a few more reassurances, he took his leave.

Miller entered with a tray of sandwiches, which he placed at his master's elbow. "Best get these inside you, Major." He bustled around, setting the room to rights, all the while watching the major from the corner of his eye.

Stafford quickly finished the sandwiches. "Thank you, Miller. I believe I will turn in now." And hope I don't dream of guns, he added to himself.

While Stafford was hoping for quiet sleep, Louise stood by her bedchamber window, thankful the long evening had ended at last. She had not danced even once, yet she would not have been more tired if she had danced until dawn. Louise had answered queries until she could recite the answers in her sleep. Her headache, which began half way through the evening, worsened when rain pelted them, as they traveled from one ball to the other.

The one bright spot came during the second ball. Louise relived those few moments.

"Good evening, my lady. It appears you had an eventful day." Simon Abernathy had edged into the crowd surrounding her. The others disappeared, as if by magic.

"A good evening to you, too, Mr. Abernathy. I would prefer somewhat less excitement in my life, at least of that nature."

"A new set is beginning. Will you honour me with this dance?"

"I am under strict orders not to set foot on the dance floor with you, sir." A grin lighted her face. "However, my grandmother made no mention of strolling along the edge of the room."

"Shall we?" he asked with a twinkle.

"Yes, if you promise not to mention my experience today. I've answered enough questions. I didn't realize being shot at could put me in such great demand." Louise struggled to keep irony out of her voice.

With an understanding nod, Abernathy changed the subject by telling her an anecdote about his own misadventure with a dueling pistol when he was a lad.

"The weapon was unloaded, otherwise the heirloom chandelier would have fallen around my ears. My father tanned my hide."

His admission had brought her first smile of the evening. She endured her grandmother's strictures with a surprising calmness.

Now, she stared out at the deserted street. Rain continued to fall in heavy sheets, noticeable in the puddles standing below the halo of the street lamps. Perhaps the rain would lull her to sleep.

It did not. Louise lay in bed, stiff with tension, for what seemed like hours. If the rain continued through the morning, perhaps visitors would not venture out of doors. She didn't want to answer more questions or listen to more exclamations of horror. She didn't even want to think about the moment the shot whizzed between her head and the major's head. She cringed at the thought he could have died in front of her eyes, after surviving his Peninsula battles.

Louise had looked for him all evening. Had he stayed away from her because of embarrassment? Or had he hurt his leg while he was protecting her? She would hate to be the cause of more pain for him. Perhaps Lady Jane was right. If she had been less enthusiastic about the picnic, they might not have gone to the heath. Louise would never know.

Chapter 12

Too Many Suitors

Her wishes for a rainy day were in vain. Louise realized this before she even opened her eyes the following morning. Bright sunlight penetrated her eyelids when Agnes pushed open the drapes. The rain had washed away the pall of smoke hanging over Town the past few days. However, Louise knew from experience that the sunshine wouldn't last. With a sigh, she pushed herself up in bed and reached for the cup of chocolate on the tray beside her.

"This is a beautiful day," Agnes announced. "Her ladyship said to let you sleep late this morning. Now you had better rouse yourself. You have time for a bite of breakfast before the visitors start arriving."

Louise heard the petulance in her voice when she muttered, "I don't want to see any visitors."

"My lady, I can see that having to face visitors' questions could be intolerable, however one does as one must. Come now. The sooner we start, the sooner the ordeal will be over."

How many times had Louise heard Matron say those same words? Try though she did, Louise could not deny the obvious truth in them. She pushed back the bedcovers.

The morning visitors were even worse than Louise had feared. She shuddered with repulsion when the first to arrive was Jasper Winningham, who held her hand longer than was proper, while he murmured his concern for her.

"Cousin, you must not put us into such a state of worry again. Your grandparents are too elderly to face this kind of situation."

"I assure you I did not deliberately set out to worry anyone." He must be all about in his head even to think such a thing.

"Who could want to kill you? Perhaps the major was the target. I understand you were standing quite close together."

"Nonsense. We were not standing at all. We were walking. Besides, I am sure the shot was a stray from a poacher, which just happened to come in our direction."

At length Louise managed to stop his questions, but they were just the beginning. The Amberlies were the second visitors. Louise could barely speak amicably to Lady Jane, who didn't hesitate to take her to task. No matter what Louise had said to herself the night before, she didn't want to hear it from anyone else, especially from this person whom she chose to avoid in any and all opportunities.

"How many more times are you going to lead Major Stafford into danger? If you had taken my advice in the beginning …."

"Lady Jane, I do not care to hear anything more from you." Louise stared at her. "I believed I had made that clear to you yesterday."

"I told you not to upset Jane," Herman Amberly warned her with a heavy frown.

Louise met his glaring eyes for a moment before turning away to greet other visitors. Major Stafford arrived with the rest of yesterday's party close on his heels. She didn't have a private word with him but did learn the reason she had not seen him the previous evening.

"Oh, this wretched limb decided to act up, which sometimes happens when the weather is inclement."

Her indignant stare showed she didn't believe his mendacity. Louise had just pleaded tiredness and declined to ride with him that afternoon, when Lord Saunderson interrupted their conversation, inquiring about her well-being in his usual flat monotone. He stood at her side, his aloofness inhibiting other callers until the other visitors had gone. When he asked her to drive with him, she started to decline until she met her grandmother's minatory stare. Therefore, at five o'clock she pasted a smile on her face when Saunderson assisted her into his open carriage.

"You are looking beautiful this afternoon, my lady."

"Thank you, my lord."

"I trust you have fully recovered from your harrowing experience of yesterday."

"Yes, thank you, my lord." You can do better than this, Louise scolded herself. "Those are magnificent grays you're driving. Perfectly matched too, if my eyes do not deceive me."

"Thank you." Saunderson studied the pair pulling his carriage. "I believe they are perfectly matched, yes. Those were the instructions I gave my agent. He always carries out my orders."

"Do you not choose your own cattle, my lord?" Surprise tinged her words.

He cast an astonished glance in her direction. "Why should I perform menial duties when I employ agents?"

His question stopped Louise in her mental tracks, unable to think of a reply. She even welcomed the questions from all who stopped them in Hyde Park. Anything was better than Saunderson's stilted attempts at conversation.

Near the gate after their second circle of the loop, Louise came face to face with Major Stafford. She gazed beseechingly into his blue eyes. How could she convey she was only here because her grandmother insisted? She didn't have the opportunity before he nodded and rode on past. She closed her eyes in a moment of despair. When she opened them again, she gazed into another pair of blue eyes, also hurt. Could this drive get worse?

Yesterday, Lady Belinda Creighton had enjoyed Saunderson's attention when he had stayed at her side. Now she bit her trembling lip, nodding at them when her mother's carriage passed.

Arriving at Chesley Square, Louise hurried into the house. Things were no better inside. The moment she closed her bedchamber door, Lady Granville entered with questions.

"Louise, my dear, how was your ride? Did you enjoy Lord Saunderson's company? He is a most amiable young man, is he not?"

Dear heaven, her grandmother was gushing like a schoolroom chit with stars in her eyes. "The ride was pleasant. I suppose you would describe Lord Saunderson as amiable."

Louise refrained from adding that she, herself, would not.

"Wonderful. Now, you must wear your prettiest gown this evening. Lord Saunderson is joining us for dinner and the theater afterwards. Just a family dinner, you understand; nonetheless, you must be in your best looks." Lady Granville hurried from the room before Louise could speak.

Louise slumped against the door. Her day was getting worse by the moment. All she needed was more of Saunderson's company to place this day in the list of the worst of her life. Nevertheless, she allowed Agnes to dress her in a new gown of mint green trimmed with Brussels lace at the square neckline. She forced another smile on her face.

Louise spoke little during dinner. When Lady Granville commented on her loss of appetite, she managed a few bites. She welcomed Foster's announcement that the carriage had arrived to carry them to Covent Gardens. As Agnes had said earlier, the sooner we start, the sooner it will be over. There will be other people at the theater perhaps with better conversation.

There were. The first person she saw after entering the Granville box was Major Stafford in the Shelburne box across from them. Louise managed a smile before Saunderson claimed her attention. The interval was a nightmare. Lord Granville urged her to stroll in the lobby with Saunderson. Louise found herself stopped beside the major in the crush of people. Before she could speak, a harsh voice intervened.

"I understand there was a little problem yesterday, Stafford," Lord Hurley commented with a smirk on his face. "You can't be too careful, can you? You should know it is never wise to turn your back on people." He pushed his way through the crowd before they could speak.

Louise turned toward the major, but Saunderson saw her intention and pulled her in the other direction.

"Time to return to the box," he announced. Without even a nod toward the major, Saunderson hurried her away.

Louise endured the remainder of the evening in virtual silence. When they returned to Chesley Square, she hurried inside with a barely civil 'good night' to Lord Saunderson. She rushed up the stairs and into her bedchamber with the hope of avoiding a session with her grandmother.

It was not to be.

"Was this not the most pleasant evening we have had since coming to Town?" Lady Granville seated herself in an armless chair near the fireplace. "Lord Saunderson was most attentive to you again this evening. I believe you have a real prospect there."

Louise's muffled reply came through the night robe that Agnes drew over her head. "You don't need to stay, Agnes."

"I must first brush your hair," the maid protested.

"Not tonight, please. My head feels as though it will burst. I don't want a brush, or anything else, touching it." Louise hoped her grandmother would take the hint when Agnes left. She did not.

"You will remember I promised you an evening when you could show your talents on the piano. I believe now is the time to put my plan into action. Do you not agree a dinner followed by your entertainment is an excellent plan? Your talent should not go unnoticed any longer."

After taking a deep breath, Louise replied, "This has been a trying day answering questions. I have a terrible headache, Grandmother. May we discuss this another time?"

"Yes, my dear. You do look all pulled about. We will discuss our plan tomorrow. Now, you get a good night's sleep." She swept out the door, leaving the hapless Louise alone at last.

Louise knew she would not sleep anytime soon. She took her favorite spot by the window and stared out into the night. When they lived in Harley Street, she had questioned why Rebecca spent so much time staring into the night. Now she understood. Most people wanted the quiet of the country at bedtime, but not Louise. Nighttime in the City soothed her with its familiar sounds. Carriages rattled by in the distance. She could hear the riotous voices of some drunken revelers.

Louise leaned her head against the windowpane, thinking of the major. She must find an opportunity to explain about Saunderson. She cringed at the thought her grandmother was pushing her toward marriage with the most boring person she had ever encountered. How could she thwart that move? She must find a way. And she would, she told herself. One way or another, Louise vowed, she would not marry Lord Saunderson, as she slipped between the sheets. Easy in her mind at last, she slept until almost noon.

"It's about time you woke up, my lady," Agnes spoke from the door. "I have been in here any number of times to check on you. Lady Granville has looked in on you too."

Carefully raising her head, Louise realized the throbbing ache had gone. Perhaps that portended a better day than yesterday. She sipped the chocolate the maid handed to her. "I'll get up now, Agnes. You may tell my grandmother I will attend her in half an hour."

When Agnes left the room, Louise studied herself in the mirror. Her face was wan with dark circles under the eyes. She bathed her face in cool water, then patted rice powder around her eyes, but to no avail. She looked like death.

Lady Granville did care. "You will spend the day either in your bed or in the back garden. If your headache is gone, the garden will be best because it might bring the roses back into your cheeks. No visitors for you today. I'll make your excuses to anyone who inquires."

Louise knew she didn't want to stay inside. Therefore, when she had eaten, she donned the spencer that matched her peach muslin gown and hurried to the back garden. There she wandered the paths for several minutes, pinching a few dead blossoms from the Michaelmas daisies. She plucked one in full bloom, slowly pulling each white petal. He loves me. He loves me not. He loves me. She soon had the flower shredded around her feet.

She had been sitting on a wrought-iron bench for an appreciable time, her thoughts on the minor key of her present life, when she heard footsteps. Expecting to hear her grandmother's voice, she didn't turn around.

"Good afternoon, my lady," a quiet, masculine voice said.

Louise jumped to her feet, a smile crossing her face, her hands stretched toward him. "Major Stafford! How did you come to be here in the garden?" She glanced behind him.

"I bribed Foster not to announce me to your grandparents," he admitted, a wicked grin settling on his face.

Louise dimpled at him, as she returned to the bench. "I want to explain about yesterday."

"No explanation from you is necessary," Stafford responded, seating himself on the bench. "After I gave myself time to analyze the situation, I realized your grandmother had made your plans for you. I am right, am I not?"

Louise nodded in relief. "There is something else. Grandmother is planning a dinner party. I'm not sure she intends to invite you. She probably doesn't, but without doubt she will invite Lord Saunderson. She prattles on about him like a schoolroom miss just making her come-out."

Stafford grinned at the image. "Will she permit you to ride with me this afternoon?"

Louise shook her head. "She has ordered me to remain either in my bedchamber or in this garden the entire day."

The major frowned. "Is she angry with you about something?"

"Oh, no. Grandmother thinks I'm not in my best looks which, after a difficult couple of days, I'm not. She believes a day of rest will revive me. A ride would help me more than sitting around moping, but she would never understand that because she has never mounted any horse, to my certain knowledge."

"To me, you're always beautiful."

Louise felt heat rise into her face but told herself not to be missish. She turned toward him. "Thank you, Major, but you do me too much honour."

Stafford shook his head and clasped her hand where it lay on the bench between them. She turned her palm in his, returning the pressure, as contentment invaded her being. Even the chaffinches singing in the tree above them seemed to approve her caller.

They sat quietly, speaking only of trivialities until Foster interrupted them with a slight cough.

"My lady, Lady Granville is asking for you in the drawing room."

"I'm just coming, Foster. Thank you."

When the butler walked away, Louise turned to the major. She would speak her thoughts, regardless of Society rules. "This has been my most pleasant afternoon since returning to Town. I hope to see you again soon."

"For me also." Stafford grinned impishly. "Perhaps you will see me sooner than you expect."

Louise hurried to the drawing room where her grandmother awaited her. They discussed the dinner party for a few minutes before Foster announced the arrival of Lord Saunderson.

Lady Granville waved him to a chair next to her. "We're planning a dinner party for a select few ...," she stopped speaking to greet other visitors. Rebecca came in on Shelburne's arm with Major Stafford at their heels.

Louise chewed her inner lip to control her laughter at his audacity. Straightening her face to a calm interest, she turned to Lady Granville. "Grandmother, you were saying something about a dinner party."

"Oh, ah, yes, I believe I was."

"Oh, what fun." Jasper Winningham strolled into the room without being announced. "I do hope I'm invited, my lady." His boyish smile didn't quite reach his sharp eyes when he glanced at Louise standing too close to the major. "I want to become better acquainted with my newly found cousin. A small dinner party would be just the ticket."

Lady Granville knew when to admit defeat. "Yes, you are invited, Jasper. Lord Saunderson will be an honored guest. I hope we will have the pleasure of your company, also." She directed her gaze at a point between Shelburne and Rebecca, but Major Stafford answered.

"You may count on our presence, your ladyship. It will be a marvelous evening, I am confident."

Louise mangled her inner lip again in an effort not to chortle, while Foster brought in a tea tray. Passing the cups, Louise found an answering gleam of amusement in Stafford's eyes, which seemed to say, "How's that for audacity?"

The following morning when Louise counted the dinner invitation envelopes she and her grandmother had addressed, they realized they would seat three dozen. Neither was sure how the list had grown, nor did they care overmuch. The purpose was to allow as many people as possible to hear Louise perform on the piano, her grandmother reminded her.

"This dinner is a good idea, Louise. We also need to reciprocate on all the hospitality extended to you in these few short weeks. A dinner party is the best way to accomplish our dual purposes, I believe."

"I've attended several balls," Louise said. "Also, various dinner parties."

"Yes, I know, as well as a few musicales." Lady Granville hesitated. "Your grandfather and I discussed the possibility of having a ball in your honour, but we have decided to postpone it until the Spring Season. By that time, I expect you will receive vouchers for Almack's. We can be sure some of the patronesses will attend, which will be the making of you."

Louise nodded, although she did not approve of the authority the patronesses had. There was no point in railing against her curtailed activities. She had learned early to tread lightly over rough ground.

After a light luncheon, Louise welcomed the appearance of Rebecca.

"I'm ready to climb the walls from boredom. What can we do to enliven my spirits?"

"Do you mean to say the mere sight of me is not sufficient for you?" Rebecca teased her old friend. "I might have a case of the vapors."

Louise laughed with her. "I have not been to Green Park since my return to London. Shall we go there?" She saw a slight shadow cross Rebecca's face. After an instant of puzzlement, Louise remembered Rebecca's earlier experience in Green Park when one of Shelburne's acquaintances tried to ravish her several months ago. "Oh dear, I am sorry I reminded you of that horrible incident. We will go to Kensington Gardens instead."

Rebecca smiled. "I would like to go to Green Park again. I enjoyed it tremendously, much more than Hyde Park. I won't allow old shadows to ruin my pleasure."

Calling to Agnes to bring her a light wrap, Louise sought her grandmother's permission. She found her in the morning room making menus for their dinner party. "Grandmother, may I go to Green Park with Rebecca Blackwell? Her maid is with her. I will take Agnes also."

Lady Granville assented, never taking her eyes from the list in front of her.

Louise made good her escape. while her grandmother mumbled about lobster patties and asparagus with lemon sauce. She paused at the door the butler was holding open for her. "Foster, we're going to Green Park for a couple of hours, in the event anyone should inquire. Her ladyship knows."

The young ladies enjoyed their stroll to the park, stopping several times to chat with acquaintances. Louise cast an apprehensive glance at Rebecca when Lord Hurley fell into step with them while crossing Piccadilly. She hoped he would not join them for long. The Duchess of Dorchester proved being democratic in one's acquaintances was acceptable, but Major Stafford held a different opinion. Louise didn't want to upset him now.

"Good afternoon, ladies. I hope I see you well." Hurley's modulated voice was in direct contrast to his usual harsh tones.

"Yes, thank you, my lord. We are well," replied Louise. Rebecca nodded.

"You ladies have chosen a pleasant afternoon for your outing. Are you perhaps going to Green Park?"

Louise glanced upward to meet the sardonic gleam in his eyes. "That is our destination."

"You don't care for my company," Hurley declared. "Stafford has warned you against me, I warrant. Probably Shelburne also."

Goaded beyond her tolerance, Louise stared him in the eyes and responded tartly, if not quite truthfully, "Major Stafford does not discuss you, Lord Hurley. My grandparents have expressed their opinions of your suitability as an acquaintance."

His harsh laughter startled her. "Oh yes, I can imagine what old Granville thinks of me. However, I don't believe Stafford has not warned you away from me. He's too starched up not to do so. You are not a good liar, my dear. Don't try it with me." Hurley turned toward Rebecca, who stared him in the eyes. "What about you, my lady? Have either Amesbury or Shelburne warned you against me?"

"There was no need, Lord Hurley," she answered. "Your reputation is on everybody's lips."

He stared at her a moment, then left them at the entrance to the park.

Louise stared after him with loathing. "I don't understand why anyone would choose to associate with him."

"He isn't important, Louise. Don't allow him to ruin our enjoyment of the park."

Entering the park, they sniffed the air before strolling inside. It was fresh, so the cows must be on the far side of the park. They strolled, their maids the requisite two steps behind them, chatting between themselves.

"Rebecca, there's something I have not thought to ask. Have you seen your parents' apparitions since returning to Town?"

She shook her head. "I saw them immediately after Lady Becca identified them for me. I can't say they gave me the blessing I wanted, but I was content in the moment. I've walked all over Green Park a few times hoping to see them but haven't found them. Perhaps my knowledge of who they are has allowed them to pass on."

"You could be right."

A boy of about ten years strode back and forth some half dozen steps each way, his hands clasped behind his back. A frown of concentration marred his forehead; his lips moved in silent conversation. Louise strained to distinguish his muttered words.

"He's conjugating Latin verbs," she murmured to Rebecca—not a usual occupation for little boys in Green Park.

"Amo, amas ... oh, why can I not remember the third person singular? Sapskull." He thumped himself on the head.

"Amat. You are not a sapskull, so don't think you are. Latin verbs can be extremely difficult to conjugate, even the simplest ones."

The boy gazed into Louise's face in stupefaction. "You're a lady."

"Yes."

"How do you know about Latin verbs?"

"I learned them a long time ago." Before he could dispute her word, she continued, "I know, females are not supposed to be able to learn Latin. Someday, you will realize females are more capable than gentlemen believe. Shall I help you learn the verb conjugations?" Louise sought a way that would allow him to accept help from a mere female without being unmanly. "Oh, I say, can you whistle?"

"Of course, I can. Anybody can whistle."

"I can't," she answered, a small frown appearing between her brows. "I always wanted to learn, but I could never get the knack of it. Do you think you could teach me if I help you with your verbs?"

He studied her for a moment, his thoughts evident on his face. She seemed to be serious. He did need to learn those verbs before his tutor shouted at him again. He made his decision. "Alright. Purse your lips this way."

For the next hour, Rebecca sat on a wrought-iron bench, hiding her amusement while the lessons proceeded. She glanced up and saw Major Stafford coming toward them. His limp was much improved now, she realized. Rebecca struggled to control her mirth when he saw Louise sitting on the ground facing a small boy, her lips pursed.

"You must not be holding your tongue right. Keep it barely touching your lower teeth. Don't pucker quite so much."

Louise tried again. This time she got out a creditable sound and grinned her pleasure. Soon they were whistling together until they collapsed in giggles against each other.

"Bravo, Louise, you did it." Rebecca's voice brought the two students back to their surroundings.

Louise gasped with horror when she saw the major watching her with a grin on his face.

"You never cease to amaze me," he assured her, helping her to her feet. "I don't believe I know any other female who can whistle. I congratulate you."

She stammered her thanks. "You see, Major, David taught me to whistle in exchange for helping him with his Latin verbs. Oh, this young man is David Hollinsworth, who is preparing for entrance to Eton. David, this is Major George Stafford."

David got straight to the point. "Why are you not in uniform, Major?"

Stafford returned his bow with aplomb. "You see it's this way. One of Boney's men put a ball in my leg. I came home to recuperate. While I am recovering, I don't wear my uniform."

"Master David." A scolding voice approached them. "I have looked everywhere for you."

The boy grimaced. "Mr. Bellows, my tutor. I must go now. Thank you, my lady, for helping me with the verbs. You're a better hand at teaching than he is."

David scampered away.

"Latin verbs?" Stafford studied her countenance.

"I learned Latin at the orphanage, Major." Did he think her a bluestocking? Heaven forbid that he ever learn she could also speak French and Greek. Louise enjoyed her intelligence, yet she hoped she didn't act the way she had heard women of that ilk did.

"You surprise me again," Stafford said. "Now, shall I escort you ladies home?"

Louise entered Granville House in a pleasant frame of mind, which didn't last beyond the first few steps. Jasper Winningham greeted her, as if this were his home and he the host.

"Your excursion out of doors put roses in your cheeks, Cousin. You must allow me to escort you on your next visit to Green Park."

"No thank you. Lady Rebecca and our maids are perfect companions while walking."

"Yet, I believe I heard Stafford's voice at the door."

Louise ignored the comment and excused herself to go above stairs to prepare for tea.

After the afternoon visitors left, Louise's thoughts returned to Major Stafford. What would be his reaction to their meeting in Green Park. Her abstraction at dinner caused Lady Granville to decree they would stay at home that evening.

"You must be sickening for something, Louise. I will send our excuses to Lady Amberly. You can get to bed early."

Louise nodded her acquiescence, thankful to avoid a confrontation with Lady Jane. The major's face blotted out the words when she tried to read. She paced the floor instead. "I am not a bluestocking," she muttered. "I am *not*."

The entrance of her maid caused Louise to stop her pacing but not her scowl.

"Ma'am, whatever have I done wrong?"

Louise didn't even hear the question. "Agnes, am I a bluestocking?"

"A bluestocking? I'm not sure what that is, but if it's bad, you're not."

Louise smiled. "Thank you for your vote of confidence, Agnes."

They were quiet, while Agnes helped her into a night robe. When the maid left the room, Louise snuggled beneath the covers. Major Stafford needed to learn females are intelligent enough to learn most things if they have the opportunity.

Louise laughed aloud at the thought of Lord Saunderson's probable reaction to seeing her sitting on the ground learning to whistle from a small boy. Besides supposedly not being able to learn Latin, a lady is not supposed to whistle. Nor sit on the ground.

The major was also pensive throughout the evening. He returned to his rooms from White's after complaints over his inattention in a card game. He sat long into the night, thinking about his growing interest in Louise. To find her sitting on the ground in a public park was beyond anything—a shocking want of decorum. As for conjugating Latin verbs, he doubted he could conjugate even one, this long past his school days. Was she a bluestocking? He was not sure he approved of educated females.

Stafford thought of his mother. She could read and write. Beyond that she had little education in anything remotely useful. He was not aware of his mother ever setting more than a few stitches, although she kept needlework beside her. Stafford almost laughed aloud at the thought of his ultra-feminine mother sitting on the ground whistling with small boys. Yet she seemed the perfect wife, the perfect mother, her mind on her men folk instead of parading knowledge.

Louise didn't hesitate to parade her knowledge. Stafford could do nothing about that. All he could do was watch her the following evening at the Granvilles' dinner party. If she were a bluestocking, her conversation would show in the dinner table conversation because Granville's known lack of patience with frivolous discourse would set the tone.

Chapter 13

Poachers in Hyde Park?

The evening of the Granville dinner party was clear and crisp. No hope anyone would decline their invitation, much to Louise's regret.

"That shade of green brings out the green flecks in your eyes," Agnes told her as she straightened tiny rows of lace around the decorous round neckline.

"Thank you. I do like this deeper shade of green," Louise replied and checked her reticule for the requisite handkerchief. "Wish me luck, Agnes."

"There's no need for you to be nervous. Now enjoy the evening."

Louise paused at the foot of the stair, took a deep breath, and then joined her grandparents in the receiving line to greet the guests. She cringed inside yet managed to smile when Mrs. Drummond-Burrell arrived accompanied by Lady Cowper, the dreaded twosome of Almack's patronesses. Maria Sefton greeted her with a quiet smile, which restored Louise's confidence to some extent, but she couldn't let down her guard.

Dinner was a long, tedious affair with course following course, each with several removes. Louise felt the major's questioning glance resting on her from across the table. She gave him a slight smile; otherwise, she confined her attention to her immediate partners, even though the conversation became general at one point. Her nerves were on edge with the patronesses so close to her, watching her every move. After a quiet reminder to the footman, she drank only lemonade. She had known the patronesses would be there, so why hadn't she pay closer attention to Lady

Granville's seating plans? Without doubt, Louise would have changed them, seating the ladies on the same side of the table as she was.

When Lady Granville led the ladies out of the dining room, she turned toward the music room instead of the drawing room. Once inside she said, "While we wait for the gentlemen to join us, Louise will entertain us with a few airs on the piano."

Louise swallowed her dismay. She had forgotten she would perform tonight as a reward for not showing up the less talented girls at the Holgarths' musical evening. With a brief smile, she seated herself on the piano bench. Louise's nervousness faded when she immersed herself in music. In only a moment, she was unmindful of her listeners, unaware of the gentlemen entering the room and the prevailing silence around her. Louise mentally returned to her surroundings only when Lady Granville laid a hand on her shoulder, a proud smile lighting her face.

"My granddaughter had the best music masters when she grew up in the Hampshire orphanage, sponsored by Elizabeth, the Duchess of Dorchester. She recognized Louise's talent and encouraged her."

With a quick nod, Louise acknowledged the loud applause awarded her, then hastened to take a seat near Rebecca. In the ensuing general conversation, Lord Saunderson joined her on the small sofa. She glanced at him warily.

"You perform in a tolerable way, my lady."

"Thank you, my lord."

They sat in silence.

"Do you play the piano often?"

"I practice most days."

"That accounts for your smoothness."

Louise racked her brain for a topic that would elicit some enthusiasm from him. She sighed with relief when people started leaving so that she could excuse herself to do her duty. She had one brief meeting with the major.

"Will you ride with me in the morning?"

Louise wondered at his subdued expression. Perhaps his injured leg was bothering him. "Yes, Major, I would enjoy a ride with you. Eight o'clock?"

After everyone left, Louise trudged up the stairs with the hope of solitude. It was not to be, because her grandmother followed her into the bedchamber.

"Our evening went quite well, Louise. Do you not agree? I watched Saunderson's face while you were playing the piano. He truly appreciated your talent."

Louise managed to say, "Thank you for telling me, Grandmother."

"Louise, my dear, I know it is early days, but perhaps we should talk about your marriage."

"My marriage?" She turned appalled eyes toward her grandmother.

"Yes. Lord Saunderson admires you. Do you think you might like to live with him? In marriage, I mean to say," Lady Granville amended with a flush covering her normally pale face.

Louise paced the floor. "Grandmother, I don't want to marry someone I might like to live *with*. I want to marry someone I cannot live *without*."

Lady Granville straightened her barely relaxed posture, her tone returning to her early severity. "You must understand people of our class do not approach marriage in that fashion."

"Lord Saunderson is the most boring gentleman of my acquaintance, Grandmother. He's always solemn. Have you noticed he never smiles? I want a husband who laughs with me."

"I suppose I never thought of laughter being a prerequisite for marriage."

Louise turned pleading eyes toward her. "One of the few memories I have of my early childhood with my parents was the laughter in our house. I don't suppose they laughed all the time; still, that is how I remember them, always merry. I want what they had."

Lady Granville's expression made clear that she did not want to hear about her son or the conniving upstart who had snared him into marriage. "Do you have someone in mind?"

"Major Stafford and I always laugh together," Louise said, after the slightest pause. "Even his eyes laugh. I've noticed he's acceptable in Society. Is he so very unacceptable?"

"Has he approached you?"

Louise answered the horror in her grandmother's voice. "Oh, no, you may be sure he would never do anything improper."

"I have come to love you, despite everything. I do want your happiness." Lady Granville rose to leave. "We will talk about it again. There is no hurry, only do not pin your hopes on Stafford. We simply cannot permit you to make such a *mésalliance*."

Louise paced the bedchamber. Marrying George Stafford would not be a *mésalliance* to anyone except the Marquess and Marchioness of Granville. History was repeating itself. Although the major had not said anything about marriage, she was confident he would. The question was—would the honourable major elope with her, if necessary? Louise cringed at the thought of the consequences of such an action, yet an elopement might be necessary if she married the man of her choice. Her mother had.

Across Town, the dashing major sat in thought. He didn't quite know what to make of Louise Mansfield. On the one hand, she could conjugate Latin verbs—unheard of in a female. On the other, she played the piano like a professional—better than many he had heard in concerts. How could one person, a female at that, be adept at two such diverse skills? Louise was challenging his views on the weaker sex. He was not sure he wanted to change them. He didn't know any other female who could whistle either. She also rode better than most men. Louise could in all probability drive to an inch, a female Corinthian, in fact.

Louise was already awake the following morning when Agnes brought a tray containing a cup of chocolate. "Good morning, Agnes. Another glorious day, is it not?"

Agnes showed some surprise to see her mistress standing at the window in her night robe. "Bless me, my lady, you gave me a turn. What are you doing out of bed already?"

"I'm riding with the major this morning. Lay out the gold velvet habit and the hat with the two plumes."

"You will look a treat for sure."

Moments later, Louise smoothed the soft fabric over her hips with satisfaction and gave her hat one last adjustment. Pulling on her soft leather riding gloves, she hurried to the stables.

The major was waiting. He nodded toward the swaying plumes. "Fetching, I must say. Bang up to the nines, right, Baker?"

The groom grinned, as he tossed Louise into the saddle and mounted his own restless bay hack.

They trotted until they entered the park, where, after one glance down the avenue, the three riders broke into a gallop. They pulled up at the other end, Baker staying a short distance away.

The other two exchanged smiles, as they began their slow return to the park gates, holding the reins loosely. About mid-way of the avenue, a sharp crack sounded, causing Juno to rear in fright before taking off through the trees at a full gallop. Louise had not been minding her business, so she was unprepared for the sudden increase in speed. She held on to the reins until they reached the trees where a low limb knocked her off Juno.

"Baker, see if you can catch the rogue," the major shouted across his shoulder, as he thundered after Louise. He found her lying dazed at the base of a tree.

Kneeling beside her, the major patted her face. "Louise, are you alright? Did he hit you? Do you hurt anywhere? Speak to me!"

She gasped with pain when she tried to raise her head. "Did someone shoot toward us again? Is that what spooked Juno?" Louise managed to sit up. "Where is Juno? I see two of everything else but not even one of her."

The major eased her back to the ground. "Take it easy, my dear," he soothed her. "We will find Juno in a few minutes." He turned his head at the sound of footsteps. "Baker, did you catch him?"

"No, Major, I regret to say he disappeared before I could see him. I did find where his horse had been standing. I couldn't catch him, although I could hear him galloping away." He gazed at Louise. "Is she alright? Without doubt, the marquess will have my head on a platter for this."

"More likely it will be mine," Stafford answered. "See if you can find Juno."

"Ah, Stafford, do I intrude? This is an odd time for a tryst, if you don't mind my pointing that out to you," Lord Hurley spoke in a silky voice, with a glance at the recumbent Louise. "Do all your ladybirds turn pale after receiving your attentions?"

"Hurley, this is not what you probably think," the major began.

"Yes, I begin to realize that. Has there been another, uh, accident?"

Stafford climbed to his feet. With a stifled groan, he leaned against his mount. "Someone shot across her mare's neck which startled her into running. Lady Louise was unable to dodge a tree limb, with the result you see. Her eyes are not focusing, always a matter of concern."

Baker rode up, leading a panting Juno. "How is she, Major?"

"I'm alright, Baker," Louise raised herself into a sitting position, leaning against a tree. "Is Juno hurt?"

"No, Miss, just winded."

Hurley offered his help. "People are arriving in the park. Unless you want more gossip, you will leave at once. I shall try to commandeer a carriage to take the lady home." Wheeling his mount, he started to ride away until Louise's voice stopped him.

"No thank you, Lord Hurley. You're very kind—I do appreciate your offer—however, I must ride Juno home. I prefer not to worry my grandparents any more than necessary." Louise turned to the major. "Help me to my feet, please."

With a shrug, Hurley departed, leaving Stafford trying to persuade her.

Louise was adamant. She would return home the same way she left, on Juno's back, which she did, after straightening her clothing. The maid might revive the crushed velvet, but the plumes were beyond repair.

Her grandparents had not come downstairs, so Louise suggested the major return later to talk with them. "I can see your leg pains you. Without doubt, you need to rest it."

Stafford could not deny her words. "Please tell Lord Granville I shall return before the morning has passed."

Nodding, she grasped the stair railing to help her up the steps.

After ringing for Agnes, Louise lowered herself into a chair. Her mind was in such turmoil that she hardly heard the maid's exclamations, before Agnes hurried away for bath water.

Louise glimpsed herself in the mirror. Her face was pale, her head throbbed, but she was no longer seeing double.

Her common sense told her she could not avoid telling her grandparents about the shooting. After her bath, Louise limped downstairs.

They had heard the servants' gossip but had forced themselves to wait for her appearance. Lord Granville studied her face and withheld his wrath. "I do not recall ever hearing of poachers in Hyde Park. Do you contend this was an accident too?"

He was not shouting. Louise breathed a sigh of relief. Her poor head could not stand that. "No, Grandfather, I must admit I cannot excuse this as an accident. Doubtless the first time was not either. Can we be sure he or they intended to shoot *me*?"

"Whatever can you mean, child?" her grandmother demanded.

"I was with Major Stafford both times. Perhaps he was the target. After all, who would shoot me? I don't know anyone well enough to have made an enemy. He probably has at least a few."

"You do have a point, Louise," her grandmother said. "Nevertheless, we cannot rule out you were, indeed, the intended target. I shall not accuse you of being heedless—you just take such risks.”

“Life is a risk,” she answered as politely as she could manage. “I could easily break my neck with a tumble down the stairs. Outside, the weather is hazardous to say the least. What about rogues and cut-purses?”

“What you say is correct,” her grandfather acknowledged. “Nevertheless, there will be no more early rides in the park. Furthermore, you are to go no place where there is not a large crowd of people. Do you understand?”

“Yes, Grandfather.” Louise gently touched her left temple. “The way I feel at this moment, I may never leave this house again.”

“Back to bed with you, my girl,” her grandmother ordered. “I sent for the doctor. We will talk again after he examines you.”

After the doctor’s visit, Lady Granville entered Louise’s bedchamber. “You have a mild concussion. A few days in bed should make you right as rain. You will be sore for several days, probably have some unsightly bruises. I imagine you will choose to remain indoors.”

Louise agreed. At this point, she could not imagine venturing from her bedchamber much less out-of-doors.

Lord Granville was in his study reading the newspaper when Foster announced Major Stafford. With a grim expression, he waved his visitor toward a chair. “Good morning, Major.”

“Good morning, my lord.” Stafford took a deep breath, then looked the older man straight in the eyes.

"I have come to talk to you about Lady Louise. I understand from Foster that the doctor has been to see her."

Granville gave a grudging report. "The doctor said she has a mild concussion and should remain in bed a few days. Now, Major Stafford, what can you tell me about the occurrence this morning? Although I have heard Baker's account, I hesitated to question my granddaughter. She was in considerable distress."

"We had given the horses their heads for the length of the avenue. Returning at a slow pace, we heard the shot." Stafford continued with the story, a slight frown on his face. "Baker attempted to catch the culprit, but was unable to find him."

"My granddaughter made a point which is worth our consideration, I believe. She believes you might be the target instead of her. Do you have any reason to believe someone is trying to kill you?"

"No, my lord, I don't. There is one thing to consider though. I have never seen Lord Hurley in the park so early. He came on the scene in a very pat manner. I've tried to remember whether his horse was at all hot. I must admit such was not the case. I believe we can rule him out as the culprit."

"Have you reason to believe he might do you harm?"

The major shrugged. "We've had our differences since our days together at Eton. However, I don't believe he despises me to the point where he would attempt my life. Besides, I am out enough on my own that anyone trying to injure me would have no difficulty finding me alone. That brings us back to your granddaughter. Who is trying to harm her? Also, why? To put it bluntly, who will benefit from her death?"

"I understand you," he responded, his voice grim. "My heir is a distant cousin of my own generation.

Succeeding generations have no surviving males until we reach another cousin's grandson, whom you have met, Jasper Winningham, who has just turned up after years on the continent. I suppose he will inherit if Louise does not produce a male child."

"My lord, I don't care to be rude about your family, but I have a difficult time visualizing Winningham generating enough energy to make an attempt on anyone's life."

The marquess released a bark of laughter. "I agree with your reading of his character. However, still waters do run deep at times. Lady Granville suggested he would more likely attempt to fix his interest with Louise than to murder her. I must admit that he has been hanging on her sleeve at every opportunity."

They discussed the matter for several more minutes but did not reach a conclusion before the major departed.

Throughout the day, visitors kept the doorknocker busy, inquiring about Louise. Only Rebecca entered the house, and that was over her grandparents' highly vocal objections. Louise's repeated requests won that argument.

"You fail to understand my situation," Louise told them, petulance coloring her voice. "Since we were six years old, Rebecca and I have always been together when we needed each other. I need her now." Her voice broke on a sob.

Her grandparents gave in to the inevitable rather than risk their granddaughter having a fever of the brain. Lady Granville intercepted Rebecca in the hallway outside Louise's door the afternoon of the shooting. "The doctor ordered complete bed rest for several days. Louise has taken a few drops of laudanum, but unless she stops fretting, the medicine will not help her. Against our judgment, she insisted upon seeing you, so her grandfather and I depend on you to calm her."

Assuring the older lady that she would do her best, Rebecca entered Louise's sitting room, her arms outstretched. "I came the moment I heard. Are you truly alright? Head injuries can be particularly bad. Tell me all about it, do."

Louise clung to her best friend for a long moment. Then, she led her to a small chair next to the bed, and settled herself against the pillows. Nothing loath to unburden herself, Louise gave considerable detail. "I believe someone means mischief to Major Stafford, Rebecca. I can't bear the thought."

"The major? I'm concerned about you, not him, no matter how estimable he is."

"There is no reason for anyone to shoot me, can you not see? As I told my grandparents, I haven't been in Town long enough to make enemies. So, it seems obvious to me that Major Stafford is in danger of losing his life after surviving his war experiences. I find it worrying in the extreme."

Rebecca was quiet for a moment, while she studied the other's face. "You're quite pale. I cannot decide if it results from your injuries or from your concern for the major."

"My head still aches a little, but the laudanum will take care of that soon enough. I am somewhat stiff too, but I don't have any actual injuries. It's Major Stafford, Rebecca. What will I do if someone does shoot him? The guilt will be mine."

"I don't understand."

Louise reminded her of her disobedience to her grandparents. "I'm supposed to obey them in all things. I can't, Rebecca. Not in this. I truly can't! It goes against everything I hold dear."

"Tell me what they want you to do."

"They want me to marry Lord Saunderson," Louise almost wailed. "I can't. I *won't*." Her voice dropped to a whisper. "The thought is beyond bearing."

Rebecca answered the anguished whisper with soothing words and soon had the satisfaction of seeing Louise's breathing calm into a deep sleep.

Closing the door softly, Rebecca assured Lady Granville that her granddaughter was asleep. "I will return the instant Louise again needs me, no matter what other plans I might have."

"I will send word if she asks for you."

The patient remained calm. On the afternoon of the third day, Louise ventured downstairs for the first time, hoping only a few people would join her for tea. Shelburne and Rebecca arrived first with the major, followed closely by the Amberly ladies, escorted by Herman Amberly. Lady Jane did not hesitate to express her opinion.

"Whatever next will happen to you? Perhaps now you will heed my admonitions. It is not safe for you or Major Stafford to be out of doors. Has it not occurred to you that fate is warning you not to endanger the major any further?"

Before Louise could form a polite disclaimer, the major interrupted. A ferocious scowl marred his countenance. His words cut like steel. "Lady Jane, I recall telling you that Lady Louise is not responsible for me. Nor are you, I might add. I will appreciate it if you will refrain from making comments about my actions. They are no concern of yours."

"Don't upset Jane." Herman Amberly stared the major straight in the face. "How many times must I say it? *Don't upset Jane.*"

"Come, Herman, we'll tell Mama it's time to leave." Without even a nod at Louise or the major, Lady Jane left the room, her family in tow.

The remainder of the day passed without incident. However, morning brought new excitement to Chesley Square.

Chapter 14

The Prince Regent Is Enthralled

Foster so far forgot himself as to bustle into the breakfast parlor, a smile on his face, a silver salver in his hand. which he extended toward his master.

A footman in royal livery had delivered an invitation for the Marquess and Marchioness of Granville and Lady Louise Mansfield to attend dinner at Carlton House.

"Oh, may we please go?" Louise's eyes were shining in excitement. "My bruises will be healed by that time."

"I do not see how we can avoid it," Lord Granville commented with a scowl. "One does not refuse an invitation from the Prince Regent, no matter how one feels about him."

"Yes, we must go," agreed Lady Granville. "I would send regrets if I could. Before we go, we will discuss proper behavior, Louise. Forewarned is forearmed. The company you will meet there cannot be considered pattern cards of propriety." Pouring herself another cup of coffee, Lady Granville expounded on what Louise could—and could not—do. Her primary warning was to stay outside the regent's pinching range.

"I understood he prefers older ladies for his dalliances."

"That is true, as far as it goes. His preference does not stop him from being too familiar with the younger ladies."

Louise accepted the instructions, knowing she must. Nevertheless, nothing her grandmother said could dampen Louise's spirits. On the night of the dinner, she dressed with particular care. Lady Granville warned her not to wear a gown with a deep décolletage.

"Grandmother, I don't even own such a gown. I wear the most modest necklines of anyone I know."

"That is as may be, young lady. You are to pay particular attention to how much skin is showing. I will inspect you before we leave."

Louise turned with a resolute expression toward her maid. "Agnes, order a bath, and lay out the new emerald green gown."

An hour later, Louise gazed at herself in the mirror. The gown, fashioned of watered silk, sported a standup collar. Long sleeves tapered into fullness over her hands hiding the elbow-length matching gloves. The gown fell in graceful folds to her ankles, encased in matching slippers. When she moved, the skirt swayed gently, giving a hint of long limbs. Not a spot of skin was visible except her face. Her eyes, turned green by the gown, held a glint of determination when she faced her grandmother who stepped into the room.

Lady Granville's eyes bulged. "Where did you get that gown?"

"Do you like it, Grandmother? I made sure to choose a gown that did not have a low neckline," Louise assured her sweetly.

"Excuse me, Lady Granville," Agnes interrupted from the corridor. "Lord Granville sent word the carriage is waiting."

Louise hurriedly wrapped the matching cape around her shoulders, which fastened with a diamond clip. "Perhaps we should not keep Grandfather waiting."

Lady Granville shook her head. "Yes, we must go. Louise. Be warned. We will leave on the instant if your gown draws you into unbecoming behavior. We will discuss this matter further when we return."

Louise winked at Agnes. "I am going to have a glorious time tonight, Agnes. I doubt I will ever be allowed to attend Almack's, so I will enjoy dinner at Carlton House, respectable or not."

Louise tried to restrain her exuberance when the Granvilles' crested carriage passed through the gates at Carlton House and pulled to a stop in front of the columned entrance. She was aware some people compared the Prince Regent's home to an ugly barn. Louise could not agree. In the partial light supplied by several flaming flambeaus, the impression was of grandness.

"Louise, stop gawking like a peasant." Lady Granville hissed out the side of her mouth, as they entered the Chinese drawing room.

Louise ignored her, feasting her eyes on the glorious gowns and fabulous jewelry around her. She felt underdressed with her only ornament being earrings. She shifted her gaze to the high ceiling with a glowing chandelier, while she waited their turn to enter the dining room. Feeling a touch on her arm, she turned to greet Major Stafford, who eyed her with a scowl, although he spoke for her ears only.

"Lady Louise, your gown!"

Her eyes glinted at the implied criticism, yet she answered in a sugary voice. "Yes, Major Stafford, this is a gown. Do you have a comment to make about it?"

Stafford restrained himself. "The gown is more daring than any I have seen you wear before."

"Daring? I am completely covered, Major," Louise said with a tight smile. "I obeyed Grandmother's injunction not to wear a low décolletage."

When the Granville party joined Lord Shelburne's party at the table, the major disappeared from Louise's view. She met Rebecca's amused smile and allowed her mouth to twitch before greeting the others.

The dinner was so long Louise soon lost count of all the courses and removes. She remembered her grandmother's instruction to eat sparingly of each offering, yet she was soon replete. Louise wondered at the amount of food passing before her. She had heard of the Prince Regent's unheeding use of public funds. Tonight, she was seeing his extravagance firsthand.

After the lengthy dinner, the guests wandered through the rooms, while waiting to see who the Regent would favor with a private visit.

Louise gazed with wonder at the furnishings, not realizing how much of a stir she created. The babble around her contained many snide remarks about her gown that might have upset her if she had heard them. When Lady Granville tapped her on the shoulder, she turned a smiling face toward her.

"The Prince Regent has requested our presence, Louise. Please remember all I told you."

Louise's heart leaped with pleasure. She had longed to meet the future king. Now she had the opportunity. She gazed toward the high-backed chair where he sat to greet his subjects. He was fat. Obese. When she approached to within a few feet of him, Louise dipped into a low curtsy, thankful for the fullness of her gown.

"Who have we here?" The Prince Regent's roving eyes caressed her when his lackey pronounced her name. "Oh, yes, I heard Granville's granddaughter had appeared seemingly out of nowhere."

Louise found her voice. Lifting her chin a mite, she replied, "Not precisely out of nowhere, Your Highness. I grew up in an orphanage patronized by the Duchess of Dorchester in Hampshire." She heard, but ignored, her grandmother's gasp at her impertinence. Louise stared him in the eyes, almost daring him to make another disparaging remark.

"I don't often see such spirit in a gel. I dare say Elizabeth Dorchester encouraged it. She was ever a spirited female herself. You're the most beautiful creature I've seen in many Seasons. I expect you to grace my dinner table again soon." He nodded his dismissal, and Louise moved away.

"We are leaving this minute, young lady. I will have words with you later." Lady Granville kept a bland expression on her countenance, but her words were not. They left no doubt that Louise was in for a fine trimming.

Louise didn't care. She had conversed with the Prince Regent, answering his remarks quite well, in her estimation. He had not said a word to her grandparents, not even a greeting. The oversight, if it was that, pleased her beyond words.

Louise sat through her grandfather's homily, which lasted the carriage ride home. She stood through her grandmother's disparaging remarks about her gown when they entered her bedchamber.

"Your disgraceful gown brought you too much attention. Did you hear all the remarks made about it?"

"I cannot help other people being envious, Grandmother. I imagine others will have similar gowns within a week."

"Where did you get the gown, anyway? Surely not from Madame Bouchet."

"No, Madame DuValle fashioned the gown for me," she answered with a quickened pulse. It was fortunate Lady Granville did not recognize the name of the modiste, whose daring creations seldom graced the ladies of the *ton*.

"You are not to wear it again, do you understand? That a Lady of The Family should court this much attention is beyond belief." One can't accuse her of slamming the door as she left, but it was close.

Louise relived her evening with Agnes, who was agog to hear all the details.

The following morning, Louise sat with a blank face when visitor after visitor made sly remarks about her unusual gown or about the attention Prinny paid to her. Inside, she was seething. Her temper exploded when Jasper Winningham took a seat beside her.

"My dear cousin, I've heard such glowing reports of your encounter with our illustrious Regent," he drawled. "He is known to be a connoisseur of beauty, although his preference is for older ladies. Don't get your hopes up of becoming a royal consort."

Louise raked him with blazing eyes. "What I do or who I attract is none of your business, you jackanapes. I don't care to hear anything you have to say."

His eyes blazed. "I don't care to be talked to like a lackey, Cousin."

"If you don't like the way I talk to you, *Cousin*, you can always stay away from me. I have not noticed the marquess has made you welcome in his house."

"You should be careful how you speak to me, Cousin. You might live to regret being rag-mannered to Granville's heir." With a smirk at her amazed expression, he moved away from her.

After the visitors left, Louise approached her grandfather in his study. "Grandfather, is it true Jasper Winningham is your heir?"

"My eventual heir, unless you marry and produce a son, who would be my heir since he would be in the direct line. Are you forming a *tendre* in his direction?"

Louise stared at him in horror. "Absolutely not! You could not want me to be leg-shackled with such as he, even if he is a member of The Family."

"Young Ladies of The Family do not use that term," Granville admonished. "However, no, I do not care to have you married to him."

"That is a relief, I must say. I would not care to cross you any more than necessary. Nonetheless, I draw the line at marrying any Bartholomew baby," she stated, albeit with a smile.

"How do you feel about being married to Lord Saunderson?"

"Grandmother asked me the same question. Grandfather, he is too solemn for my preference. I enjoy laughter, a bit of light-hearted fun. Do you realize I have never even seen him smile? Besides, he has not one iota of conversation."

"Town is thin of company at present," Granville said. "Perhaps the Spring Season will give you more of a choice."

Louise gathered her courage in her hands. "Grandfather, is Major Stafford truly beneath your consideration? We share many of the same thoughts. We even laugh at the same things." She eyed him pleadingly.

"Has he spoken to you?" Granville's harsh voice filled the room. "He should approach me first."

"No, no, Grandfather, he hasn't even hinted at marriage. I promise you, the major is much too decorous to speak to me before applying to you for permission. I don't even know if he has given it any thought. After his reaction to my gown last evening, I dare say he has washed his hands of me."

"Am I to understand you contemplate marriage to someone who has not even indicated an interest?" Granville's mouth gaped in astonishment.

Louise did not drop her gaze from his face. "Yes, I am. Do you not see, Grandfather? He must believe you will not consider his suit, so he says nothing."

"Stafford is right," he informed her. "Perhaps you will see the error of your ways in the not too distant future." He dismissed her with a nod.

As they finished a light luncheon, Foster handed a note to Louise with the information that Lady Rebecca's footman waited for an answer.

Louise scanned the message before passing it to her grandfather. "Rebecca Blackwell wants to take me up in her carriage for a drive in Hyde Park this afternoon. May I go?"

Granville studied the situation for a moment. "You will have the protection of her coachman. I doubt anyone will fire any shots in such a crowded place; still, I prefer Baker accompany you on horseback."

Louise turned to Foster. "Send word I will be ready at five o'clock, please."

When the Amesbury carriage stopped for Louise, she saw that Marie Haverford was also there.

Louise laughed off some light teasing about her conquest of the Prince Regent. After they entered the park, the carriage stopped often while various people greeted them. Louise managed a tinkling laugh at the innuendoes cast in her direction. A particular one amused her.

"Good afternoon, ladies." Simon Abernathy brought his bay mare alongside their carriage. His companion was a lady who controlled her showy mount with ease, a slight smile playing around her lips. Abernathy addressed Louise with a twinkle in his eyes. "I can see why Prinny succumbed to your charms, Lady Louise. I wonder if those gold-flecked eyes shot flaming darts at him, as they are doing at me."

"Actually, Mr. Abernathy, last evening my eyes probably shot green darts at anyone who crossed my path."

"I heard about your unusual gown. I wish I had seen it. I suppose my invitation to Prinny's gala got lost in transit," he remarked with a grin, even as his companion laughed.

Louise dimpled up at him. "Sir, I cannot imagine how that could have happened."

With a chuckle, Abernathy saluted her with a tip of his hat, then rode on, the lady riding alongside.

Louise turned to her companions. "Do either of you know who his companion was? I admire her sapphire habit."

"I don't know her," admitted Rebecca. "I wonder why he failed to introduce us."

"He would not dare." Marie told her in a low voice. "She's the notorious Lady Brooke, whom the *ton* does not recognize."

Louise sniffed. "I doubt if she has done anything the other Society ladies have not."

Marie riposted, "Only she was caught doing it," causing the others' laughter.

There was a spectator to this encounter. Major Stafford had watched from a distance of a few yards. He could not hear the conversation, only saw Louise's reaction. Now he swung in beside their carriage.

Rebecca and Marie returned his greeting. With a bland face, Louise curbed her enthusiasm. "Good afternoon, Major Stafford."

He turned to Louise with a slight smile crossing his face. "My lady, I am pleased to see you in the park this afternoon."

Louise began to relax at his cordial voice but stiffened with his next words.

"I believe you have forgotten what Shelburne told you about Mr. Abernathy's reputation. Being seen conversing with him cannot help your consequence. Quite the contrary."

Louise lowered her long lashes to hide her hurt.

Stafford continued. "I really must warn you against being in conversation with Margaret Brooke. She's notorious, therefore quite beneath your notice."

Rebecca and Marie sat in stunned silence at such a public reprimand. Rebecca, at least, recognized Louise was about to give him a sharp set-down.

"In the first place, Major Stafford, what I do is no concern of yours. Secondly, I was not in conversation with Lady Brooke, but only because she did not speak. Had she spoken to me, I would have conversed with her. I am not shallow like some people I know."

She ignored Rebecca's gasp.

"Furthermore, Major Stafford, I informed you on a previous occasion when you had the nerve to reprimand me, that I am acquainted with some of Mr. Abernathy's family, besides finding him a very pleasant person. I will not give him the cut."

Louise raised her voice to tell the coachman to put the horses in motion. They left the major with a flush on his face.

Louise spent the rest of the day in a foul temper, sitting in the back garden going over the events of the last twenty-four hours. How dared Major Stafford reprimand her and in public too? She'd hardly had the courage to face her friends after leaving the park. They had refrained from making comments. Louise wondered if they had agreed with him. Had she in truth told her grandfather she was contemplating marriage with that overbearing rudesby?

Chapter 15

Good, Bad, and Unwanted

Louise woke to the sound of rain driving against the windowpanes. Her head throbbed. Her dreams had been of George Stafford. Awaken with him on her mind did not ease her discomfort. He would not venture out on such a day. She could not expect an apology for his interference yesterday.

You are the one who should apologize.

Louise pushed aside the bed curtains and gazed around the room. No one was there. She realized the little voice was in her head. She tried to shush it.

You know you should not have spoken in such a way to him yesterday. He was only trying to be helpful.

"Oh, be quiet."

"What did you say, my lady?" Agnes entered the bedchamber in time to hear the muttered words.

"What a miserable day it is, to be sure," Louise improvised.

"I imagine the rain will continue this way all day. Were you planning to go outside?"

"At the moment, I can't remember what plans I had for today. Whatever they were, I have changed my mind. I am about half inclined to stay in bed all day."

Agnes grinned. "I could bring you a breakfast tray, but what will her ladyship say?"

"I shan't even think about that. Instead, I will go down to breakfast. Lay out a warm gown for me, Agnes. I feel chilled to the bone just thinking about getting out of this warm bed."

"Beyond doubt, we have been spoiled by the long spell of warm weather. Most days seemed almost like summer," Agnes chattered as she rummaged through the closet and pulled out a long-sleeved muslin gown with a high neckline circled with a narrow band of lace.

Hurrying into the breakfast parlor, Louise wished her grandparents a good morning, smiling her thanks to Foster when he poured her coffee. Helping herself to buttered eggs, she broached the subject closest to her heart at that moment.

"Grandmother, this miserable weather reminds me autumn coolness is here. I need some warmer gowns."

"I trust you will go to Madame Bouchet for them," Lady Granville remarked.

Thankful that the older lady was in a good humor, Louise ventured a small chuckle. "I doubt Madame DuValle fashions warm gowns. I will plan to visit Madame Bouchet tomorrow, by which time I hope the rain will have stopped."

"What are your plans for today?"

"I intend to stay indoors, perhaps in the music room, unless you or grandfather wish me to accompany you some place."

Lord Granville lowered the newspaper. "I am promised to Hallsworthy for luncheon. We intend to discuss the possibility of an Oxford Classics Society. I expect to be with them all afternoon. I'm not sure what our evening plans are."

"I do not believe we have plans for the evening, do we, Louise?"

"No, Grandmother. Since I have spent so few evenings at home since we came to Town, I shall be happy to recoup my energies."

"You have been running off your limbs, Louise. I admit I'm thankful I have trusted your chaperonage to others for some evening functions. Today, I promised to confer with Lady Russell. She is attempting to trace an obscure branch of her family, which she believes crosses my maternal family."

"That sounds interesting, Grandmother. Do you know if it is true?"

"I do not know for certain, no. I have my doubts because I have spent many years studying our family tree. The possibility does exist. Finding a new line on our family tree would prove interesting."

Thus, Louise was alone when Major Stafford came to call in mid-morning. Foster believed Lady Louise would welcome the major. With proper deference, Foster showed the major into the music room and sent for Agnes to play propriety.

Lost in a Chopin concerto-rondo, Louise did not realize she was not alone. When the last notes died away, she whirled around at the sound of applause. The major stared at her, while Agnes watched in the background.

"Major! I did not realize you were here. Agnes, will you ring for tea, please?" Louise was flustered at the admiration she read in the major's eyes.

"I heard you play at your dinner party. Your performance then did not compare to this one. I stand in awe. How can one so young become so adept?"

"Practice, Major, practice," Louise answered. "The duchess allowed me as much time as I wanted to practice. She only stipulated I must not neglect my other studies or duties."

"I was never exposed to music while I was young," the major admitted. "My mother didn't play an instrument. In adulthood, I've avoided young ladies' efforts to entertain. However, even I can see you are no ordinary schoolroom chit."

Breathing in his masculine scent of sandalwood and leather, Louise studied his face for a moment. The music had calmed her nerves. She realized what she had to do. "Major Stafford, I must apologize to you for my outburst yesterday afternoon. My reaction was uncalled for, because I know you were only trying to help me."

"No, no, my lady," he protested. "I am the one who must apologize. I had no right to speak as I did. I don't want there to be any strain between us."

"Shall we forgive each other and forget our contretemps ever occurred?" Louise put out her hand. She didn't want to be out of temper with him either.

Stafford clasped her hand but released it when she tugged gently. With equal lightness, he replied, "Alright, yesterday afternoon is forgotten."

With that agreed upon, they moved from one subject to another, hardly pausing in their conversation when Foster set up a small table for their lunch. He stayed with them, while Agnes went to the kitchen for hers.

When the afternoon lengthened, Foster took it upon himself to remind them of the time. "Excuse me, my lady. It is almost time to dress for dinner."

Louise stared at him in amazement. Where had the day gone? "Goodness, Foster, I had no idea this much time had passed."

"Neither had I," the major said. "I must be going." He held Louise's hand for a long moment. "I don't know when I have had a more enjoyable afternoon."

"I, too, have found our afternoon pleasant, Major."

"Do you not think we are sufficiently acquainted to use first names, Louise?"

"Yes, George, I do. I am tired of being 'my ladyed.' At least, when we are alone," she amended, mindful of her grandparents' opinions.

George smiled his understanding. "Will you ride with me tomorrow afternoon? Weather permitting."

"I plan to spend the morning shopping, so a ride in the afternoon will be delightful, George." She savored the sound of his name on her lips.

With a nod, he flicked a careless finger across her cheek and departed.

Louise went to her bedchamber to dress for dinner. Her headache was gone. She didn't know when she had more enjoyed a day. She was more determined than ever to marry Major, no, *George* Stafford. Laughing together was such a joy, worth any effort to overcome the obstacle of her grandparents' wishes.

Louise penned a note to Rebecca and handed it to a footman with instructions to wait for a reply.

Over dinner, Louise mentioned Rebecca Blackwell would accompany her on a shopping expedition the following morning. "To Madame Bouchet's salon," she added with a grin.

Lingering in the music room after Louise had gone to her bedchamber, the Granvilles discussed their granddaughter.

"Louise has settled down quite well, I believe," Lady Granville commented. "Perhaps the threats on her life have had a calming effect. I cannot decide if she is in danger, or if it is the major."

"Major Stafford was right when he pointed out he is an easy target a great deal of the time when he is alone. I must believe Louise is the target, although I cannot fathom why."

"Even if the target is the major, Louise is in danger because she spends considerable time with him," Lady Granville said. "He misses few opportunities to be with her, which is something else we need to discuss. Bringing her to Town to get her away from him did not work. I do not believe forbidding her to see him would accomplish our purpose either."

"No," Granville agreed. "Neither of the two men who hang on her sleeve the most is acceptable to me. I must admit Stafford is preferable to that man-milliner cousin of mine. My sources tell me he was in dun territory almost the moment he reached Town. Clothing establishments, I understand, not gaming hells, for which I am thankful."

"The only eligible gentleman she has met is Lord Saunderson. She rejects him because he is too somber." Lady Granville sighed for what might have been. "We can only hope that during the Spring Season Louise will find someone appropriate with whom she can laugh, since she considers laughter of paramount importance. She informed me the other day Major Stafford's eyes laugh, if you can grasp such an idea."

On that incredulous note, they retired to their separate rooms, neither of them attempting to remember the last time they laughed together.

At the luncheon table the following day, Louise regaled her grandparents with her morning shopping expedition. "The light weight woolen gowns are just what I need. Even with a pelisse over my muslin morning gown, I was not comfortable in the chill air."

"Did you order a warmer pelisse too?" her grandmother inquired.

"Yes, in a dark green. Also, a blue woolen evening cloak with a chinchilla collar and muff."

"You should be well-pleased with your shopping expedition," Lady Granville congratulated her.

Louise nodded and gave herself over to enjoyment of her meal.

She seemed to spread good will throughout the day. Her pleasantness caused Jasper Winningham to linger by her side during his afternoon visit.

"Cousin, you look charming this afternoon. A new gown?" He peered at the jonquil muslin with two flounces edged in lace matching the lace around the neckline.

"Thank you, Cousin, I'm pleased you approve. You always dress to the nines, yourself. Your purple coat sets off the orange striped waistcoat to a nicety," she said with mendacious smoothness.

When Winningham left her side, he was preening, his narrow chest puffed out as far as it would go. Louise had taken to heart his admonition about the way to treat the future head of the family.

Winningham might appear a little dimwitted. In fact, he was awake upon every suit, at least the ones which mattered to him. He had hoped for an allowance from old Granville but had learned the futility at their first meeting. He was already in dun territory before he approached his distant relative. He was even now living on his expectations.

Winningham left Chesley Square with the supreme confidence his position as eventual heir to the marquess was safe. How he kept the position was not important. Only his inheritance of the Granville estate mattered. He would go to any lengths to accomplish that, even marriage. He certainly did not want to be leg-shackled to his arrogant cousin. He didn't even like females anymore, quite the contrary after his years on the continent. Nevertheless, his debts were becoming more pressing with each passing day. He must bite the bullet to secure his future. He would approach Lord Granville the following day for his permission to pay court to Louise.

He proceeded down the street with a malicious grin on his face. The chit would soon learn not to cross her lord and master. She needed to learn obedience. He would positively enjoy bringing her to her knees.

Louise was unaware of her cousin's interpretation of her friendliness, thus was in high spirits when she joined George for their ride. After entering the park, they made little progress as they greeted friends. Their lighthearted gaiety didn't last long.

"My lady, I trust I see you well on this beautiful day?" Lord Hurley pulled his mount into place beside her.

"Yes, thank you, my lord." She peeked at the major out the corner of her eye. Dear heaven, his face was like thunder.

"My dear Lady Louise, are you perfectly certain you're safe with Stafford? After all, it appears someone is trying to put a period to his existence." Hurley cast an oblique glance at the major, then grasped Louise's hand. "Perhaps you should accept my escort for the remainder of your ride. Remember, there were no unfortunate incidents when I accompanied you to Green Park a few days ago."

Reclaiming her hand from his, Louise looked at him with cool contempt. She spoke with spurious sympathy. "Is your memory failing, Lord Hurley? As I recall the occasion, both Miss Blackwell and I declined your escort when *she and I* went to Green Park."

With a sly grin, Hurley spoke in a loud whisper. "What a convenient memory you have, my dear. You can trust me to keep your secrets." He chuckled at her disgusted expression, before turning his mount away.

"Pay him no heed, George," she said for his ears alone. "He seems bent on making mischief. Do not allow him to succeed." Louise watched his grim face soften into a smile, as they continued their ride.

Returning to Chesley Square, Louise greeted her grandparents with shining eyes and chattered like a magpie about the people she had seen in the park.

When she grew quiet, her grandfather cleared his throat. "Louise, I had a caller this afternoon who might interest you. Jasper Winningham."

Louise turned astonished eyes toward him. "Considering I avoid him whenever possible, why would I be interested in knowing of his visit?"

"He asked my permission to pay his addresses to you."

"He did *what*? I hope you sent him away with a flea in his ear."

"I could not. He is not ineligible. Therefore, his suit deserves your consideration. I told him he may wait upon you tomorrow morning at ten o'clock."

"You did tell me you don't want me to marry him," she reminded him in an anxious voice.

"No more do I. Do you not think it is only polite to refuse him in person?"

"I will make short work of the meeting, you can be sure."

The following morning promptly at ten o'clock, Louise entered the drawing room with a determined air. She found her cousin lounging at his ease on a small sofa, a smug expression on his face. She stood one step inside the door, her brows raised at him. "I believe it is customary for a gentleman to rise when a lady enters the room."

He flushed yet remained where he was. "I see no reason to stand on ceremony with my future wife."

Louise gazed around the room. "I don't see your future wife. Therefore, your rudeness does not apply."

His eyes blazed. "You are my future wife, my dear. Did old Granville not tell you?"

"Lord Granville told me you had the audacity to approach him. He did not tell me I am going to marry you. Nor will he, I might add, because he knows I have no intention of entertaining such a ridiculous notion." Louise had planned to be polite when she refused him. His brazen rudeness changed her mind. She gave her temper a free rein.

"Oh, you will come around to my way of thinking when you have given the matter some thought," Winningham assured her. "I believe I pointed out to you once before the inappropriateness of treating the future head of the family without due respect, Cousin."

Louise held open the door when he minced his way across the room, bringing his stifling cologne with him. "I will never marry you, Mr. Winningham. Whether you ever become the head of this family is open to question, which you will realize when you have given the matter some thought."

Her deliberate use of his choice of words caused him to tighten his lips. She stepped outside the door and beckoned to Foster.

"Foster, Mr. Winningham is just leaving. In future, I will never be at home to him should he have the effrontery to inquire for me."

"You will regret this, Cousin," Jasper stated *sotto voce.* He gave her a glance of undisguised hatred before leaving the room.

Louise released a sigh of relief. The interview was over. She found her grandparents in their small sitting room at the back of the house.

They studied her face when she entered but waited for her to speak. When Louise sat on a small sofa without speaking, Lady Granville ventured a question.

"Did he propose marriage to you?"

"No. What he did was tell me I am his future wife. Very smug about it. According to him, Grandfather, you had already agreed on this marriage."

"Did you believe him?"

"No, yet if you had, I still would not agree to the marriage. He did not even stand when I entered the room. When I pointed out the error of his ways, he informed me there is no reason to stand on ceremony with his future wife. Can you credit such rudeness?"

"Jackanapes." Lady Granville sniffed. "All three of us are agreed that you will not marry that nodcock. Put him right out of your mind."

"Winningham told me again that I would regret being rag mannered to the future head of The Family. It almost sounded like a threat." Louise sat in silence, unaware her grandparents had exchanged worried glances. "He heard me tell Foster I am not at home to him if he should inquire. Perhaps he will stop coming."

Lord Granville snorted. "I wager he will be back here not later than day after tomorrow, making himself quite at home. I cannot refuse him admittance to the house since he is, in fact, at this moment the eventual Granville heir. I believe I have made clear he is not welcome. Nothing stops him from coming, it seems."

Foster interrupted their conversation to announce visitors in the drawing room.

Her unwanted suitor slipped from Louise's mind throughout her activities the rest of the day. He returned to plague her that evening at the opera.

Winningham entered the Granville box with an insouciance which amazed Louise. She cringed when he made himself comfortable in the chair beside her. He nodded to the Granvilles but occupied himself by whispering in Louise's ear.

She made a real effort not to create a scene. At length, Louise had tolerated his babble long enough. She pushed him away. "Mr. Winningham, you will please keep your distance from me, unless you care to be pushed over the railing."

"Louise," Lady Granville whispered in horror. "Lower your voice, please. You are attracting undue attention."

Louise saw the people in the adjoining box laughing at her. That added fuel to the flame of her anger. When the program was over, she pushed everyone out of her way in her haste to leave. One of those people was Major Stafford, who stared at her in consternation when she shoved him aside with a muttered, "Get out of my way."

What was she going to do about Jasper? Was the threat in his words this morning simply that he would annoy her until she consented to marry him, or something else? Louise thought of the two shots which had been so close to her. Where did culpability lie?

Chapter 16

Another Accident?

Louise stood beside the window when the maid brought her chocolate. She released a long sigh. "I would love to ride this morning, Agnes. There is enough nip in the air to make it enjoyable."

Agnes murmured in sympathy. "What will you wear this morning?"

"It does not matter." Louise's first thought upon waking had been her rudeness to George Stafford the previous evening. In truth, she had only realized later that it was he. How could she take out her temper on him of all people?

"Certainty what you wear matters. I can see you are in the dismals. You will feel much better if you wear your prettiest gown to greet the morning visitors." With those words, Agnes took from the closet a jonquil muslin with green leaves embroidered around the neckline. "This will surely brighten your spirits considerably," Agnes declared.

"Perhaps." Moments later, without even glancing in the mirror, Louise joined her grandparents in the breakfast parlor without speaking.

They glanced at her and at each other with raised eyebrows. Lady Granville spoke. "Good morning, Louise. What plans do you have for today?"

Louise nodded her thanks to the footman for the toast. "I hope to ride in the park this afternoon. I believe we're committed to the Beauchamps for dinner, followed by the Leatherwood ball." The Beauchamps were old friends of the Granvilles. Louise would be surprised if anyone present at the dinner were on the sunny side of fifty. She kept that opinion to herself.

"If Baker accompanies you, I see no reason why you cannot ride this afternoon, my dear." Her grandfather sounded almost sympathetic.

"Good morning, Lord Granville, Lady Granville, Cousin." Without invitation, Jasper Winningham sat next to Louise at the breakfast table.

Lord Granville motioned for the footman to serve the younger man.

Silence reigned while Winningham took the edge off his appetite, the sight of which made Louise push her plate away in disgust.

"I did not realize you ever arise this early, Cousin," she taunted. "You must have been out of your bed for several hours to achieve such a high degree of elegance in your apparel."

Winningham smiled in her direction. "Cousin, I would arise before dawn each day if it meant I could see your face across the breakfast table."

"I would not want to put you to any bother," Louise said rising to her feet. "Excuse me, please; the breakfast table palls." She hurried to the music room. The nerve of him.

Life had turned to a minor key again.

Louise managed to lose herself in a Bach fugue until Foster advised her visitors were in the drawing room. "I will be there in a few minutes."

Returning to her bedchamber, Louise pulled a comb through her short curls. Perhaps George Stafford was here. That meant she would have to apologize to him again. Would there ever be a time when they could be together without one or the other of them having to apologize first thing?

Louise entered the drawing room in a pensive frame of mind. She greeted several visitors before she reached the major, who was standing by himself to one side of the room.

"Good morning, Louise."

Their eyes met for a moment. She flashed him a dazzling smile. He did not appear to be angry. "Good morning, George. I am glad you came because I owe you an apology for my rudeness last evening. I can only say I was too angry with someone else to behave in a rational way. I will strive not to let it happen again, although I make no promises on that head!"

The stiffness left his shoulders. "I could not fathom why you were angry at me. I am glad someone else ruffled your feathers this time." He paused, his voice diffident. "Do you care to tell me who caused your anger? Someone I know?"

Louise chewed the inside of her lip. Did she want the major to know Winningham intended to marry her, regardless of her wishes? There was no reason not to tell him.

"Jasper Winningham. He's my grandfather's heir. To make sure he inherits the estate and receives an allowance in the meantime, he's determined to marry me."

The major appeared speechless until he said, "Surely Granville isn't importuning you to accept that … that ridiculous fop!"

"Oh, no," Louise assured him. "Grandfather is completely against the idea. However, I told him that I won't marry Jasper under any circumstances. He didn't ask me to temper my words."

"I can't imagine Winningham married to any female, but certainly not to one of your spirit!"

With an easier heart Louise agreed to ride with him that afternoon.

Louise and the major, together with Baker, guided their mounts from the mews behind Chesley Square into the street. They held the horses with an easy rein in the light traffic. Baker's shout alerted them to danger seconds before a closed carriage, pulled by galloping horses, came upon them from a side street. Louise fought to control Juno until Baker grabbed the reins subduing the frightened animal.

"Louise, are you alright?" The major came alongside and clasped her shaking hands.

Louise managed to nod.

Of one accord, they returned to the stables, where Baker took charge of the horses while Stafford supported Louise into the house. Shouting for Foster to bring a restorative, the major led Louise into the study where he found the Granvilles, who stared at their granddaughter in consternation.

"*Another* accident?" The marquess pounded the desk with his fist. "This cannot be a coincidence! What happened?"

Lady Granville urged Louise to drink the restorative the anxious butler presented on a tray.

After a couple of sips, Louise pushed the glass away. "I'm alright now, Grandmother."

"Was it an accident, Stafford?" Granville eyed him closely.

The major shook his head. "I can't be sure about that, but the horses did move from a standing position to a gallop in a matter of seconds. Yet, for another reason, I don't see how the occurrence could have been a deliberate action against your granddaughter, my lord. Still, I must admit the driver's actions are open to question."

"A deliberate action against you, perhaps?" Lady Granville asked. "That has been of a concern in the two previous incidences."

"No, my lady, I do not believe so. My reason for believing the action was not a deliberate attempt toward either of us is that, to the best of my knowledge, no one knew we would ride that way. It isn't our usual direction."

"I didn't mention it to anyone, although I suppose someone could have overheard us making the arrangements," Louise shrugged. "Grandfather, how could the occurrence have been anything except an accident? I don't ride every afternoon. Unless a carriage stands in the street every day waiting for me, it had to be an accident, an inexperienced coachman, perhaps."

"Despite my earlier belief, I now must admit that I might be the target after all."

Louise turned to the major in consternation. "Why? Who would attempt to kill you?"

He grasped her outstretched hand but quickly released it when he recalled where they were.

"Yes, do tell us, Major Stafford." Granville ignored the familiarity.

"I have been accosted a couple of times recently by what I thought were footpads determined on robbery. Several other people came along both times, and the footpads disappeared into the shadows."

"Were you hurt?" Louise scanned his face. With his crippled leg he could never get away from his attackers.

"Not at all," Stafford soothed her. "They never got in more than a couple of swings at me. They only used their fists. They didn't have weapons either time. I found it easy enough to dodge them."

"Have there been any other attempts on your life, which we do not already know about?" Lady Granville, too, chose to ignore their intimacy, at least for the moment.

Louise noticed their restraint and breathed a prayer that they would refrain from stating their oft-given objections until she was in a better frame of mind.

"I believe it is a possibility," the major admitted. "I left my horse unattended for a few minutes in the stable yesterday. When I returned, I automatically checked the girth—a habit left over from a childhood tumble. The girth was loose—perhaps loosened while I was riding, although I have never known it to happen before."

"Was there anyone about?" Granville questioned him before Louise could speak.

"The stable boy said he saw one or two people around, but he didn't believe anyone could have tampered with the girth without his noticing. I decided I should mention those occurrences to you, even though they might have been mere coincidences, which I thought at the time."

They discussed the matter a few minutes longer before the major departed. Louise went to her bedchamber to rest before dressing for dinner. Could the culprit have been Jasper? Or was someone trying to kill George? Lord Hurley, perhaps? He certainly did everything he could to antagonize the major. Yet, Louise failed to detect any real animosity between them. More like a standing feud that had lasted so long neither remembered the reason.

Her grandmother joined her a short time later. "Louise, are you sure you want to go to this dinner tonight? Should you not better stay at home after your ordeal? The Beauchamps will understand if we cry off."

"By no means should we stay home, Grandmother. I quite look forward to the dinner. Besides, if word gets out that I had another near accident, my presence among the *ton* this evening will allay any exaggerated gossip."

Louise was pleased to find that the Beauchamps had dinner guests who were close to her in age. Much to her surprise, Lord Hurley proved to be a witty conversationalist on her left. Louise had to smother her laughter when he related the outrageous behavior some of the dinner guests had indulged in during their misspent youth.

"My lord, surely you jest. No one would permit horses to eat at the dinner table. As for stabling them in the attics, absurd even to contemplate. How could they climb the stairs?" Louise shook her head at him in mock reproof.

Hurley grinned and turned to his other dinner partner.

Soon after the meal, carriages arrived to take the group on to their various other commitments. The Granvilles went to the Leatherwood ball. Louise had met these old friends of her grandparents and again wondered if she would find friends there.

Stepping into the ballroom after greeting her hosts, Louise gazed into a pair of smiling blue eyes. "Good evening, Major," she murmured sedately.

"You are quite recovered from our afternoon contretemps, I see. Shall we join this dance?"

Before she could acquiesce, they heard a familiar harsh voice.

"Contretemps, Stafford? Another accident?" Hurley greeted him with a sardonic glint in his eyes. "Lady Louise, I did tell you that you would be safer with me."

"It was only a coachman who failed to watch for traffic, my lord," she answered with quiet emphasis, pressing the major's arm in warning.

Hurley's companion laughed, drawing Louise's attention to her. "Coachmen can be quite careless, can they not?"

Louise ignored the tug of the major's arm when he tried to pull her away. She smiled at the lady and raised her eyebrows to Hurley. "I don't believe I have had the pleasure of meeting this lady, my lord. Perhaps you will introduce us."

"Please forgive my neglect." Hurley bowed, his face alight with amusement. "Lady Louise, I am pleased to introduce Lady Brooke."

Louise smiled. "I am pleased to make your acquaintance, my lady. I admired your seat on a horse when I saw you in the park."

"The music is starting, Lady Louise." Stafford guided her into a set forming near them.

Louise flashed Lady Brooke a smile across her shoulder, but she sneaked a peek at the major's stern face from the corner of her eye. She didn't want to upset the major. Nonetheless, she would not cut a fellow guest. Would Stafford rake her over the coals again?

Stafford relaxed his tight lips when their steps met in the *contradanse*. She sighed with relief. There would be no public reprimand, for which she was thankful.

Louise tried to keep the peace by avoiding both Lord Hurley and Lady Brooke. However, the latter caught her unawares at the close of a dance.

"Do you go to Almack's this week, my lady?"

"Neither this week nor any other," Louise admitted, a rueful smile lighting her countenance. "I offended the patronesses' sensibilities when I first arrived in Town. They denied me vouchers. At least for this Season, although Lady Cowper said she will consider me again in the Spring if my behavior improves."

"Whatever did you do?"

"Several things," Louise shook her head in disgust. "I really cannot understand how seven ladies can hold sway over the entire *ton*."

"I agree with you. I imagine you find other activities more enjoyable than you would find Almack's."

"Do you attend?"

Lady Brooke laughed aloud. "Child, my behavior has gone so far beyond the pale that I will never be allowed inside those sacred portals again."

"I'm not the first person to be wholly ostracized, am I?" Louise's light tone belied her true feelings.

"I dare say your illustrious grandparents will make certain that does not happen. Speaking of them, I believe Lady Granville is trying to attract your attention."

Louise felt her heart sink. She smiled at Lady Brooke, excusing herself without undue haste. Was she in for another scolding? Probably. Louise joined her grandmother near the door.

"We will leave now," Lady Granville said. They entered their carriage in silence, which lasted until they arrived at home.

Entering Louise's bedchamber the moment she removed her cape, Lady Granville motioned for Agnes to leave. "Louise, I will say this only once. Lady Brooke is not a fit person for anyone to know, least of all a member of The Family."

Louise struggled for calmness in the face of her grandmother's harsh words. "Lady Brooke was an invited guest of your friends. I don't understand why you do not consider her acceptable."

"I have no control over whom my friends invite to their balls. You do not need details of her behavior. You will not seek her out nor converse with her if you happen to meet her at any function at any time. Do you understand?"

"Yes, Grandmother."

"Furthermore, while we are on the subject, Lord Hurley is not a proper person for you to know either. I noticed you talked with him over dinner." She held up her hand when Louise opened her mouth to speak. "Yes, I know. He was your dinner partner. Therefore, you could not give him the cut direct. Nevertheless, you did not need to prolong his conversational gambits the way you did. He would consider it encouragement. No female is safe with him. You will stay away from him also."

Without waiting for an answer, Lady Granville left the room, closing the door behind her, leaving her exasperated granddaughter grinding her teeth.

Louise rose early. Without bothering to dress, she made her way to the back gardens, clutching a shawl tightly around her shoulders. She paced along the graveled path, while she tried to make sense of Society's restrictions. When the cool air penetrated the woolen shawl, she returned to her bedchamber, where Agnes waited.

"I wondered where you could be, my lady." Agnes bustled around the room, keeping an eye on Louise, who sat staring into space. "Which gown will you wear?" After a moment, Agnes repeated her question, "My lady, I asked which gown you will wear."

At length the maid's voice penetrated Louise's thoughts. "I'm not going out this morning. Any gown will do."

Other than brief good mornings, there was no conversation between Louise and her grandparents. Hardly aware of their presence, she pushed buttered eggs around her plate, picked up a slice of toast but returned it to her plate without taking a bite. They left the breakfast table one by one without even a nod. Louise spent the remainder of the morning in the music room, even though she could not have named the airs she played if anyone had asked.

At the luncheon table, Louise received a note from the major, asking if she would drive with him. She scanned the message before handing the paper to Lady Granville. "May I accompany Major Stafford on a drive this afternoon? A *drive*, not a ride."

"After the events of yesterday afternoon, I am not sure I should allow you out of the house for your own safety and our peace of mind. I cannot consult your grandfather, who is at his club. I do realize we cannot keep you immured inside the house for the rest of your life. So, you may go for a drive with the major if Baker accompanies you. The carriage will give more protection than would a horse."

"Thank you, Grandmother."

Across Town, Major Stafford had spent the morning in his rooms, his injured limb propped on a cushion. His thoughts centered on Louise Mansfield. He hadn't been ready to love or even be attracted to a female for many years. "There is no point in setting artificial times to do something. Something always intervened," Stafford realized when he said the words aloud.

Stafford admired Louise's beauty and was growing accustomed to her intelligence. Most important of all, though, was her quick laughter. He didn't want to face a somber face across the breakfast table every day for the rest of his life. George realized he thought of her not only as a prospective wife but also as a friend. A *female* friend? The idea intrigued him. He didn't know of any man who would even consider such a relationship.

There were two drawbacks to their marriage. The most obvious was the opposition of her grandparents, yet they did not forbid him the house. They probably realized their headstrong granddaughter would defy them at every opportunity.

The other was Louise herself. She was heedless of conventions, willing to associate with people whose existence she should not even acknowledge. She did not appreciate efforts to point her in the right direction. Driving down St. James Street in an open carriage, she had even nodded to several passersby. Stafford acknowledged she did not realize where she was. Yet, her lack of attention did not excuse her behavior, rather it made the situation worse. Remembering her obvious enjoyment of Lady Brooke's company sent a shudder down his spine. He must make another effort to guide her into a better understanding of what Society expected of young ladies.

Louise, too, was in deep thought. Regardless of her grandparents' opinion of the major, she wanted to be with him. They laughed together. His lineage could not compare with laughter. They'd had a pleasant time the previous evening, so his somber expression surprised her when he arrived for their drive. Louise hid her surprise when he passed the turn to Hyde Park. When she realized that they were going to the quieter Green Park, her heart quickened as she thought of what it might mean.

Inside the park, they drove in silence until they reached a deserted area. There, Stafford left the carriage in Baker's care, while he strolled with Louise to a wrought-iron bench under a large beech tree. Louise was exultant, as she spread the skirts of her jade green carriage gown and waited for him to speak.

Gathering his wits, the major cleared his throat. "Perhaps you are wondering why I brought you here instead of going to Hyde Park. Green Park is quieter, allowing us to converse more easily."

Stafford was leaning over, his arms resting on his buckskin-clad knees, staring at the ground. He didn't seem disposed to continue, so she gave him a hint.

"Was there something you wanted to say to me?"

"Yes, there is. I'm afraid you might take my words the wrong way; still, I mean them for the best."

Giving only a nod Louise schooled her features to a blank expression.

"I'm concerned about the way you attract the attention of undesirable men. Females too. Both Hurley and Simon Abernathy are far beneath your touch. Furthermore, I am appalled you insisted upon meeting Margaret Brooke last evening."

Stafford was into his grievance, rushing on without noticing her tightened lips. "Being reared in an orphanage you cannot be expected to know how to go on in the polite world. There are some things you simply must not do. Your grandmother should have instructed you, even if the orphanage people did not."

Rising to her feet, Louise gave her temper full rein. "Grandmother has done little except preach at me since the moment she laid eyes on me. She has the right to scold me—you do not. Please return me to Chesley Square on the instant." Louise marched to the carriage and climbed in without waiting for Baker's assistance.

Stafford's own temper flared. Muttering "hot-tempered chit," he climbed into the carriage and unwound the reins from their peg.

Baker's gasp alerted them to possible danger. He rushed toward some shrubs where he had seen movement. He came out holding a boy by his shirt collar. "Explain yourself."

The boy stared at the groom, his eyes wide with fright. "I wusn't doin' nuthin', Guv'ner, honest. I jus' wanted ter see them horses. They be proper good 'uns." He stared in awe at the phaeton. "That be a bang-up rig, yer got there, Mister."

If he had not done anything else, the urchin had eased the tension. They sent him on his way. When they reached Chesley Square, Stafford turned toward her.

"Louise, please pardon me for placing you in danger again. It was stupid of me."

She nodded without looking at him, then allowed Baker to assist her out of the carriage. Hurrying to her bedchamber, Louise paced the floor. The major didn't approve of her or her chosen companions. He was worried about his reputation, not hers. That was the truth of the matter, if he would admit the truth. She would show him he could not dictate her behavior.

Driving away, the major berated himself for being so intent on his grievances against Louise that he had forgotten the recent incidences. He not only had not protected her—he had placed her in danger. True, only a harmless urchin this time, but it could have been someone bent on attacking her. Stafford shook his head in disgust at himself.

Over the next few days, Louise ignored Stafford whenever they met. She flirted with every male she met, including crossing sweepers. She refused to acknowledge his presence at the Opera, where she kept Mr. Abernathy at her side throughout the intermission. For that, Louise received a reprimand from her grandmother.

Lady Granville was in something of a dilemma. She continued to hold her granddaughter on a loose rein, using Lord Granville's phrase. She was thankful Louise had come to her senses about the major. Still, encouraging Mr. Abernathy was even worse. The major at least was not dangling after her fortune.

Simon Abernathy was, which he admitted to himself, if to no one else. The wealthy chit was beautiful. Yet neither her fortune nor her beauty kept him at her side. Her naturalness did. In the hands of the wrong man, Louise Mansfield would lose her spontaneity, which would change her out of all recognition. Therefore, his obvious duty was to rescue her. She would be a rare handful for any man. He was up to the challenge. His encounters with her might appear accidental. They were not. He had watched her behavior toward Stafford. Now was the time to make his own move.

The morning after he had remained by her side throughout the opera, Abernathy paid a visit to Chesley Square. He waited patiently, while Foster stared at him with askance before admitting him into the drawing room. Abernathy watched with amusement as Louise flirted with a couple of young sprigs of the nobility, while Stafford glared from across the room. When the major moved in her direction, Abernathy moved faster. The dandies faded away when he arrived.

"You are always enchanting, my dear." Abernathy lifted Louise's fingers to his lips in a brief salute.

Louise flashed him a bright smile. "Mr. Abernathy, it is always a delight to see you."

"Tell me something, my lady," he murmured. "Have you succeeded in putting Stafford in his place?"

She twinkled at him. "Are you helping me, Mr. Abernathy?"

"It would be my distinct pleasure, Louise." Her quick frown warned him he had gone beyond the line of what she would permit. "Ah, forgive my familiarity, Lady Louise. Basking in your intoxicating smile drives coherent thought from my head," he confided with an outrageous leer.

Louise tapped her fan against his sleeve. "Mr. Abernathy, you are a rogue. A charming rogue to be sure. Still a rogue."

Abernathy's eyes flashed a wicked twinkle, as he bowed himself from her presence, relieved he had redeemed his *faux pas*.

Chapter 17

The Masquerade Ball

Louise intended to behave with discretion. Truly she did. She might have succeeded, except for one invitation among the stack on the breakfast table one morning. Her eyes gleamed, as she waved the missive excitedly in her grandmother's face. "May I accept this invitation, Grandmother? I'm certain the evening will be marvelous above all things."

Lady Granville scanned the card. "Attend a masquerade ball? I should say not, Louise. Only riffraff attends those things."

"Grandmother, dressing up in a costume is fun. At the orphanage, we often dressed up for charades. This will be even more fun because there will be more people, and they will wear a larger variety of costumes than we had."

Peering at her over the top of his newspaper, Granville commented with rare tact. "Charades are rather different from masquerade balls, young lady. The games those people play are not the charades you played as a child."

Louise turned to him with appeal. He shook his head.

"Your grandmother has spoken, Louise. Young Ladies of The Family do not attend masquerades. Let us hear no more about it." Granville returned to his newspaper. His edict closed the subject.

The Granvilles believed they had settled the matter. Louise had a different opinion.

Breakfast over, she went to the back garden, where she sat on a bench in the sun to give the matter some serious thought. What could possibly be wrong with going to a masquerade ball? After all, everyone would be in costume and wearing masks. It would be fun to see adults wearing historical costumes, which children could not do.

From there, it was only a step to convincing herself that if she left before the midnight unmasking, no one would know she had been there so could not tattle to her grandparents. This would take some detailed planning. Louise nodded. She would attend Lady Adelaide Weatherby's masquerade ball, come what may. If her grandparents did learn of it—she didn't see how they could—she would at least have had the pleasure of participating in an adult masquerade before accepting her punishment.

Thus, she rationalized her disobedient behavior.

Perhaps Louise should have listened to the scolding chaffinches above her head.

The next problem was figuring a way to get there. She must decide upon a costume, which brought her up short. No, she must decide on a costume first. Louise chewed her lip for a moment. An elaborate costume was out of the question, for how could she arrange it without anyone's knowledge? There was nothing else to do. She would have to wear a simple domino and mask. With that thought, Louise rushed to her bedchamber and rang for her maid.

"Agnes, I need for you to accompany me shopping this morning."

"Certainly, my lady. Are you shopping for anything in particular?"

Louise replied with a deviousness she employed on rare occasions. "I need to match some ribbons. I also thought to search for a lace fichu."

At the drapery shop, Louise sent Agnes in one direction to match the ribbons, while she strolled the other way. She could carry a mask in her reticule, but how could she smuggle a domino into the house? Louise gave brief consideration to taking the maid into her confidence. No, she could not trust even Agnes in this matter.

Browsing through a shelf of masks, she felt someone staring. Glancing around, Louise spotted Lady Brooke. Did she dare approach that notorious lady? It was not necessary because the notorious lady approached her.

"Good day, Lady Louise. Are you choosing a mask for the masquerade party tonight?"

Louise replied with unaccustomed caution. She could not be sure how much of a gossipmonger Lady Brooke was. "I have given some thought to attending but have not made a decision."

Lady Brooke smiled with understanding. "Why don't I pick you up in my carriage at the corner nearest Granville House? You can put on your domino when you are inside." Seeing Louise weakening, Lady Brooke pressed her advantage. "I will loan you one of mine, so you will not have to be concerned about getting the domino into and out of Granville House."

Louise succumbed. Everything had fallen into place, a good omen. She could enjoy herself.

Louise hid her excitement throughout the day. At dinner, she pleaded a headache and went to bed early. Her grandmother looked in on her twice during the evening. Finding Louise apparently asleep the second time, she did not return. Louise began to dress when the house grew quiet. With a determined glint, she pulled a gown from the back of her closet. Louise had gone to Madame DuValle's salon because she wanted gowns which did not make her look like a schoolroom miss. After the sensation the emerald green creation had caused, Louise decided tonight would be her only opportunity to wear this one.

Holding a branch of candles near the mirror, Louise gazed at herself with a nod of satisfaction. No Society miss would dare to wear this ensemble, she thought with a smile. Madame DuValle had fashioned the gown like a Roman toga in a shimmering gold. One shoulder was bare, while the other side had a long sleeve ending in a band at her wrist. Her only ornament was a wide gold bracelet above the elbow of her bare arm. She wore a matching scarf, wound turban style around her head, completely covering her telltale hair. Gold sandals peeked out from the ankle-length skirt. Louise shrugged off momentary disappointment when she acknowledged that a domino would hide the gown's splendor. She admitted she wanted people to admire it. Perhaps she wouldn't wear Lady Brooke's domino after all.

At a few minutes before midnight, Louise left the house through a side door with the devout prayer no one would rob the house while she was gone. That would put the crowning touch on her evening. Louise approached the waiting carriage, with a sigh of relief when Lady Brooke stuck her head out the window to greet her in a soft voice.

Louise had not realized the difficulty of entering a carriage while wearing a straight gown. Lady Brooke's escort stepped to the street. Louise glanced into the face of Lord Hurley. She should have known. He lifted the embarrassed girl into the carriage, where she donned the domino and mask.

Her night of adventure had begun.

Louise tried to appear at ease, glancing around Lady Weatherby's crowded ballroom. She gathered her courage to mingle with the crowd when her escorts left her on her own upon arrival. Observing the antics of the dancing couples, Louise was grateful for her disguise. She squelched the thought that this was not exactly what she had expected. She wandered around the room, managing to evade groping hands until someone grabbed her from behind. This was her undoing.

"Come on give me a kiss, sweetings." A man wearing an eye mask leered down at her, his wine-soaked breath hot on her face.

Louise twisted and turned but could not get loose. She kept her lips clamped together, trying to ignore the jeers from the crowd. After what seemed an eternity, she broke free, losing the domino in her struggle. The obscene remarks about her gown brought tears to her eyes. At this point, her grandmother's strictures did not seem unreasonable. During Louise's struggle to reach the door, her scarf came loose, leaving her well-known auburn curls exposed.

A murmur of recognition rose as a strong arm clasped her around the shoulders and pushed through to the door. Louise was too terrified to speak until she looked upward into the amused eyes of Simon Abernathy.

"Out of your depth, aren't you, love?" He hailed a hackney. "If you had told me you wanted to come, I would have escorted you. Who did bring you?"

"Lady Brooke," Louise replied with a gulp. "I didn't know a masquerade would be like that. I thought it would be like charades."

"I'm afraid the damage is done, Louise." Abernathy held her trembling hands in his strong grip. "Lady Brooke will spread this all over Town. Your reputation will be in shreds."

"Why would she?"

"Did you not know? I suppose not. It happened before my time, but it's common knowledge. She wanted to marry your father—even got him into a compromising position—but failed in her attempt. He slipped her leash by the skin of his teeth, you might say."

Louise interrupted him. "Surely Lady Brooke is not of my father's generation. She appears far too young."

"Oh, she employs all the arts known to mankind to appear younger than her age," Simon commented. "Anyway, the marquess called her some choice names, said she would never get a shilling of his funds, even if he had to disown his son."

"He did, anyway."

"The difference is that your mother loved your father. From what I have heard of her, she would have lived in happy poverty with him. Lady Brooke only wanted access to the Granville money, so she ditched him in a hurry." Simon chuckled. "I understand your father threw a party to celebrate when she gave him his *congé*."

The hackney stopped at the corner. Abernathy walked with her to the door, keeping in the shadows. He cradled her face between his hands for a moment and pressed a gentle kiss on her trembling lips. "Better get some sleep, little one. You're in for a rough time tomorrow."

Louise slipped into her bedchamber, exhausted yet too keyed up to sleep. She put away her clothing, flinging the mask onto the remains of the fire. She stood by the window, staring at the night sky until the first rays of light appeared over the rooftops.

The morning was clear with the promise of a pleasant day. Anyone in Hyde Park would have recognized the young lady on the back of the galloping mare. Her riding habit of green cloth with braiding and epaulets bore a striking resemblance to a Hussar uniform. Her tall-crowned hat, shaped like a shako, boasted two curled ostrich plumes. Louise was trying to shake off her feeling of impending disaster. She had not yet succeeded.

She had managed to saddle Juno without waking the stable boys and slipped through the mews without an escort. She was riding neck or nothing down the broad avenue when a strong, gloved hand grasped the reins, pulling her horse to a stop. Hazel eyes flashing, Louise brought her riding crop down on the hand that had dared to interfere. Louise stared into the worried dark eyes of Lord Hurley.

"How dare you stop my horse?"

"She was running away with you!"

"I had her under perfect control. I don't want any more interference from you. Do you understand me?" Louise's voice rose in a crescendo.

"Yes, I understand you." Hurley stared at her, a sneer on his harsh face. "You are determined to set the *ton* on its ear, are you not? Between last night and this morning, you have succeeded. I wonder how Granville will react to these escapades." He rode away with one last comment across his shoulder. "And Stafford."

Louise soon learned Stafford's reaction.

"Very pretty behavior, I must say." The cutting voice of Major George Stafford broke across her tumultuous thoughts. "You show a decided want of conduct."

She whirled on him, raising her riding crop, her intentions obvious to the meanest intelligence.

"Oh, no, you don't. No disreputable hoyden is going to strike me." Stafford broke the crop, which he threw aside. "Hurley will spread this episode all over Town. You will be fortunate if Granville does not beat you. Come, I will escort you home."

Louise raced toward the gate, rage boiling through her veins.

At Granville House, the major gripped Louise by the elbow while marching her into the marquess's study, bypassing the startled butler.

Granville studied the grim face of one visitor, the rebellious face of the other. His expression was steady, a bit impatient.

"Is there some way I can serve you?" The silken voice held a note of steel.

Louise stood with her hands clenched at her sides. Her breasts heaving, her face white with rage, she trembled but didn't speak, while the major gave a succinct account of her morning's activities.

The marquess sat in silence until the major finished the tale. Granville shifted his gaze toward his granddaughter. He spoke with a deadly calm she had not heard since her earliest days in his household.

"Am I to understand you were foolish enough to go to Hyde Park without your groom, even after those attempts on your life? This incident is the last straw, young lady. Three reports have come to me already this morning about your presence at the masquerade ball last night. The ball we specifically forbade you to attend, I might add."

Louise gave no indication she had heard him. Stafford stared at her in open-mouthed horror at the reference to the ball.

Granville took a deep breath. "For the past few weeks, I have considered sending you out of Town for your own safety. We were not sure your leaving was the answer. Now, you have taken the decision out of our hands. You have shown beyond any doubt that we cannot trust you to behave with discretion. Your heedless actions dictate we must send you away until we can be certain you are not in danger. Also, until your conduct shows marked improvement. You will remain in your room while I make arrangements for your journey."

Louise walked with measured steps out the door.

"What do you have in mind for her, if I may ask?"

Louise heard the major's words as the door closed. She stepped into the next room and crept to the inner door to hear her grandfather's answer.

"I shall send her to a cousin of mine in Yorkshire. Lavinia will not stand for any nonsense. Also, no one will know where she is. She will be safe from whoever has been attacking her."

"You can depend on me to keep your confidence regarding her whereabouts, my lord. When do you intend for her to leave?"

"I will need a week to make arrangements. For now, I will put it about that she is ill. No one will believe it. They will not have the audacity to tell me to my face, though."

Louise had heard enough. She hurried to her bedchamber, where she paced the floor, her thoughts racing. Go to Yorkshire? Absolutely not. Whether for punishment or for safety did not matter in the least, because she had no intention of going to the northern wilds of England. Life there didn't bear thinking on at any time but especially not in winter. How could she avoid going there? She had truly gone too far this time. Louise spent the day alone, her thoughts directed toward what she considered an escape from prison. Agnes returned the dinner tray to the kitchen, without commenting on how little of the meal Louise had eaten.

Louise continued her pacing, fanning the flames of her wrath. They were unreasonable. They should have told her about her father's acquaintance with Lady Brooke. Louise would have known not to trust her. The whole situation was their fault. They were punishing her when they should be apologizing for their dereliction of duty. Louise dismissed the nagging voice asking if that was either reasonable or logical.

The house grew quiet as the night deepened. What should she do? What could she do? Louise sank onto a *chaise longue*. This required rational thought, not continued temper.

Louise could not return to Harley Street. That would be the first place her grandparents would look for her. She could change her name again, resume the music lessons, but where would she live? She could become a governess. No, that would not do—no references— besides, who would hire a person with her besmirched reputation? No one.

Enlightenment came with the dawn. She would go home. Home to Matron, whose twinkling blue eyes belied her scolds, home to the dearly loved Triple D, who understood the pitfalls of Society. Her heart eased as she remembered her last conversation with the duchess. Several months had passed since Louise and Rebecca left the orphanage, yet it seemed only yesterday the duchess had called Louise into her private sitting room.

"Come in, dear." The duchess poured a cup of tea for the nervous girl. *"You leave us today, Louise. I'm confident you're ready to enter the adult world. You have done well during your years with us. I am proud to point to you as an example to the rest of our girls."*

Louise smiled with gratitude, wondering if the duchess said the same thing to each girl when she left.

The duchess continued. "You have an honourable profession to keep you, one for which you received excellent training. You might not find obtaining piano students easy because too many people believe that only men are capable of teaching. My dear, I have complete confidence in you. You leave with my blessing."

The duchess placed her teacup on a table and stood with a proud smile on her face.

Louise faced the reality of leaving the only home she had known since she was six years old. She stood. Was she dismissed? Did she just walk away?

The Duchess of Dorchester opened her arms when she read the uncertainty in her pupil's face. She held the trembling girl for a moment before moving apart from her. "My dear, please remember this is your home. If anything goes wrong in your new life, you are to come home. We will find the solution to whatever the problem is."

With a trembling smile, Louise had left the duchess and set out on her journey to London eager to learn whatever life had to offer in the big City. Anticipation battled with nervousness—and won.

Now, in the wee hours of the morning, almost a year later, a reminiscent smile crossed Louise's face. She had not been obedient to her advice, but she would take the Darling Duchess of Dorchester at her word.

Several hours later, Louise awoke when Agnes brought the breakfast tray. After finishing the buttered eggs and toast, Louise sipped tea for a moment. With resolution, she addressed the maid.

"As you have no doubt heard, Agnes, I'm confined to my bedchamber for a considerable period. I will put my banishment to good use by catching up on my rest. There is one thing I wish you to do for me."

Agnes cast a suspicious glance at her. "What is that, my lady?"

Louise laughed at her expression. Gossip was undoubtedly rampant in the servants' quarters, so her maid's hesitation was natural. "Nothing horrible, I promise you. I only want you to tell me when both my grandparents are out of the house, so I can go down to his lordship's library. I want to get some books to read while I pass the time."

Agnes nodded in quick relief. In late morning, she returned with the information the way was clear for Louise to get the books.

Within a few minutes, Louise returned to her bedchamber, carrying randomly chosen books, no one the wiser. She read throughout the afternoon, again had supper on a tray, and continued reading into the evening. She'd been right when she told her grandfather that reading the classics in the original language is better than the English translation, no matter how well done.

The marchioness looked into the room on two occasions, without speaking. She shook her head, her face settled into the harsh expression that was common when Louise first entered her life.

Louise continued this behavior for the two days she had conjectured would be sufficient to lull the household into carelessness.

On the third day, she listened to Agnes chattering about the schedule for the evening. She was bubbling over with the servants' plans.

"We are to have the evening off, my lady. The master and mistress are going to Woodvale for a dinner party."

"I haven't heard of Woodvale, Agnes. Where is it, do you know?"

"I only know Woodvale is some distance outside London. They will leave at four o'clock and don't expect to get back until quite late."

Louise congratulated her on having some extra free time. "What are your plans for the evening?"

"We're going to Vauxhall Gardens."

"I've heard of them. You'll have a marvelous time, I'm sure, although I have never been there."

Louise had asked permission to go to the Gardens with Rebecca, but her grandparents had refused. No amount of persuasion worked, which was one more thing to hold against her progenitors. "You must tell me all about the gardens tomorrow."

Louise had not spent all her time reading. She had thought of plan after plan, discarding each in turn until she had hit upon one that would work. Her plan included purchase of a seat on the Hampshire stage, which she must do today. To do that, she must obtain the help of her maid by some devious means.

"Agnes, I realize you cannot leave until after my grandparents have gone. Can you run an errand for me afterward?"

The suspicious expression returned to the maid's face. "What do you want me to do?"

"I'm tired of reading these dull tomes from my grandfather's library. Would you obtain some novels from Hookham's for me? The Lady who wrote *Sense and Sensibility* might have a new one out by this time. Also, someone named Lady X has been raising quite a stir with her scandalous stories about members of the *ton*. That ought to keep me amused."

"Yes, I can obtain the books. Will there be anything else while I am out?"

With a twinkle, Louise held up an embroidery frame. "Boredom has reduced me to needlework, if you can believe that, knowing me as you do. I need this shade of yarn matched."

"You're taking this situation better than I would have expected," Agnes admitted

"I haven't really enjoyed making a spectacle of myself, Agnes. Both the duchess and the matron would be disappointed in me, would they not? Maybe I can come back to Town next Season.”

“The terrible person who has been trying to kill you might be caught too. You can really enjoy the Season.” Agnes left the room, the yarn in the pocket of her gown.

Chapter 18

Louise Asserts Herself Again

The stage pulled away from the White Horse Inn, slowly winding its way toward the outskirts of London and southwest toward Hampshire. Louise had boarded early, acquiring a corner seat where she sat far in the shadows. She would arrive at the orphanage before dark. In the meantime, she would pretend to sleep to avoid talking to her fellow travelers. Louise was thankful she had worn a poke bonnet with a brim wide enough to conceal not only her recognizable hair but also most of her face. Forcing herself to breathe evenly, Louise thought back over the past several hours, while she waited for the other passengers to arrive.

After hearing her grandparents leave Granville House, Louise returned to the *chaise longue*. She was deeply engrossed in a book when Agnes came in a few moments later.

"I'm going now, my lady. Your errands should not take more than an hour."

"Are the other servants waiting for you to join them before they leave?"

"They are all down in the servants' hall, having tea and resting their feet until I return. Everyone can't leave, so there will be someone to prepare your supper." Agnes hurried out the door, carrying Louise's tea tray.

Louise put on a drab pelisse and a bonnet, which covered her flamboyant hair, then waited at the window until she saw the maid hurrying through the alley. Louise tiptoed down the stairs and left by the side door. Around the corner, she glanced around. Seeing no one, she hurried to the next corner and hired a hackney, which she directed to the stage office. There, she purchased a ticket on the stage, leaving at five o'clock the following morning. Thankful she had saved so much of her pin money, Louise returned to her bedchamber with ten minutes to spare before Agnes came in with the books and embroidery yarn. After a quick smile, she hurried away.

Louise passed a quiet evening, enjoying the antics of the *Beau Monde* as regaled by Lady X. She ate the supper brought by the kitchen maid and read until the maid returned for the tray. Louise heaved a sigh. She should not be disturbed again, giving her ample time to organize the items she intended to take. She did not dare pack her portmanteau until she was ready to leave.

She retired to bed at the early hour of ten o'clock, admonishing herself to wake at three. She dozed but was aware when Agnes slipped into the room, leaving quickly. Louise wondered if the maid checked on her every night, whether from being certain she was not needed further or from instructions given by either of the Granvilles.

Louise woke when she heard her grandfather's deep voice but feigned sleep when her grandmother entered the bedchamber. She made a small snoring sound when Lady Granville moved the bed curtains aside to observe her granddaughter. Moments later, Louise smiled when her grandmother reported from the passage that the chit was sound asleep and was not likely to wake before mid-morning.

Sounds from her grandparents' rooms died. The house became quiet. When the clock on the mantel indicated a few minutes past three o'clock, Louise packed a portmanteau with the few items she would take with her. She glanced around the room which had become a prison. Now that she was leaving for the last time, Louise felt some regret for what might have been. But most of all, she regretted deceiving Agnes, who had been the perfect maid. She sent out a silent plea for forgiveness.

Rebecca's image passed through her mind. She would know Louise had gone home. No one else mattered. She knew her oldest friend would never reveal her whereabouts. Nonetheless, Louise was glad the Amesburies had taken her to visit out-of-town relatives for a week.

As the poet Horace said, *'Carpe Diem'*—she must seize the day, the hour. Nay, she must seize her life. Taking a steadying breath, Louise snuffed out the lone candle she had used and eased open the door. Hearing no sounds, she left the house the same way she had done in the afternoon. Louise doubted she would ever know if burglars entered the house through the door which she left unlocked. On second thought, when her grandparents learned she had gone, they would hunt her down for yet another scolding on her thoughtless behavior.

Now came the difficult part—getting to the stage stop on foot without interference from gentlemen—or ruffians—on the prowl. The early morning fog muffled footsteps, so Louise strained to hear the slightest sound. She stayed in the shadows, several times shrinking behind a tree until danger passed. She stood in the shadows of the White Horse Inn until the stage arrived, then climbed into the coach, hardly daring to breathe until they were on their way. The fog changed into a heavy mist and gradually into rain—a perfect fit for her mood.

Granville House began coming to life, as the stagecoach moved at a slow, ponderous pace over the rough road surfaces on its way to Hampshire. Servants went about their duties, allowing the family to sleep.

In mid-morning, when Louise had not rung her bell, Agnes entered her bedchamber. The rumpled bed covers were flung back. Turning toward the adjoining sitting room, she called, "Lady Louise, are you ready for breakfast?"

Receiving no reply, Agnes glanced into the empty sitting room. "She's probably in the music room. I didn't think she would stay away from the piano for long."

While straightening the bedchamber, Agnes paused, one hand in mid-air, staring at the dressing table. Where were the brush, comb, and mirror, which normally graced the top? The jars of cream? The perfume bottles? After a glance into the drawer, Agnes ran to the wardrobe. At first glimpse nothing appeared to be missing. Lady Louise must have a reason for moving those other items. When Agnes could not find them in the dressing room, however, she hurried down the stairs, looking for Lady Louise in each room. She even ventured into the garden.

At length in near desperation, Agnes asked Foster if he had seen Miss Louise this morning. At his negative reply, she said, "I can't find her anywhere, and some of her belongings are missing from her bedchamber. What am I to do?" Agnes wrung her hands as her eyes darted around the hall, seeking guidance from spirits living there.

Foster had been afraid of this. Just last night he had discussed the situation with Mrs. Foster. They reached the conclusion the young lady was assuming a docile air for her own purposes just like their Jonny had done. They had been right. Lady Louise was too much like her father to submit to what she surely considered unreasonable commands.

A thorough search of the house by all the servants failed to disclose the young lady, although it did disclose the unlocked door. Foster sent a footman to the stables to see if Juno was in her stall. Perhaps Louise had gone for an early ride. She had not.

Now Foster must apprise his master of the situation and withstand the same situation he did when the Marques's son left home. After a deep breath, he tapped on Lord Granville's dressing room door.

"What do you mean, my granddaughter is gone?"

"She isn't inside the house or in the grounds, my lord." Foster related the staff's activities.

"Gone!" The roar sounded over most of the house, bringing the marchioness hurrying to his rooms.

"Whatever is the matter?"

Granville glared at her. "Are you sure you saw Louise in bed this morning? Did you walk right up to the bed? Look at her?"

"I'm sure. I moved the bed curtains aside. Louise was sound asleep and snoring. What has happened?"

"The ungrateful chit has gone. She's nowhere in the house or grounds. No note. Just gone."

Lady Granville's harsh voice filled the silence. "Send her maid to me in Lady Louise's bedchamber. At once!"

"Agnes is already there, my lady."

Indeed, Agnes was already there, standing white-faced in the middle of the room, too terrified to think or speak clearly. She babbled her movements but was able to speak with confidence when Lady Granville asked what personal effects were missing.

"Lady Louise took the items normally on her dressing table, two sets of undergarments, two of her old gowns, one pair of shoes, a pelisse, and a poke bonnet."

"Tell me the truth. Are you sure you did not know what she was planning?"

"Oh, yes, my lady, I am positive. I did not know." Relieved she could be truthful, Agnes chattered. "She seemed to accept the necessity of leaving Society for a time. Just yesterday, Lady Louise told me she realized she deserved punishment. Even said maybe she could return to Town in the spring. I can't believe she has gone." The last words were a wail, ending only when the marchioness left the room.

Questions directed at each member of the staff brought no enlightenment. At last, the Granvilles were alone in the study.

"Granville, what do we do now?" Lady Granville's harsh voice filled the room. "I thought we were getting along together quite well the past several weeks. Ungrateful chit. We should never have brought her to London or relaxed our restrictions on her."

"Like father, like daughter. Not an ounce of sense, either of them." Granville fumed a moment. "We cannot just ignore her—that would give the *ton* a field day. We certainly do not want to go through that again. The gossip was bad enough when our son eloped with that red-headed wench."

"I suppose you're right. Rebecca Blackwell might be giving her shelter at Amesbury House."

"Surely not in the wee hours of the morning."

A sigh greeted those words. "She must have gone to the woman in Harley Street. I suppose we start there."

They found no trace of her there or at Amesbury House, where they learned the family had left Town a few days before. Granville sent footmen to the stagecoach offices and to the various stables where it was possible to hire horses or carriages, all to no avail. No one recognized the description of a beautiful young Society miss with short red curls, with or without a poke bonnet.

Major Stafford arrived in midmorning and asked permission to see their granddaughter.

The marquess glanced at his wife. "You cannot speak with her because she isn't here."

"Not here? I thought you were not sending her away for a week. Did I misunderstand?"

"No, Major, you did not misunderstand. Those were, indeed, our plans. She seemed to accept the necessity of leaving the social scene, yet this morning her maid found her gone." Bitterness tinged his voice. "We should have known she was plotting mischief. We have been unable to find any trace of her. We do not know which way to turn. Unless we go to Bow Street, which we prefer not to do."

The major sat in stunned silence, looking from one to the other. "When did you see her last? You questioned her maid? Are you sure the girl doesn't know Lady Louise's whereabouts?"

The marchioness spoke for the first time since the major entered the room. "I saw her for myself at two o'clock this morning when we returned from Woodvale. She was sound asleep. Her maid found her missing at about nine o'clock."

Granville's harsh voice took up the story. "Her maid *appears* mystified. However, we can never be sure about the lower orders. Lying is a way of life for them. They don't know better."

"I feel responsible. Do you mind if I try to find her?"

"I have no idea what you can do which we have not already done, Major. However, people may talk with you rather than our emissaries. I trust you will be discreet. I do not want the *ton* to learn Louise has disappeared." Almost as an afterthought, he added, "You will let us know if you learn anything."

With a nod, the younger man left the room.

Louise had brought sunlight into the darkness Jonathan left when he married that upstart female. The chit had rejected everything they held dear, just as her father had done. They had survived without Jonathan. They would survive without Louise.

Stafford left the Granvilles in their study, fuming over the Granvilles' attitude. They didn't want the *ton* to know. All they cared about was their precious reputation—no thought for the welfare of a girl alone in this vast City. Louise probably thought no one cared about her. He cared. He had realized how much he cared during the long, wakeful night, which had ended at daybreak when he was finally able to sleep. Throughout the night, the major had paced the floor, thinking of Louise. He relived his horror over the conversation he had overheard at Woodvale the evening before.

Stafford had stood beside a potted plant in the large ballroom, his eyes scanning the crowded dance floor. His auburn-haired beauty was not present, nor had he expected she would be. Would he ever see her again? Yes, he would, even if it meant going to the northern wilds. Would life in Yorkshire change her beyond all recognition? Female voices had penetrated his doleful thoughts.

"I notice the Granvilles' granddaughter isn't here. Wonder what kind of scrape she's getting into tonight."

The matron's shrill laughter grated on the major's ears.

"I heard she's unwell. Burned to the socket, I suppose," a second voice proclaimed.

A third voice broke into the laughter. "You both have it wrong. A footman at Granville House told my maid the young miss has behaved so badly the Granvilles have banished her to relatives in Yorkshire or somewhere equally far out of Town for an indefinite stay, possibly forever."

"Oh, the chit will find some kind of mischief to get into, regardless of where Granville sends her. I wonder if she took that scandalous gown with her!"

Stafford had slipped away unnoticed by the people beyond his hiding place. Scandalmongers should have their tongues cut out. He returned to his rooms, too upset to relax. Throughout the rest of the night, Stafford castigated Louise for her behavior, yet he excused her excesses as high spirits. For the first time in her life, she had gained a measure of freedom. Unfortunately, freedom had gone to her head.

The major had talked himself into a determination to beg her pardon. He would intervene with the marquess, try to get her punishment mitigated somewhat. She could be safe somewhere closer. Yorkshire in the winter was no laughing matter, according to all he had ever heard. Stafford was too late. It was his fault she ran away.

Now, leaving Granville House, Stafford mounted his horse with a nod toward Baker.

"Major, I don't know how she could have taken Juno out the other morning without my hearing her. I've always been a light sleeper. I don't know why I slept so hard that night."

"I hope his lordship didn't give you too much of a trimming."

"Lord Granville is a rare one when he's in a temper, sir. I at least have my job, which I wondered about while he was blasting me."

There was nothing the major could say to that, so he nodded and turned his mount toward Hyde Park. He wondered how much time would pass before the news of Louise's disappearance became common property. He knew servants would talk and soon learned their gossip had already started.

"Your filly has kicked over the traces, has she, Stafford?" Hurley's harsh voice held a distinct note of glee. "It is most comical to think of Granville's servants, chasing all over Town looking for her."

"I'm surprised she was not banished after the little episode at the masquerade ball." Lady Brooke, who accompanied Hurley, watched the major with a smirk on her face. "What a show she gave us, to be sure. Especially through her ripped gown."

"I'm certain you enjoyed it, Lady Brooke," the major answered calmly, although he wanted to plant her a facer. "Did your spite make up for losing the Granville fortune?" He rode on, leaving stunned silence behind.

Stafford tipped his hat to a few acquaintances but didn't linger to chat. When he reached the midpoint of the long avenue, he jerked his mount to a stop at the spot where Louise fell off Juno after someone shot at her. Could she be with him, whoever he was? Did she trust the wrong person with her plans, thereby playing right into his hands? Maybe this was not a simple runaway after all. Oh yes, Louise had run away alright, but had she become someone's prisoner? The major shuddered at the thought, as he gave his mount the office to start again.

"Major Stafford?"

Stafford brought his wandering thoughts under control to answer Simon Abernathy. "What is it?"

"I spoke to you twice, Major. You seemed miles away." Abernathy hesitated only a moment. "Is the *on-dit* true? Has Lady Louise run away?"

"Where did you hear that?" Stafford evaded a direct answer, while he debated the wisdom of confiding in this man whom he preferred to ignore.

"The news is all over Town," Abernathy replied. "Is Granville taking steps to find her? Has he called in the Runners?" Seeing the answer in the major's face, he laughed, albeit with contempt. "No. Granville would rather let his granddaughter disappear into oblivion than admit to authorities she is gone."

They rode back toward the gate, each recognizing the truth of that condemnation of the Marquess of Granville. The Granvilles paid too much attention to Debrett's, not enough to the reality of family ties.

"Stafford, I gather she ran away because of the contretemps at the Weatherby masquerade?"

"What do you know about that?" the major asked.

"I took her home after I rescued her from the jeering crowd. Louise was out of her depth. Hurley and Maggie Brooke ought to be strung up for taking her there." Abernathy shook his head. "I tried to see her at Chesley Square the following day. The butler denied me. I've been looking for her ever since. I understand she was in Hyde Park the following morning, so she had some freedom."

"I believe Lady Louise has not been out of the house since her early morning ride in Hyde Park." The major could not bring himself to confide in Abernathy, who seemed to realize the hesitation.

"I like Lady Louise and don't care to think of her on her own in Town. I can see you're not going to tell me anything. If you change your mind, just remember, I stand ready to help in any way possible." Abernathy turned away without waiting for a reply.

The major rode on. He wondered how many days would pass before the Granvilles left Town. They would not stay long, once they learned everyone knew their granddaughter had run away. Had they accomplished anything by their efforts to find her? The marquess said he had contacted the people she might have gone to for sanctuary, but would they tell him the truth? By Granville's own admission, people might prefer not to answer his questions. After all, it was no secret to most people they had been too strict when they first came to Town. Stafford would contact her friends again. He might get a different answer.

Chapter 19

On The Hunt

The one thing the Marquess of Granville had accomplished was to raise consternation at Amesbury House as well as in Harley Street. The moment Rebecca returned to Town and learned that Louise had disappeared, she had hurried to consult with Amelia Peters, now Mrs. Rogers. She learned Granville's servants had already been there.

"Oh, Rebecca, I've been sitting here, praying you would come. The marquess sent word Louise has run away, seemed to think I might be harboring her. Have you ever heard of such a dimwitted thing?" Amelia babbled on without waiting for an answer. "If that poor little lamb has run away, Lord Granville is at fault. I shall tell him so, even if I have to invade his house. See if I don't!"

Rebecca clung to her a moment. "They've been getting along much better in the last few weeks. I cannot believe she would run away. Where can she be? What could the Granvilles have done to cause her to leave? What am I going to do without her, Amelia?" Rebecca's questions ended in anguished sobs.

They comforted each other, promising to stay in touch. Rebecca returned to Amesbury House, her thoughts in turmoil. She paced her bedchamber throughout the day, castigating herself for not making sure Louise was happy. She would not have run away if she had been happy, Rebecca argued to herself. The Granvilles are at the bottom of this.

This situation was all her fault. Rebecca had promised Louise she would help. What had she done? Nothing. She had listened, true, but that was not enough. She should have done something. Rebecca's bitter thoughts kept pace with her striding back and forth across the Aubusson carpet. Rebecca was pleased with her own life, wrapped up in her dreams of life with Shelburne. She had let day follow day, night follow night, without doing anything to help her dearest friend, nay, her almost-sister. Why did Shelburne have to be out of Town right when she needed him? He would know what to do.

Rebecca hurried downstairs when the footman announced Major George Stafford's presence in the drawing room. The major strode the length of the room until the butler brought the tea tray and left the room. Only then did he speak.

"Miss Blackwell, I know you are a close friend of Louise Mansfield, so I come to you with a question. I don't mean to offend you in any manner, but I must know. Do you know where she is?"

"No, I am sorry to say, I do not. She couldn't come to me because I was not here. I will never forgive myself for failing her. Louise knew this would be the first place her grandparents would inquire for her, so she would not come to me."

"Where would she go for help to escape the wrath of her grandparents?"

Bitterness crept into Rebecca's voice. "Louise was unhappy for several weeks until her situation with her grandparents improved. She still felt confined after they reduced their strictures, but everything turned bad again. I promised to help her, yet I haven't done one thing to make her life easier."

"What could you have done? I could have helped. I feel responsible for her running away."

With a puzzled frown, Rebecca asked why he would feel responsible for Louise's leaving Granville House.

"I told the marquess about finding her in the park the other morning, riding as though the devil was after her. He was angry because she had gone out without her groom. Granville confined her to her room with the intention of sending her to a relative in Yorkshire. However, to give him credit, Lord Granville thought she would be safer there too, away from whoever caused her injuries."

"Yorkshire?" Rebecca couldn't visualize Louise being in the wilds of that far northern area. "What is all this? I haven't heard a thing about her going there or anywhere else for that matter."

Stafford assumed a noncommittal voice as he told her about the Weatherby masquerade ball, ending with the last incident in the park.

"She went to the masquerade ball?" Rebecca asked in a surprised tone. "Oh, dear. I can see how she would want to go to something entirely different from what she has known." She shook her head in dismay at a masquerade ball. "I'm sure that her grandparents gave her a thorough trimming."

"Lady Louise must have learned he was sending her to his cousin, then bided her time until she could leave. Her behavior truly was beyond bearing, Miss Blackwell, besides placing herself in danger again. I couldn't just ignore it, could I?" The major resumed pacing the floor. The carpet would never be the same.

Controlling her own anxiety, Rebecca patted the chair next to her, urging him to sit. "Louise really is not the hoyden you seem to think her."

"Hoyden, Miss Blackwell? She goes beyond that. She is harum-scarum. You should have seen her riding in the park. Her hair was flying in all directions, her face flushed—she looked like Haymarket ware." Stafford's voice broke as he finished his rant. "Lady Louise didn't seem to realize she was riding a thousand pounds of strong-willed muscle. She could have been killed. You do realize that?"

Rebecca made soothing noises. "Louise feels unwanted by her grandparents. Oh, they do their duty. They consider their first duty is to their family name however, not to an individual person, especially not a female. Louise—truly no one—can live up to their expectations of perfection."

The major listened without interruption.

"The Granvilles are family-proud, more concerned about how Louise reflects on their name than they are about her as a person. At least Louise believes so. Shelburne's mother told me about the Granvilles' obsession when I received a letter from Louise explaining why she could not visit me."

Rebecca could imagine what he was thinking. Well-bred females did not attend masquerade balls. Well-bred females did not ride *ventre à terre* in the park. Well-bred females did not run away. Well-bred females accepted the dictates of their guardians until they married, after which they bowed to the wishes of their husbands. Everybody knew that. Therefore, Louise's actions were deliberate.

"Louise was content in our lodgings in Harley Street, never did anything to cause raised eyebrows. She is the only red-head I have ever known who simply never loses her temper. She is not happy. In a nutshell, that is why Louise has behaved in such a questionable manner. She is not happy."

"Where can she be?" The major did not appear to have heard Rebecca's words. "Granville thinks he looked everywhere. I don't know where to start."

"Why do you want to find her?" Rebecca gazed into his eyes. She made the instant decision to thwart him if he was simply going to return Louise to her grandparents.

The major's mouth opened and closed. He swallowed before he answered. "I had no idea her grandfather would behave in such a drastic manner. I want to make amends."

"How can you?"

Instead of answering, Stafford pursued the main question. Where could his love have gone? "Would any of her other friends take her in?"

Rebecca shook her head. "We have always been the only close friend either of us needed or wanted all the way back to being six years old. You heard our story of being 'bestest friends' for always."

Stafford nodded, although his thoughts were on Lady Louise's whereabouts now. "Can you not tell me anything that will help me find her?"

Rebecca sat in silence a moment. "My brain is numb. I cannot think. You will call upon me daily?"

With a nod, Stafford left the room.

During the following days, the major rode in Kensington Gardens, thinking she might try to lose herself among the nursemaids with children. Stafford flinched at the memory of his last visit to Green Park but knew he must search for her there also. He sent his tiger to maintain a discreet surveillance of the house in Harley Street.

The major sat over dinner at Brooks' Club on the second evening, reviewing his efforts to find Louise. When he heard his name, he glanced up to see Simon Abernathy, standing beside his table.

"May I join you, Major?"

Stafford waved him to a chair. He could use some company, even this man.

"Have you learned of Lady Louise's whereabouts? You're so downcast I must suspect you have not found a trace of her."

"You're correct," Stafford assured him. "I'm at my wits' end. I don't know where else to look or what else to do since Granville refuses to call in the Runners."

"He would, would he not? A more stubborn man I hope never to meet." Abernathy eyed the major for a moment. "I don't suppose you have investigated the brothels?"

Stafford glared at him. "How dare you even suggest such a thing? Lady Louise would never go to one of those places."

"Not of her own volition, I agree. Major, we can accept that Lady Louise left home on her own accord. It does not follow she reached her chosen destination. I don't need to remind you of the attempts on her life."

"I agree. Those attempts bother me the most. I must admit I had not thought of looking for her in a brothel." A moue of distaste crossed his face, causing Abernathy to chuckle.

"Your fastidiousness in that respect precedes you, Stafford. Therefore, I will assume the duty of visiting them. I will let you know if I learn anything about Lady Louise." He rose to leave. "I'm known in several brothels, so I should have no difficulty finding her if she is in one of them. After all, my penchant for red-heads is common knowledge." With a nod, Abernathy left the room to begin his search.

Abernathy's efforts failed. Louise was not in any brothel he visited, nor did he hear even a whisper about a new auburn-haired beauty on the tiles. He knew

Stafford had consulted Rebecca Blackwell, who professed to have no knowledge of her friend's whereabouts. She knew the major would report to the Granvilles. Would she have told Stafford the truth?

Abernathy decided to call upon Rebecca Blackwell himself, using his relation to his brother for his entrance gambit. Without doubt, Shelburne wouldn't approve his visit. Nevertheless, Simon approached Amesbury House a little later. The footman left him cooling his heels in the hall for several minutes before escorting him to a small sitting room on the first floor, which Rebecca entered after only a few minutes.

Abernathy bowed over her hand. "Thank you for seeing me, my lady."

"Please be seated, Mr. Abernathy," Rebecca asked the footman to bring tea. "Ask Dulcie to attend me, please."

Moments later, the maid slipped into the room, followed by the footman with a laden tea tray.

Simon took a cautious sip of the steaming brew. "I understand you met my brother, Michael, during the summer."

"Yes, Louise and I spent a pleasant fortnight with his family." Rebecca's eyes were shining. "Oh, please tell me about Miranda. She's such a precious child. Does she still have Fluffy? Has she again tried to ride her pony while standing up?"

Simon chuckled. "I don't believe so. I would not be surprised in the least if she did. Yes, Fluffy is still a member of the household, as is Brownie. Miranda chatters like a magpie about Miss Rebecca and Miss Louise."

Abernathy didn't want to upset her but felt he must. "I know you told Major George Stafford that you didn't know Lady Louise's whereabouts, but have you heard from her since?"

Rebecca blinked away the tears he'd glimpsed. "No, sir, and I'm truly worried. I know she'd be in touch with me if she could. Oh, what could have happened to her?"

Simon grasped her outstretched hands. "We'll find her. Stafford is also searching. We'll find her," he repeated.

Despite his assurances, Abernathy left Amesbury House with a heavy heart, unable to believe his own words.

The major consulted with Rebecca every day, receiving the distressing news of her own efforts. Each evening he visited Chesley Square to report his lack of progress. The marquess had stopped his own efforts. Now he listened with only partial attention to the major's reports.

The major did solve one problem, leaving him with a feeling of relief after his temper had cooled. Riding in Hyde Park one afternoon, he stopped when Lady Amberly hailed him.

"Major Stafford, is there any news of Lady Louise?" Genuine concern colored her voice.

"Nothing yet, my lady. Thank you for inquiring." Stafford nodded to Lady Jane and Herman Amberly who were in the carriage.

"Whatever happens to her serves her right," Lady Jane sniffed. "I told her …," she stopped in confusion when the major rounded on her.

"Silence, you troublemaker!"

Herman Amberly shouted at him. "I'm warning you, don't upset Jane. I told Miss Mansfield not to upset Jane. Just look what happened to her."

Stafford turned toward him, ignoring the gathering crowd. "What do you know about what happened to her?"

"She left Town because she knew I would kill her if she stayed."

Those words were his undoing.

The major dismounted and jerked him out of the carriage with one swift movement. Stafford roared while he shook the hapless youth until his head flopped. "Are you behind those attempts on her life? Answer me before I kill you!"

Lady Jane jumped out of the carriage and commenced to beat Stafford on the arms, screaming at him to stop hurting Herman.

Abernathy, who had followed Stafford into the park, watched the commotion with some amusement for a moment before dismounting. He laid a hand on the major's shoulder. "Yes, Stafford, I believe you had better turn Amberly loose. He cannot answer while you shake him."

The major gave Amberly one last shake before setting him on his feet. "Talk."

Rubbing his arms where the major had grasped him, Amberly muttered, "What I did was her own fault. I told her not to upset Jane, but she didn't listen."

Before Stafford could get his hands on Amberly again, Abernathy intervened. "Are we to understand you shot at Lady Louise? That you attempted her life on three different occasions?"

"She didn't listen," Amberly repeated. "I don't allow anyone to upset Jane."

A gasp ran through the crowd, and Lady Jane drew back in horror at her cousin's words.

Lady Amberly denied any knowledge of the situation. "Major Stafford, I assure you I had no idea of Herman's perfidy. I knew of his partiality for my daughter, of course. After all, they have grown up more like brother and sister than distant cousins. I must tell Lord Amberly of this. Come, Jane."

"I won't leave without Herman," her daughter said with a glare at the major. "That lunatic will murder him."

The major clenched his fists, causing Abernathy to intervene. "I believe it will be best for us to escort all of you home and turn the matter over to Lord Amberly."

Stafford whirled on him. "He tried to murder Lady Louise. *Three times*. I intend for the Bow Street Runners to take him in charge."

"Easy, now, Major," Abernathy spoke. "Young Amberly appears to have some mental difficulties. I'm sure we can convince Lord Amberly to confine him in the country."

At length the major consented. After Lord Amberly had agreed his young cousin would live permanently on his country estate, the major hurried to Chesley Square to inform the Granvilles.

Foster escorted him to his lordship's study, where he found both Granvilles. After explaining, he said, "We've solved one mystery. Lady Louise is no longer in danger from Amberly."

Lord Granville shrugged.

Lady Granville sniffed. "Louise's behavior placed her in danger, Major Stafford. She is at fault for whatever happened to her."

He stared at her in stunned amazement. "You do not appear to be at all relieved to know your granddaughter is no longer in that particular danger, my lady." Receiving only a supercilious stare, Stafford stormed out of the room to continue his efforts to find their granddaughter. They were not trying.

Encountering Winningham on the strut in Hyde Park didn't improve Stafford's temper.

"Stafford," called the dandy. "Well met."

The major tried to pass him by with only a nod, but the numskull blocked his path.

"Have you located my cousin? Pulled a fast one, didn't she." When he didn't receive reply, Winningham blundered on. "Granville is hiding in his study, refuses to see anyone, even me—his heir."

Still the major didn't comment.

"I don't know why Louise thought she had to run away," Winningham complained. "I offered marriage, which no one else will do after her mad escapades. From what I hear she caused quite a sensation at the masquerade ball."

Stafford allowed a sneer to settle on his face. "Lady Louise preferred to disappear rather than be leg-shackled to you. Now, move out of my way. I've wasted enough time on you."

Several days had passed since Lady Louise disappeared. The major had to confess his failure to find any trace of her. One moment he cursed her for worrying him; the next he vowed to protect her from her grandfather's wrath, if only he could find her.

Stafford sat one evening in his rooms, his aching leg propped on an ottoman. He ignored the brandy snifter at his elbow, as he went over his efforts to date. Try though he did, the major couldn't think of another action to take, another place he could search.

Shelburne spotted George Stafford walking along Bond Street. After speaking to him twice without an answer, he grabbed the major's arm.

"Why the brown study?" Receiving no answer, Shelburne urged him toward White's. "Come where it's quiet, and tell me what's bothering you."

In a dim room of the club, George related the story once again. "Edward, I cannot find a trace of her anywhere."

Shelburne had returned that day from Shelburne Park, so he had heard nothing about Louise's disappearance. Now he asked a blunt question. "Why do you want to find her?"

George repeated the reasons he had given Rebecca but flushed when he met his old friend's cynical smile. "Oh, alright, I'm besotted by the chit. Louise drives me wild, yet I cannot stay away from her. She's caused me more sleepless nights than pitched battles ever did. What am I going to do?"

The anguished whisper was just audible, but Edward heard.

"Louise Mansfield is a minor, you realize. Do you mean to return her to her grandfather?"

"No, I mean to marry her out of hand, if I don't throttle her first." Stafford grinned. "That from a man who has avoided parson's mousetrap for all these years."

"Louise is not quite in your usual style, is she? Aside from her auburn hair."

"She's heedless of limitations, headstrong, resents guidance, goes from one extreme to another, and has a dreadful temper." Stafford admitted, "Louise is everything I despise in a female. I don't even like her, yet the idea of living without her is unbearable. I believe one good thing has come out of this, though."

"What would that be?"

"Without doubt, Granville will be happy to get her off his hands if—no, *when*—I find her. For the first time, I have confidence he won't refuse my offer."

Shelburne studied him a moment. The major's face was as gaunt as when he had first returned from Spain with the leg injury. His friends had hoped never to see him in such condition again. Should he or should he not tell the distraught man where to find his love? Surely Rebecca knew. Perhaps Louise had sworn her old friend to secrecy.

"Have you talked to Rebecca Blackwell about this? I've just this moment returned to Town after some days at Shelburne Park and have not talked with her."

"I've talked to her every day. She is worried to the point of sickness."

"We'll go together to see Rebecca. Maybe I can jog her memory."

The major showed surprise at the choice of words but agreed.

They found Rebecca in her sitting room at Amesbury House with her hands idle, her vacant gaze lost in space. A touch on her shoulder brought her back to her present surroundings with a start.

"Edward!" Without conscious thought, she threw herself into his arms. Flushing rosily, she pulled away from his loving embrace. "I do beg your pardon. May I offer you some refreshment?"

They talked for a few minutes of the earl's visit to Somerset before Shelburne brought up the subject they needed to discuss. "My dear, I understand you told Stafford you don't know where Louise has gone. Is that true—forgive me—or did she ask you not to tell?"

She gazed at him in surprise. "Certainly, it's true. Shelburne, she couldn't confide in me because I was not here."

"Have you truly thought about this?" Shelburne questioned. "Have you not thought of the one place above all others where she would go?"

"I visited Amelia Peters, rather Mrs. Rogers, as she is now. I'm convinced she does not know where Louise is. I asked the parents of her former piano students if they supplied references for her. I even sent a discreet messenger to Granville Manor to see if she has taken refuge with her father's old nanny. As far as we know, her maternal family no longer exists. I don't know what else to do." Rebecca buried her face in her hands, her shoulders shook with sobs.

The earl took her in his arms. "When we find her, I might murder her for upsetting you. Now, my love, dry your tears."

"I can't even think any more," she whispered.

"Rebecca, love, you do know where she is or, at least, have a very good idea. You're one of the most intelligent people I have ever known, but in this instance, your brains seem to have deserted you."

She shook her head in denial. "If I knew where she is, I would have gone to her. Nothing—no one—could keep me away from my best friend when she needs me. We're almost sisters!"

"Do you remember telling me about the duchess last summer?"

"Of course, I remember. My memory has not failed that much."

Shelburne smiled at her indignation, waiting for her to make the connection. When she did not, he reminded, "What did you tell me was the best thing about the duchess? When she found places for her charges, I mean."

Enlightenment flashed into Rebecca's face. "Stupid beyond permission, that's what I am, stupid. A regular nodcock, as Amelia Peters would say. Of course, she's there. I, of all people, should have known on the instant. Louise is safe." Rebecca burst into tears again.

The major had been sitting quietly, his gaze moving from one to the other, but now his patience deserted him. "How nice you have remembered, Lady Rebecca, after several days of worry. Now, would you mind telling me?"

Stafford's sarcasm was lost on his companions, whose attention centered on each other.

"I said ...."

"Oh, Major, I truly am sorry about all this. I rarely think about my old life because my new one occupies all my thoughts. Shelburne reminded me that the duchess, who sponsors the orphanage, encourages all her charges to return there if their lives outside prove unbearable for any reason. I should have remembered this information immediately and told you at your first visit. I don't understand why it slipped my mind. I suppose the stress of hearing that she had run away was the cause of my forgetfulness. I can only apologize for not remembering this sooner."

"I know about the orphanage from Lady Louise, of course. She has often mentioned the duchess who supports it. In Hampshire, I believe?"

Stafford jumped to his feet when Rebecca gave him the direction.

"Wait, Major," Rebecca said. "You can't start out at this hour. You would arrive in the middle of the night. Besides, you must consider the dangers of traveling in the dark."

The major sat down again. "You're right, of course. I suppose I should report to the Granvilles before I go after her. I will talk with him this evening and then leave for Hampshire first thing in the morning."

"Do wait for daylight, Major," Rebecca implored.

The major insisted upon admittance at Granville House at eight o'clock that evening, despite the butler's efforts to deny him. "I believe I have news of Lady Louise, Foster."

The butler opened the door further, gazing at him with anxious eyes. "I hope you have good news, Major. Everyone below stairs is worried about her."

"His lordship should hear my news first, but I will set your mind at rest. Her closest friend believes Lady Louise has returned to the Hampshire orphanage. I plan to go there first thing in the morning."

Foster so far forgot himself as to hit his forehead with the heel of his hand. "Now, why did we not think of that? It's logical Lady Louise would go to the only home she could remember." With a disgusted shake of his head, Foster tapped on the door.

"Foster, I believe I ordered we not be disturbed." The harsh voice penetrated the closed door. "Go away. Get back to your duties."

The butler put on his haughtiest expression and opened the door. "My lord, Major Stafford is here with possible news of Lady Louise. I believed you would want to see him, so I permitted him to enter." With those words, Foster stepped aside so the major could enter the room.

After closing the door behind him, Foster hurried to the kitchen quarters to apprise the others. "The major is going to Hampshire tomorrow morning to find Miss Louise," he finished with a delighted smile to the vocal pleasure of the others.

"Oh, why did I not think of that?" Agnes wrung her hands with anguish. "The duchess told me if anything went wrong, I could return, and she would find me another place. It simply never occurred to me she told Miss Louise, as she was then, the same thing, because she isn't a servant."

"Now, now, Agnes, don't agitate yourself," Mrs. Foster soothed her. "There has been so much upset, it is no wonder to me that you forgot."

Agnes turned her attention to Foster. "Sir, do you think Major Stafford might allow me to ride to the orphanage with him? I have the funds to ride on the stage, but I'm afraid to ride with strangers."

Foster studied the anxious face turned toward him. "Agnes, I'm not in favor of girls riding the common stage either, so I will ask the major his opinion." He returned to the front hall.

While Foster was giving the good news in the kitchen, the major was not having an easy time with the Marquess of Granville in the study.

"My lord, I have just come from Amesbury House and a conversation with Lady Rebecca. She has realized your granddaughter might have returned to the orphanage in Hampshire."

"Yes, I know she did."

The major gaped at him. "Did I hear you right, my lord? Did you say you know that your granddaughter is there?"

"That is what I said, Major." Granville glared at him from beneath bushy eyebrows.

"My lord, how did you come by this information?"

"The duchess sent me word when the chit arrived there."

Major Stafford swallowed twice before he was able to speak. "Do you mean to tell me you have known this for several days yet did not bother to inform me? You knew I was scouring London for her. I reported to you daily. Why did you not tell me?"

"I do not consider it necessary to account for my actions to you, Major Stafford, not on this subject or any other. Now if you will excuse me, I am busy." Granville's astringent words fell on deaf ears.

"Wait just a moment, my lord." The major's voice was grim. He struggled for calmness. "What are your intentions toward your granddaughter?"

Granville's eyebrows climbed his high forehead. "What business is that of yours?"

Stafford spoke through clenched teeth. "Are you going to return her to London?"

"No, why should I? My lady and I will return to Granville Manor tomorrow."

"Is she going to join you there?"

The marquess answered with one blunt word. "No."

"Are you going to send her to Yorkshire?"

"You are impertinent, Major Stafford. Now cease these endless questions."

"Impertinent or not, you will listen to me, my lord. I am going to Hampshire tomorrow, where I pray I will find her. I intend to marry her, with or without your permission. Have you anything to say?"

"Nothing. To put the matter succinctly, Major, I have no intentions of any description toward the rebellious chit. Louise is a disgrace to The Family. She no longer exists."

The major stared at him in disbelief. *Louise had been right. The Granvilles care more for their family name than they do for her. The arrogant bounder. We will see how fast he comes down to earth.*

"When our first son is born, I believe you will find it necessary to change your mind on that point, my lord." Stafford had the pleasure of seeing his host's face whiten. He threw caution to the wind. "How do you feel about the next Marquess of Granville bearing the name Stafford?"

Without waiting for a reply, the major quitted the room and found Foster waiting.

"Major, may I speak with you a moment?"

In normal circumstances, Major Stafford would not discuss family matters with servants. Now, in his irritation, he made an exception. "Foster, are you aware his lordship has known for several days that his granddaughter is at the orphanage?"

Foster's mouth dropped open. His eyes widened. "Major, he has not said a word about Lady Louise to anyone. I have even inquired each day if he had received any news."

"The patron of the orphanage notified him immediately after she arrived there." The major took a deep breath. "I agree with you, Foster. I could not believe Granville's perfidy myself when he told me."

"I don't know what to say, Major, other than to express my surprise. I assure you that, had I known, you would have received the news immediately."

The major nodded. "Now, you wanted to talk with me?"

"Yes, sir. I hesitate to ask a favor from a gentleman, but her ladyship's maid wants to return to the orphanage. She asked me to ascertain if she could ride with you. You see, sir, Agnes is afraid to ride the common stage by herself." Foster did not acknowledge Louise had probably traveled that way to Hampshire.

"She should be. Am I to understand Lord Granville terminated her employment?"

"Yes, Major, he has. He does not blame her for Miss Louise leaving, you understand. He and Lady Granville prefer older maids in their household. They did supply Agnes with a reference. She should have no difficulty finding another position."

"I see. Yes, she may ride with me. I intend to drive my landau. There will be space for her box. I will be here to take her up at nine o'clock tomorrow morning, Foster." With a nod Stafford departed into the cool night air. He waved his coachman away. Perhaps the long walk back to Jermyn Street would cool his temper.

Chapter 20

Home at Last

Louise wandered around the gardens, those same gardens she had loved playing in as a child. As an adult, she did not find them appealing. Her feet moved along without her conscious thought until she seated herself upon a bench in the rose garden. Louise was home. She was welcome. Everything looked the way she remembered. Had the orphanage always been this quiet? At this hour the children were inside. All Louise could hear was the sound of birds chirping.

Louise's heart had lightened when the hired carriage that brought her from the stage stop to the orphanage arrived at the gates almost a week ago. She was home. Safe. Her problems would go away.

A group of small girls had stopped their play to stare, wide-eyed, at the beautiful lady descending from the carriage. Louise joined them, giving a hug here and there. She paused by a child with a mass of red curls.

"I was a little girl like you when I first came here." Louise studied the small face. "I believe I had more freckles than you do. What is your name?"

"Mary. You don't have any freckles now. What is your name?"

"Louise. They went away when I grew up."

"Will mine go away too?" the child asked.

"Oh yes, you can be sure they will when you are older. You must remember to wear your sunbonnet."

Louise chuckled when Mary rounded on her friends. "See, I told you they would go away!"

With a wave Louise had run up the steps, lighthearted for the first time in weeks. Her life would go back to a major key now.

Matron had met her with open arms, asking no questions until they could be private. Over teacups, she listened with care to the story her former charge told. She used the same words of comfort the Duchess of Dorchester used later in the evening. "There, there, child, everything will come out right in the end. We can trust God to take care of everything."

Neither lady said anything about notifying Lord Granville, which Louise had been ready to challenge. She excused herself and went to the bedchamber assigned to her. It is as well Louise did not hear the conversation the duchess had with the matron after she left the drawing room.

"Do you plan to notify the Granvilles?" Mrs. Dysart hesitated to disturb the duchess, who sat in thought.

"Yes, I must. I admit to the low thought I would rather let them fret some first, which would not be right." Few things roused the duchess to anger. Under these circumstances, her wrath overflowed. "Louise has lost her merry heart. How dare they treat her so shabbily? Such behavior is just like Hortense Tracy. We were young girls together. She was already toplofty beyond words—family proud, just like her parents. We did not think she would ever find a husband to suit her."

"I suppose she found one just like her. Rebecca will tell them Louise has returned here. Our failure to contact the Granvilles would show us in a bad light, though."

"Yes. There is another essential thing to do—keep watch on Agnes. They might put her out on the street if they take it into their heads that she knew about Louise leaving there."

Mrs. Dysart nodded her agreement, as she reached for the bell to summon a footman.

On the first night, Louise had welcomed the privacy of a small bedchamber, while she twisted and turned in the narrow bed. Her eyes refused to close as scene after scene of her recent behavior flitted across her mind. Louise cringed in memory of the jeering voices at the masquerade. As for that final gallop in the park— why, oh why, had she acted in such a madcap way? She knew better.

If only Rebecca was here .... Louise moaned with a sudden recollection of a conversation they had in the summer. Louise had admitted to her dearest friend that she could not imagine being besotted with any man. Now she knew she not only could be but was. There would be no happy ending for her. No gentleman could ever forgive her. Forgiveness from just any gentleman would not bring happiness to Louise. Did she even deserve it? Probably not. Her behavior over the past several weeks precluded happiness.

After a near sleepless night, Louise woke with a renewed determination. She would stay busy doing anything that came to hand. Even cooking, she thought with a grimace. Anything was better than confronting her thoughts.

First, Matron insisted Louise recoup her energies in the quietness of Hampshire, after the noise of the metropolis.

On the first day back, Louise had visited the stables to greet old friends, both human and equine. Her favorite mount, Starlight, had welcomed her home, but she had taken the mare out only twice. Both times

Louise relived every ride she had shared with the major. Each ride on Starlight ended with tears sliding down her cheeks.

Louise made an early visit to the music room, where she had spent many happy hours throughout her childhood. Her fingers moved through a Beethoven sonata, her mind far away. Why could she not forget George Stafford? She vowed she would not think of him, but to no avail. As the sonata gave way to a Bach fugue, smoky blue eyes stared at her from the keyboard.

Louise deserted the music room. Long hours in the gardens followed, even those where the blossoms were gone. She had to face it. She was bored, waiting for something to happen.

Louise gave herself a mental shake when a cheerful countenance topped with fair hair flashed into her mind. Why was she attracted to him? He didn't care for music. She loved it. If George had ever read even one of the classics, he had not mentioned it. He appeared displeased with her education. She was proud of it. He didn't care for the hustle and bustle of Town life. She thrived on it. He was particular about acquaintances to the point of rudeness. She was much more relaxed in greeting people, as the duchess had demonstrated in her own life.

Face it, Louise told herself. She would enjoy being anywhere, doing anything, if Major George Stafford were there despite their differences. She must accept she would never see him again. Never sit quietly in the garden with him again. Never laugh with him again. Laughter was the key. No one else laughed with her in the same way. In childhood, Louise had often wondered what Matron meant when she told the duchess that Louise had a merry heart. Now she knew. God had given her a match for her merry heart. She had thrown it away. Louise buried her face in her hands stifling sobs.

Footsteps approaching on the gravel penetrated her consciousness. Louise wiped her eyes with the back of her hand before glancing to her right. She stared, blinked her eyes, stared again.

"Are you really here, or am I dreaming you?"

"I'm really here." The major dropped down on the bench beside her, never taking his gaze off her face. "I have never been so glad to see anyone in the entirety of my life. I didn't quite believe you would be here."

Stafford's lips tightened for a moment before he relaxed them. "I brought your maid with me. The Granvilles decided they had no further need for her services. She was afraid to ride the stage by herself. You did, though, did you not?"

Still staring at him, Louise only nodded.

The major cradled her hands in his. "I told myself not to lose my temper or shout at you. Will you please explain to me why in the name of sense you just disappeared? Can you not understand the turmoil you left behind? Rebecca Blackwell was upset to the point she could not think, your maid was in hysterics, Amelia Rogers swooned, your grandparents were beside themselves with worry."

His last statement brought an unladylike snort. Louise pulled her hands free of his grasp. "My grandparents care for nothing except their precious family name. If they worried about anything, it was that, not me as a person."

Louise was determined to be civil at any cost, although she felt her temper rising again. "Why will people not understand I can take care of myself? I was taught that here at the orphanage."

"Yes, I imagine you were," Stafford agreed. "They certainly taught you independence."

Louise shrugged. "Rebecca should have known I would come home. Where else would I go? If she is too upset to think, how did you know where to find me?"

"Shelburne returned to Town. He knew at once where to find you."

"How would Shelburne know?"

"He remembered Rebecca telling him some months ago that the girls were encouraged to return to the orphanage if they had problems with their lives." Stafford again forced himself to calmness. "No matter how your grandparents have behaved toward you, they do have a sincere concern for your well-being."

A hoot of derision met that ridiculous statement.

In a burst of candor, the major continued. "I will admit, though, I had not expected the marquess to react in quite such a strong manner. Yorkshire in the wintertime is extreme, even though I understand the area is quite pleasant in summer. Nevertheless, I should think they could find a closer place to keep you safe as well as to monitor your conduct."

"They did seem to care when I had the accidents."

"They were not accidents anyway. You were the target of a disordered mind." Stafford told her of his conversation with Herman Amberly. "He cannot bear for Lady Jane to be upset. You were cutting up her peace, so he did the only thing his limited brain could conjure. He tried to kill you."

Louise stared at him open-mouthed.

"Even though I was not the intended target, I was the reason you were in danger," Stafford said. "If I had not shown my decided partiality for you, Lady Jane would not have berated you, thereby inciting Amberly's efforts to kill you."

Louise picked up the important phrase. "How could you be partial to me? You think me headstrong and willful."

"I hesitate to contradict a lady, but I do not think you are either," the major answered with aplomb, exercising a selective memory. "You are impulsive and careless about the consequences—most of which is caused by your kind heart. Rebecca Blackwell has known you longer than anyone whom I know. All her comments are positive. On the way down here, Agnes became quite loquacious on what your life has been like with your grandparents. I do see you were sorely tried."

"What are you going to do—return me to my grandparents? I cannot imagine they would want me back, though, under any circumstances. Another runaway family member goes beyond what their pride will permit."

Although Stafford didn't comment, Louise saw confirmation in his face. All she felt was relief. "They don't want me. They never will."

"We can't be sure, Louise. When they have been back at Granville Manor for a time, perhaps they will recognize their own shortcomings. The transformation might take longer than we would like, yet while they live the possibility exists."

"I would like to have loving grandparents," Louise admitted. "They started to care for me toward the end. My behavior ended the hope for more. Perhaps if I apologize to them, they will begin to care for me again."

"That, too, is possible," he assured her. "I now regret some things I said to them before I came to find you. They were preparing to leave Town. When we leave here, we will visit them in the country. We can offer our apologies there."

"What happens now?" Louise asked.

Stafford answered in a roundabout way. "Shelburne asked me my intentions. I told him I intended to wring your neck for worrying me."

Hazel eyes met smoky blue for a long moment before she looked away. Stafford had to strain to hear the soft words. "I'm not such a terrible person, truly. At least, I never believe so."

"No, you are not terrible, my dear. I have come to realize you have had much to provoke you. How can I expect you to be perfect when I am so far from perfection?"

Louise didn't want him to be perfect. She only wanted him to love her.

The major picked up her hand, caressing it with both of his. "Louise, I know I said some rude things to you. Do you think we could start over from this point? I will be more understanding in the future."

"I suppose you think I should spend my time sitting in a corner with my embroidery frame." Belligerence sharpened her voice.

The major chuckled. "Don't work yourself into a temper. I cannot imagine your being quiet enough to do needlework."

Louise believed in being direct. Taking a deep breath, she looked him straight in the eye. "George, you do realize my grandparents do not approve of you. I mean, if you have more than friendship in mind ...,"

Her voice trailed off, her face grew hot, but her gaze did not falter.

His eyes softened, and a gentle smile appeared on his face. Leaning forward, he moved his lips across her parted lips. Their kiss deepened when she slipped her arms around him, drawing him closer. At length, he drew away from her.

"Oh, yes," George murmured. "I have more in mind than friendship. I told Lord Granville I'm going to marry you, with or without his blessing."

"Marry me? Did it not occur to you I might have other ideas? Might even want a proposal in proper form?" The dancing mischief in her eyes denied the outraged words.

The chirping birds applauded as the major knelt on one buckskin-clad knee and proposed in due form. "My darling Lady Louise Rebecca Marie Mansfield, would you do me the honour of becoming my wife?"

"Hmmm, I need to think ...." With a gleeful shout, Louise threw herself into his arms. They landed in a heap on the ground, convulsed with laughter, thus setting the tone for their life in a major key.

Author's Note

Your opinion matters, so if you enjoyed The Merry Heart, please spread the word by posting a short review on Amazon, Good Reads, and other sources to which you have access. Reviews are enormously helpful to the reading community, and your support really does motivate me to keep writing. Thank you!

♥ Peggy ♥